Praise for Hannah McKinnon and
The Lake Season

"Seasons of change take us home to the places and the people who shelter us. Well-told, and in turns sweet and bare, *The Lake Season* offers a compelling tale of family secrets, letting go, and the unbreakable bonds of sisterhood."

—Lisa Wingate, nationally bestselling author

"A delicious tale of sisters and secrets. Hannah McKinnon's writing style is as breezy as a weekend at the lake, yet her insights into the murkiness of family interactions run deep. The takeaway of this compelling read is clear: you can know someone your whole life and not know them at all."

—Mary Hogan, award-winning author of *Two Sisters*

"Hannah McKinnon's lyrical debut tells the story of a pair of very different sisters, both at a crossroads in life. McKinnon's great strength lies in her ability to reveal the many ways the two women wound—and ultimately heal—each other as only sisters can."

—Sarah Pekkanen, *New York Times*
bestselling author of *Catching Air*

"This is a beautiful tale of sisters, a heartfelt journey of truth and choices that will leave you deeply satisfied."

—Linda Francis Lee, bestselling author
of *The Glass Kitchen*

"Family and secrets colliding at a lakeside wedding . . . [a] must-read."

—*Cosmopolitan*

"Charming and heartfelt! Hannah McKinnon's *The Lake Season* proves that you can go home again; you just can't control what you find when you get there."

—Wendy Wax, *New York Times* bestselling author of the Ten Beach Road series and *The House on Mermaid Point*

"Hannah McKinnon's *The Lake Season* is a pure delight. Iris Standish is such an appealing woman, handling an overload of family calamities with good sense and good will, not to mention a few really good times. It's a bonus that the setting on Lake Hampstead is as enticing and refreshing as McKinnon's voice."

—Nancy Thayer, *New York Times* bestselling author of *Nantucket Sisters*

"*The Lake Season* is one of those rare gems of a book that's both impossible to put down and emotionally complex. Do yourself a favor and put *The Lake Season* on your summer reading list: you'll love getting to know Iris Standish and her family, and Hannah McKinnon's writing is so beautifully evocative that even the most landlocked of readers will swear s/he can smell the fresh New England summer air."

—L. Alison Heller, author of *The Never Never Sisters*

"Sometimes funny, sometimes sad—but always bursting with compassion and sly humor. *The Lake Season* is a joy to read for anyone who cherishes the complexity and richness of family dynamics. Impossible not to be swept along by the characters. The perfect book to spread out with luxuriously on the beach."

—Saira Shah, author of *The Mouse-Proof Kitchen*

"Charming, absorbing, and perfectly paced, *The Lake Season* is as full of warmth as summer itself. Don't blame Hannah McKinnon if this cinematic tale has you glued to a beach chair until it's finished!"

—Chloe Benjamin, author of *The Anatomy of Dreams*

"An emotionally charged story about returning to yourself."

—K. A. Tucker, *USA Today* bestselling author

"Here is sisterhood in all its complexity, rich with tenderness, resentments and shared jokes, disappointment, admiration, and profound love. Those who have a sister will read this book and pass it on to them; those who do not, will wish more than ever that they did."

—Gabrielle Donnelly, author of *The Little Women Letters*

"Two sisters, a glittering New England lake, and one desperate, last-chance summer set the stage for Hannah McKinnon's emotionally affecting new novel *The Lake Season*. The story features the complex Iris and her unpredictable sister Leah but its power extends well beyond the beautiful, heartbreaking bond between these two women. A memorable rumination on life, loss, and how to find a path home."

—Michelle Gable, nationally bestselling author
of *A Paris Apartment*

"Breezy . . . Summer isn't summer without an enticing beach read, and Hannah McKinnon delivers just that."

—*InStyle*

"A multilayered, nuanced portrayal of modern divorce . . . McKinnon is a talented observer of the family dynamic, weaving disparate personalities together as they navigate relationships, self-preservation, and redemption. Fans of Allison Pearson's *I Don't Know How She Does It* (2002) and Maggie Shipstead's *Seating Arrangements* (2012) will love this romantic yet realistic novel."

—*Booklist*

Mystic Summer

◆ a novel ◆

Hannah McKinnon

EMILY BESTLER BOOKS
—
ATRIA
NEW YORK   LONDON   TORONTO   SYDNEY   NEW DELHI

ATRIA PAPERBACK
An Imprint of Simon & Schuster, Inc.
1230 Avenue of the Americas
New York, NY 10020

First Emily Bestler Books/Atria Paperback edition June 2016

EMILY BESTLER BOOKS / ATRIA PAPERBACK and colophon are trademarks of Simon & Schuster, Inc.

For information about special discounts for bulk purchases, please contact Simon & Schuster Special Sales at 1-866-506-1949 or business@simonandschuster.com.

The Simon & Schuster Speakers Bureau can bring authors to your live event. For more information or to book an event contact the Simon & Schuster Speakers Bureau at 1-866-248-3049 or visit our website at www.simonspeakers.com.

Manufactured in the United States of America

10 9 8 7 6 5 4

Library of Congress Cataloging-in-Publication Data is available.

ISBN 978-1-4767-7769-6
ISBN 978-1-4767-7773-3 (ebook)

In loving memory of Michael Reese.
Brother-in-law, uncle, godfather.

The music in my heart I bore
Long after it was heard no more.

—WILLIAM WORDSWORTH

One

"Just how are you planning to fix this?" Mrs. Perry's hands are clasped on the desk, the hand adorned with the colossal diamond resting pertly atop the other. Her fixed smile belies the parental rage I detect in her blue eyes, which, despite their lovely azure color, are boring holes through me across the student desk that buffers the narrow space between us. "My son is an A student. I will not allow you to fail him."

I take a deep breath. "Mrs. Perry, Horatio has to complete his assignments in order to receive an A on them."

I am determined not to squirm in my own classroom. I have found myself seated across the desk from Mrs. Perry too many times in the last eight months, and each time I've come up with the perfect retort to her complaints. Each time being the very moment after she clicked out my classroom door on her designer heels: a moment too late. Now, I dig deep, summoning the voice of Dr. Dwight, my favorite Boston College professor, whose classroom I exited just five short years ago. Whose kind demeanor and sensible pronouncements had convinced me that teaching was an altruistic path to guide children to their full potential. How wrong he was. "All parents truly want is for their child to be happy." Sure, if happiness is defined by an unwavering 4.0 grade point average, however undeserved.

"Horatio does not have time for homework," Mrs. Perry informs me curtly, as though this explanation will magically sweep away the requirement that each of the other forty-eight fourth graders in our school is expected to meet. "It interferes with his tennis lessons at the club. Did you not realize that he has qualified for the regional tournament in the Hamptons this summer? He's first in his division." She drums her manicured fingernails, which I notice are a tasteful shade of nearly colorless pink.

"That's wonderful. However—"

"Furthermore, Horatio's father and I will be sending him to Camp Pendleton at the end of the month. It's an esteemed program instructed by a Pebble Beach pro. So you'll have to excuse Horatio from the last week of school, as well." She checks her watch with a brisk flick of her wrist, as if to signal that this meeting is now over.

"Attendance is a different matter. You'll need to speak to Dean Hartman about that. But in regard to the science grade—"

"Miss Griffin. It is still *Miss*, correct?" I have taught Mrs. Perry's son all year; she knows my name. This reference to my single status is a cruel deflection, tossed masterfully in my path, no different from the critical once-over she now inflicts. Still, I flinch as she makes a cursory examination of my naked left ring finger, before her eyes roam over my off-the-rack sweater, screeching to a halt at my sensible black loafers, which I tuck quickly beneath my chair.

Thrown momentarily by her impromptu fashion findings,

Mrs. Perry pauses, and I seize my chance to regain parent-teacher-conference control. "Mrs. Perry, I can't give credit for work that isn't done. I'm afraid the F stands."

Mrs. Perry's blue eyes have narrowed so that her dark pupils are mere pinpricks between her dense lashes. "Brilliant children should not be hampered by regulations set by the simple-minded administration for the weak-minded majority." Professor Dwight's voice is quick in my ear: "Parent teacher conferences are a wonderful opportunity to let parents know how much you enjoy working together as partners in their child's education." I shoo the professor away, before Ainsley Perry can squash him with her manicured hand.

We are at a stalemate. As I have sadly come to realize, there is no rationale for the unbalanced expectations of many of the parents in this privileged community in which I teach. Darby is a day school in the Belmont section of Boston. When not confined to their Duxbury and Hingham saltboxes, these children inhabit the New England stomping grounds of the post-Mayflower generations, adroitly wielding tennis racquets and toting monogrammed golf bags by the age of three. During summer, they log serious sailing time, tacking and jibing away the month of August off either Nantucket or the Vineyard.

Despite the fact that I was offered two other teaching positions, I was smitten by the New England façade of the Darby Day School the first time I drove through the granite pillars. These kids came to school already on an Ivy League track. Gone would be the heartbreaking struggles I'd encountered during my student teaching stint in a neighborhood where most children were on government welfare and arrived to school hungry, frustrated, and grossly behind, if at all. Though I'd embraced the assignment initially, stalwartly hanging on to those green beliefs about making a difference in each individual whose life I hoped to alter, I soon faltered, exhausted by the harsh realities of the system. I was just one more lofty-minded education graduate plunked in an urban jungle with nothing more than a newly printed diploma stashed in her messenger bag. As my father said when I accepted the Darby position, "Don't think twice, kiddo. You're a scrapper. You'll still find ways to make a difference, no matter where you teach."

Now, as I sit across from Mrs. Perry, who drums her nails on the desk, I am questioning just what kind of difference I am making here. I do not wish to embroil myself in academic litigation with Mrs. Perry, or her husband, who has yet to grace my classroom with his presence, though he routinely clogs my email box with bullet-pointed lists of complaints, as he is mostly overseas engaged in some form of exporting business. But my principles will not allow me to give in. I wonder how happy Mrs. Perry and her husband are with each other, or in general. Despite their racquet-wielding son and his success in the tournament world of their country club, what kind of parents show up only to demand unnecessary special treatment? I have yet to see either one attend the fall harvest picnic, or our spring school play. Forget a fund-raising event like a bake sale. Instead, they are perpetual no-shows who also failed to alert the music teacher of Horatio's absence the night of the fourth-grade play, leaving poor Mrs. Riley, the music teacher, scrambling to fill his lead role minutes before curtains opened. These are not parents who consider for a moment the long hours I stay late at school, grading papers, personally disinfecting their children's desks with Clorox wipes (purchased by yours truly), or the two hours spent waiting on the front steps for parents who simply "forgot" to come pick up their child after a field trip. (Who forgets their own kid?)

And then there's Horatio, the boy himself, whose upturned nose wrinkles when I ask him to take out his homework each morning, and who blithely opens his empty folder, displaying it for all the class to see with such misplaced chagrin I have to bite my lower lip. I have always taken pride in my skill to find good in all of my students, no matter their weaknesses or unkind tendencies. Even when I have to dig deep. But as I sit across from his impeccably dressed mother, I admit that Horatio Perry has challenged that dig-deep skill. I'm an elementary school teacher, not an archaeologist.

Now it's my turn to look at the large white clock on the wall. It's no Rolex, but it tells me what I need to know: I am finished here. It's four thirty on Friday afternoon. Despite my sensible black loafers, my feet hurt from running back and forth across the building to the multipurpose room, where I sacrificed both my prep period and lunch to paint backdrop scenery for the fifth-grade theater production.

In the rear of my classroom the crayfish click audibly across the glass botom of their crustacean tank; a science unit that I tend, because let's face it, they smell and none of the other teachers wanted them. Beside me is a bag full of ungraded social studies essays that I will have to finish by Sunday, and on my desk there is a note from Sadie Jenkins telling me that Melissa Bates has been calling her Butt-Face in gym class. Back at home my cat, Mr. Kringles, is probably sharpening his claws on the corner of my new couch, the only new piece of furniture in my overpriced and undersized Back Bay apartment, where my unwatered plants are sporting the final shades of pre-death yellow. I'm certain that my best friend and roommate, Erika, has left at least five voice mails on my cell. And that Evan has called between filming scenes to see if we can meet for happy hour. Because even though I sometimes feel like I have no life outside this classroom, I manage to have friends and a boyfriend who do. Right now I want nothing more than to sit with Evan at a bar and take a deep sip of a salty margarita, or collapse on my couch at home, even if it does mean listening to Erika fret about her crazy in-laws-to-be, or her couture gown that needs yet another alteration because she's still losing so much weight. And I'm not letting Mrs. Perry suck another moment of that from me.

"I'm sorry, Mrs. Perry, but I have an appointment. Here is Horatio's science assignment. I expect it by Monday." I set the folder between us.

Mrs. Perry looks as if I have slapped her. "You will be hearing from my husband about this," she says, yanking her purse over her shoulder.

Which reminds me of another delightful encounter I shared with Horatio, just the other day: I had warned him that I would phone his father in regard to some colorful language Horatio had tried on for size in the lunch line. When confronted, Horatio had smirked, reached into his pocket, and handed me the newest iPhone. "I dare you to call my dad. Here. You can use my cell."

With that tidbit fresh in my mind, I look Mrs. Perry in the eye. "I look forward to it." Round One: Maggie Griffin.

◆　◆　◆

When I finally get home, Erika is reclining upside down on our couch, reading an edition of *Martha Stewart Weddings*. Her blond head hangs off the armchair, and her legs are tossed carelessly up over the designer hand-stitched pillows she talked me into going halves with her last week. Mr. Kringles, who has draped himself across her tummy, purrs audibly.

"Doesn't that make you dizzy?" I ask, dumping my keys on the Pottery Barn knockoff nesting table. Our apartment, a 1920s brick walkup, is tiny. But what it lacks in square footage it makes up for abundantly in charm. When you enter off the main hallway, you step into our living area, which boasts high ceilings and a modest fireplace. The hardwoods are a rich honey hue, and the old windows, while drafty in winter, let in loads of sunlight. On one side of the living area is a galley kitchen that fits one person comfortably at a time. On the opposite side of the living area is Erika's bedroom, an itsy-bitsy bathroom, and just beyond that the alcove, also known as my room. The tight living quarters have had their challenges, and Erika claims she can't wait to move out to Trent's spacious two-bedroom Brighton apartment at the end of July when they get married. But I disagree; we've made so many memories here. From our first jobs to late-night movie marathons with just us girls, to hosting standing-room-only wine and cheese parties with the few neighbors we could squeeze inside. The thought of moving out makes my heart ache, like I'm saying goodbye to a part of who we were these last poignant years.

Erika holds up her magazine. "Did you know that French birdcages are back in style?" she says dreamily. "Nineteen-twenties chic."

"You're getting a bird?"

"No, dummy. I meant the veil. They're all the rage in bridal couture." Since Erika became engaged she's become a register of bridal facts. Sometimes to the point that I don't think I can bear to listen to another. She sits up and surveys me curiously. "What happened to you, anyway? I've been waiting for you forever."

"Mrs. Perry," I mumble, kicking off my shoes on my way to the kitchen.

"Parents. They're all nuts. Which is why I will never be one."

"You're joking, right?" I pull a glass from the cupboard and fill it with water. It's not atypical of Erika to make shock-value statements. I have a momentary flashback to our elementary-school days when we pushed matching pink strollers, our plastic baby dolls tucked safely inside.

"Not really. People who have kids are certifiable. Look at your sister. She's never been the same." She squeezes past me in the kitchen, takes my water glass, and dumps the remains down the drain. "Ever since Jane started down the family trail, the girl has been lost deep in the woods. And she hasn't come out yet." Erika pulls a bottle of pinot from the fridge and refills my glass. "Here. You look like hell."

"Thanks." She is right about Jane, I have to admit. My sister, older by four years, has remained our measuring stick for all of life's significant milestones. As kids, Erika deeply envied my having a sister, especially an older one. As Erika and I spent our childhood trailing Jane's wake, simultaneously admiring and despising her, Jane's age gap provided us with a wealth of knowledge and experience that we eagerly stowed away. Jane was both smart enough and pretty enough, and not too shabby on the soccer field, which added up to a decent ranking on the popularity scale. Which meant that while she had the metaphorical keys to the car of teenagerism, Erika and I got to stow away in the backseat for the ride. Through Jane we learned how to shave our legs, which new CDs to buy, and how to navigate the halls of high school without standing out too much in either direction. By eighth grade, Erika was practically obsessed with Jane, then a senior, gleaning as much data for our upcoming freshman year as an understudy would to shadow a Broadway star. I still remember several occasions where I retired to my room with a good book, while Erika remained moony-eyed at Jane's vanity table, scrutinizing her expert application of Maybelline mascara in the little green-and-pink tube.

Although we're almost nearly all in our thirties now, nothing has really changed in Jane's role as measuring stick. Though, for Jane, things have changed a lot. Through Jane, we have most recently experienced engagement, marriage, pregnancy, and birth. She lives back home in Mystic, Connecticut, with her husband and three kids. Jane is a stay-at-home mom to Owen, age five; Randall, three; and Lucy, six months. The kids are great, and Jane loves motherhood, but I can't argue Erika's point. My formerly put-together, on-the-ball sister has never been the same since. And it's got nothing to do with looks so much as with the look on her face, an expression that teeters between dazed happiness and faded consciousness, always with a diaper bag and a stroller in tow.

"So what's on for tonight?" Erika asks me.

The wine is settling warmly in my stomach, and if I have another, I will end up on the couch in my sweats with Lifetime TV. Which actually sounds pretty good, because Evan has messaged me to say that unfortunately he has to work late tonight. But I know Erika won't stand for it.

"Trent got us a reservation at the new tapas place on Boylston," Erika says.

"Are you informing me or inviting me?" I tease.

She pours herself a glass and I follow her to the couch. "Peyton and Chad are coming, too. It got great reviews in the *Globe*."

Peyton, Erika, and I have been friends since moving to Boston the summer after graduation. She and Erika met at a Women in Law luncheon, when Erika first joined Cramer and Bosh. But of greater consequence than their shared profession, Peyton Whitmore Adams is a newlywed. Married last spring to Chad Adams, a former varsity crew captain she met at Skidmore, this marks her as highly desirable bridesmaid material, given her recent nuptials. As Erika says, best friends are eternal. But former brides are indispensable. And since she couldn't combine both in me, I've been asked to share my maid of honor duties. I don't take offense to it. Really.

The indispensable newlyweds live in a refurbished bungalow in Cambridge. Their Copley Plaza wedding set the stage for many a late-night rehashing in our apartment. Despite our differences, I like Peyton. She's a straight shooter with a dry sense of humor. And she's got a designer-label wardrobe that I try my best to take notes from, if only through last season's late-night bidding wars on eBay.

"The tapas bar sounds great, but Evan has to work late on set tonight," I remind her. Good as a night out sounds, I am staking out my spot on the couch. As if reading my mind, Mr. Kringles leaps up and joins me.

Erika regards me curiously. "So? You're free."

Lately, I've sort of gone underground in the social department. But not without reason. Spring is my cramming season at school with report cards and curriculum wrap-up. Plus I've been searching, albeit halfheartedly, for a new apartment, none of which seems to match the neighborhood vibe or old-time charm of our own. Let alone its affordability. And then there's Evan. We've been together a year now, and when you're settled comfortably in a long-term relationship, the idea of getting dressed up after a long day at work and dragging yourself into town for what always turns out to be a late night loses some of its appeal.

"I'm pretty beat from work," I tell her, stroking Mr. Kringles behind his ears. "And I've got to get up early tomorrow. I'm driving home for my mom's birthday party, remember?"

Erika slumps into the couch cushions and gazes sadly out the window, a pose that is supposed to inflict guilt. "I was looking forward to all of us getting together. Trent had to pull out all the stops just to get these reservations. And with all the stress of the wedding, I could really use a night out with you. Especially since you're getting away for the weekend."

I give her a level look. "Getting away? A full-blown family reunion is going to be anything but a vacation getaway."

"Besides," Erika continues, "I already touched base with Evan. He's going to try to meet us there after he gets off work." She smiles coyly.

"You got Evan to leave work early?" I throw up my hands. "Okay, okay. I give in. Ceviche night it is."

I grab my glass and head to the fridge. Another glass of pinot is clearly in order.

Two

J ane? Are you there?"

There is a sudden crash, followed by loud barking. Followed by the shrill cry of a baby.

"Jane?" I'd hoped to catch her at a quiet time between the dinner and bedtime rush, but apparently not.

"What on earth? Randall!"

I hold the phone away from my ear. I should be used to this. My sister Jane's three children were born in rapid succession, and since then, any attempt at uninterrupted communication with her has been something akin to navigating a minefield. Add to that a 110-pound Great Pyrenees, a house renovation, and a husband, Toby, who works sixty-hour weeks, and you can begin to piece together the picture.

"Who put crayons in the *dishwasher*?" Jane's voice is not exactly hysterical. Rather, it is what we jokingly refer to as her mommy voice. A high-pitched tone of urgency, followed by long periods of what she calls "wait time," during which the child in question is supposed to respond with honesty and regret, given sufficient time to contemplate the wrongness of his or her doings. I have yet to see it work.

"Sorry," she groans, returning to the phone. "The inside of my new Bosch dishwasher is shellacked in rainbow wax. Toby's going to have a coronary when he gets home.

"Randall?" I ask.

"Who else."

Randall is their second-born, and like most seconds, he is the busiest. Randall doesn't walk. He races from room to room. Likewise, he approaches games and crafts at the same breakneck pace, never slowing to replace the lid to a jar of red paint or the top to the hamster cage. Small disasters erupt in his wake with a regularity that makes him consistent if not careful. But Randall's dimpled smile is just as quick, as is his endearing giggle, and he gives hugs that rival a bear's. In the end, he's pretty hard to resist.

Owen is probably my favorite, even though, just as in teaching, I'm not supposed to have one. He's the eldest, and also the most thoughtful. Since babyhood, Owen has been an observer. He sits contentedly for long periods of time watching the birds in their backyard, or slowly turning the pages of his favorite books. Owen is the one who stacks LEGOs with the precision of a surgeon and who fretfully guards them from demolition whenever Randall is in close proximity. I love how he takes small bites of his cookies, savoring each morsel. In some ways he reminds me of a little old man; careful and courteous, fussing over the lineup of his toy cars, considering the colors of the backyard rocks he collects. But most of all I love him because he is mine; the baby who crawled to me first, who first deemed me "Anny Mags," and the one who still lets me hold him on my lap without wriggling away, even though he is now five.

Jane sounds frazzled. "They just woke up Lucy. So now I'm

trying to nurse while unloading the crayon-covered dishwasher. What's up?"

I've seen her on days like this. I can just picture her placing Lucy in the cupboard and tucking a dish in her nursing bra. "Sorry. Just wanted to do a final check-in before Mom's birthday. Is there anything else I can help with?"

I can hear the clattering of dishes as Jane thinks out loud. "Let's see: the cake is ordered. We've got a baked ham, au gratin potatoes, and a salad if Cousin Ellen remembers to make it. Everyone's coming, as far as I know. All that's left is for you to pick up Aunt Dotty on your way tomorrow."

I groan. "She's coming?" Aunt Dotty is my grandmother's sister. Her percentage of cantankerousness is equal to her age, which is eighty-nine. And she requires restroom stops at least every four highway exits. "Can't you or Dad pick her up?"

"Excuse me. What's that foreign sound on your end?" Jane pauses dramatically to make her point. "Ah! It's the sound of silence. Almost didn't recognize it. Tell you what, how about you come over here and bake a twenty-pound ham, clean the house, decorate, walk the dog, and entertain three kids? I'd be thrilled to drive two hours alone in the car to pick up Aunt Dotty." There is another crash, then the clatter of a pan. "Randall. Please!"

She's got me there. "Okay, okay. Anything else?"

"Yeah. We need to get something for Mom. Something nice."

"You haven't gotten Mom a present yet?"

"Can you not hear what is going on over here?"

It's not worth pushing the subject. "Okay. I can share my gift."

My mother is a consumer-martyr. That affliction, however, does not apply when it comes to treating her daughters: a set of antique silver candlesticks for Jane's last dinner party; an auburn cashmere sweater for my school harvest fair last October. We gladly accept her offerings, which means that when holidays or birthdays arise, we make a sound effort to track down her latest yearning.

Jane pauses. "So, what are you up to tonight?"

And then we are in the danger zone. Jane holds her status as a former Bostonian the way a veteran reveres their purple heart. Like me, she spent her postgraduate years there, working in marketing. She swore she'd never set foot beyond Cambridge. Until she met Toby, a junior associate at a Providence law firm, during a friend's Christmas party back home in Mystic. One year later, she was engaged, back in Mystic, and picking out kitchen subway tiles. Since then, even though I know Jane is happy back home, she can't help but inquire about city life as if it were a former lover. "Got any big plans tonight?" she presses.

What Jane doesn't realize is that as hard as her life is right now, it's exactly what I dream of someday. The husband, the kids, the dog, and the house—even the crayon-covered dishwasher interior—sometimes so badly I can taste it. Which makes it even harder when Jane makes her weekly inquiry about my weekend plans. Because I know she's peering over that proverbial fence at the grass, or in this case city sidewalks, on my side.

"Nothing, really. Erika mentioned something about this new tapas bar on Boylston."

Jane exhales like she's been punched. "Oh. I miss real restaurants."

Erika swears that once an urban dweller gets married and gives birth, crossing the city border is just a matter of time. And the ability to put your finger on the pulse of anything, beyond the suburban throbbing in your temples, is forever lost.

"You've got great restaurants in Mystic," I remind her.

"Mags. I live in the land of lobster rolls."

I keep to myself that living in the land of lobster rolls is precisely what keeps the Mystic Chamber of Commerce thriving.

"I miss ceviche," she adds with a sigh. "Maybe I should drive up for a visit."

Inviting her will only remind her that this is not really a choice within her reach at this time, and I don't want her to spend the rest of her already haggard day regarding her offspring as anchors. However, if I don't ask her to come, she will think I don't want her. That she has somehow lost her edge, and is (in her own words) too old, too fat, or too lame to be seen with us. None of which is true or will ensure a happy ending to our phone call.

I know what will follow next: it is a dance we do each time. A complicated routine in which Jane feels left out and out of touch from her former svelte and fun pre-motherhood self. I will then listen quietly, passing metaphorical tissues of reassurance as she gets misty-eyed for the good old days. During which I will turn the tables, and invite her. This will be followed by a quick rebuttal, as she realizes she hasn't the time or the strength or, let's be honest, the desire to shed the nursing bra for a black push-up and a pair of heels. But the winning ticket is that it's a realization she usually arrives at on her own, as though the choice to dance the night away in a club is still within her realm of possibility. If I can only get her to the end of the phone call without tears. Here we go.

"Tell you what. I'll check the tapas bar out, and if it's half as good as you think, we'll plan a night when you can come into the city."

Jane scoffs. "Yeah, sure. In about six months, when Lucy weans and it's no longer cool."

And so here we are. I choose my words carefully. "Or . . . you could call Toby at work and tell him to come home early. Pump breast milk for Lucy, and leave Toby with a bottle. They're his kids, too, after all. What could possibly go wrong?" It's the last five words that seal the deal.

Jane doesn't miss a beat. "Oh. No. I couldn't. Lucy nurses every four hours, and by the time I got out the door and into the city, Toby would already be down one bottle for her. Plus, Randall is going through this thing at bedtime where he wants both of us to lie down with him. And of course we've got Mom's party tomorrow. No, no, I couldn't possibly. But thanks for asking."

I breathe a sigh of relief. Jane is happily restored to her role of mother, and I am now free to go out with Erika and the guys, guilt-free. If I only had something to wear.

◆　◆　◆

Although it's only May, the evening is mild and there's the fragrant smell of lilac trees as we head out of our neighborhood on foot. I love living in Back Bay. I love that I can walk down

Boylston Street to Fenway Park in the summer, or to bars and restaurants, like we're doing tonight. But I'm also keenly aware that nights like this are coming to an end for me. As is the neighborhood lifestyle I've come to love.

It was Erika's father who, upon hearing that we were both moving to Boston, insisted his little girl reside in a safe, clean area. At first she was incensed—she loved the thought of being downtown in a high-rise. But when we first visited our two-story brick bungalow with its hardwood floors and small corner fireplace on a quiet street, she caved. Mr. Crane foots half our rent, and she and I split the other half. It's the only way I've afforded living here.

Tonight, Bostonians are out in force with the warm weather, and the sidewalk tables are clogged with both students and the mixed after-work crowd of suits and boat shoes. Inside the restaurant we find Peyton and Chad already ensconced in a corner booth with Trent.

"So what can I whet your palate with?" he asks. That's one thing about Trent: he's quick with the drink orders, and just as quick to treat.

"She'll have a vodka tonic, lime twist."

I spin around to face Evan, who is grinning at me. "You made it!"

He pulls me in for a hug and kisses my forehead. "Couldn't miss a night out with my girl." I know Evan is fresh off twelve hours of filming on the set, but he still manages to look crisp in his collared shirt and jeans.

"You didn't have to come," I say, grabbing his hand and pulling him into the booth. But I'm thrilled he did. His schedule has been so busy that I haven't seen him all week. "You must be exhausted."

Evan's acting career always takes people by surprise. It still surprises me. Upon graduation, he told his parents back in New York that he wanted to be an actor. Confused and somewhat dismayed by his sudden announcement, because outside of a small part in a high school production of *Our Town* he had never set foot on a stage, they put on a brave face and did not question when he quit his well-heeled position as a congressional intern in New York and packed a duffel bag for a summer with the Berkshire Theatre Festival. Supporting himself with modeling and catalog work when he could get it, Evan worked three years behind the scenes and eventually onstage at various New England theaters, going on auditions and casting calls in between. After a singular but lucrative stint in an Ivory Soap commercial, Evan got a call-back for a new Boston crime pilot. The rest is recent history. *First Watch* aired its pilot last fall to strong reviews, and Evan snagged one of the main roles as Officer Jack Brady. It's gotten so he's starting to be recognized when we go out. He has struggled to get used to it, and it's something I'm still working on.

"How's life on the set?" Trent asks. "Looks like you missed a spot of blush on your cheek there, buddy." Trent likes to tease Evan relentlessly, especially since his show has been picked up for another season. But it's in that mock-hassling way guys cajole one another, and I know he's just as proud of him as I am.

Evan smiles. "Did you hear that Angela Dune landed the new part?"

The guys burst out in a hoot of approval just as a large bite of *chopitos* gets stuck in my throat.

"You didn't tell me she got it," I manage to choke.

Evan puts a hand on my back. "You okay, honey?"

I force a smile and take a swig of his beer.

But Peyton is on it. "The *Sports Illustrated* model? She acts?" she asks doubtfully.

Chad, the consummate fraternity boy in our group, puts his hand up for a high five. I'm relieved when Evan waves it away.

"She seems cool," he says, casually. "I've only met her once."

Erika is looking at me now, taking the temperature of my end of the table. "So are you in any scenes together?"

They're just actors, I tell myself, running a hand through my hair and sitting up straighter. But this is my question, too.

"Not yet," Evan says. "She's playing the role of a new detective in the department. They've only contracted her for four shows so far."

I take a deep breath and nod appreciatively like this is good news. It's silly. Evan is a professional. Angie Dune is just a swimsuit model. And my food is getting cold.

"Who wants to try the chopitos?" I ask, changing the subject. We spend the evening catching up and sampling tapas. Garlic shrimp, mussels, and chorizo *croquetas*. Jane was right about the ceviche. The drinks are strong and I start to feel a little buzzed, despite my full stomach. But everyone orders another round. Erika tells a funny story about a divorce case she's working on. Though she has divorce clients of both genders, Erika has a penchant for taking the woman's side.

"My new client, a well-known lobbyist I'll call Sandra, heard rumors that her husband was hiding a mistress at their BVI vacation house."

Evan squeezes my hand. "I'd never do that to you."

Erika rolls her eyes and continues. "So Sandra charters a plane hoping to surprise the two in the act, and instead finds this girl sunning herself alone on the pool deck. Topless, no less."

Chad and Trent exchange mock-horrified looks. "Her husband, Dominic, is nowhere to be seen. Rather than confront the girl, Sandra decides to pretend that she thinks the girl is a new housemaid that her husband just hired. Just to mess around with her until the husband returns."

Peyton frowns. "I'd drown the girl in the pool!"

Erika holds up her hands. "Wait, it gets good. So Sandra sashays out to the patio, introduces herself, and tells the girl that she's thrilled Dominic was able to hire new house help. She invites the confused girl into the kitchen and takes out a pineapple and a huge knife. Tells her she's going to make them a little snack and that they can go over the housekeeping schedule. As Sandra's hacking away and the fruit is flying, she tells the mistress how she's been looking for trustworthy, honest help for months. And that the last maid they employed had flirted with Dominic so much that Sandra had to 'take care of her.' Which is all made up, of course, but remember, Sandra's telling this story with a cleaver in hand."

Everyone's jaw drops. "The girl didn't make a run for it?" I ask.

Erika grins. "Too chicken. So, three hours later, the idiot husband arrives home.

And he finds his mistress on her knees scrubbing toilets in the guest quarters, while his wife sips brandy by the pool."

Chad claps his hands. "No way!"

"And that's after she's already bathed both schnauzers and cooked dinner."

"Sandra's got balls," Peyton says admiringly.

"Not her husband. Apparently he was so rattled by the whole scene that he sat down at the dining room table with Sandra and went along with the whole charade. When the mistress brought out their supper, Sandra dumped the tray in his lap, threw a drink in the girl's face, and tossed them both out of the house."

By now everyone's laughing. It's an outrageous story, but as always, Erika's delivery is just as impressive.

The server brings the check, which Trent snatches, despite Evan's quick hand.

It's late but Erika's not tired. "Let's hit some bars," she says.

"I've got an early morning," I remind them, standing. The room is swirling, just a little, and Evan gently pulls me back onto the bench beside him.

"You okay, sailor?"

"She's fine!" Erika insists. "She's just getting started."

As a rule, Erika doesn't quit until we've hit at least three places on a Friday night, and this night is no different.

We hit a club on Commonwealth, and when the rest of our group heads to the dance floor, Evan grabs my hand.

"Come here," he says, pulling me over to a dark corner. "I want you to myself for a minute." He pulls me in for a long kiss, and I feel myself relax into him.

"I've missed you," I tell him above the music.

"I'm sorry. I know these late-night shoots are killer." He tucks my hair gently behind my ear.

"It's okay. I've had a bit of a crazy week myself."

He nods empathetically. "Report card season?"

I'm always struck by Evan's understanding of my profession. While everyone likes to repeat the slogan "Teachers are heroes!" I've never met anyone, beyond my mother, who really means it. Usually people just comment on all that money we make for part-time work (peanuts), all those summer vacations we get (unpaid, and spent tutoring in the local library), and what a cushy job it is (year-round professional development, planning, and grading at home).

Evan shakes his head in admiration. "So what ever happened with that shy student you were telling me about—what was his name, Tim?"

I smile. "Timmy Lafferty."

"The one who writes all those stories?"

"How do you remember all this stuff?"

Evan shrugs. "It's important to you."

I place my hands on either side of Evan's face and kiss him again. Later I will tell him about school and about Timmy. And we'll catch up on our weeks. But right now I want to catch up on us.

For our last stop, we settle into an Irish pub, which is much more my scene than the loud club we thankfully just left. The guys start a game of darts in the corner, and we girls grab a table.

"I can't believe I'm getting married in a matter of weeks," Erika says, pulling up a stool.

We clink our glasses and toast Erika's July wedding, but my

heart isn't quite in it. It might be the late hour, or the long week. Or maybe that nagging feeling that lately everything about our tight little group is suddenly changing.

"One down, one to go," Peyton says. She and Erika clink glasses, once more, grinning slyly.

"Meaning?" I ask.

"Meaning you're next down the aisle." Erika winks at me.

"Oh come on," I say. "Not you guys, too." Why is it that as soon as one girl in a group of friends gets a ring, the starter horn blares? If all of us were still single, we'd be sipping drinks and talking about work and summer rentals with that casual air of those who are well armed in the girlfriends department. It used to be that we were bulletproof. Nothing could penetrate our youthful optimism. Not your inquiring grandmother who squints worriedly at you across the Thanksgiving table, or your mother's remarks about her friend's daughter's tacky wedding dress (the unspoken gripe being that at least there was cause for a tacky dress to be worn). Not even your own self-doubt that finds you on a sleepless night, causing you to wonder if indeed there is "the one," if you're really with "the one," or, God forbid, if you already lost "the one."

I narrow my eyes at Erika, whose arm is draped around Peyton. It wasn't so long ago she was on my side of the table. "You two are insufferable," I tell them. I do want to get married. But being the last of our tight-knit group to do so does make me feel a little bit like an outsider at times.

"Every dog has its day," Erika tells me. She was first to have a boyfriend in the fifth grade, first to be kissed in seventh, and first to have her mom march her into what our mothers called the "training bra" section at Macy's. She leans forward on her elbows and smiles. "Remember when you used to say you were going to marry Cameron Wilder?"

"Who's Cameron?" Peyton wants to know.

Just hearing his name brings back a flood of memories: the smell of pinecones, the frayed flannel shirtsleeves rolled up his tan forearms, the drives along Mystic River in his old Jeep Wrangler. Cameron Wilder was my first love. And yet we shared a relationship as intense as it was long, following me through college and into graduate school. I always thought he would be the one who lasted.

"He was an old boyfriend from home," I say now, counting back the years in my head. "I haven't seen him since he left Mystic for California." It was both our decisions to go to different coasts for graduate school. But it was my decision to call it quits. I've always regretted that I was too stubborn to drive over and say goodbye that last morning.

Peyton smiles nostalgically over her martini glass. "There's something about those hometown boys."

Later that night, back at my apartment, I can't sleep. Erika has gone back to Trent's place, as she does on most weekends. I turn over and press my nose against Evan's back. His breathing is slow and heavy with sleep. It's not the alcohol that's making the lights outside the window spin. It's the list in my head. My mother's surprise birthday party is tomorrow. There are two more weeks of school left, the hardest weeks of the year. Most of all, there is the great countdown for Erika's wedding. It occurs to me that so far my summer consists of living everyone else's lives. My students' lives, my family's lives, and that of my best friend. And though I groan inwardly when I think of all these commitments I have to follow through on, I realize there's one thing bothering me most of all; beyond them, where are my own?

Three

The drive home to Mystic should take the average person about two hours. I picked up Aunt Dotty at eight thirty. It's now eleven. And so far, we've made four bathroom stops since Providence, the last of which I probably could've avoided if I hadn't bought her a coffee at the stop before.

By the time I finally exit I-95 for Mystic, I should be drained. But I brighten the moment we turn toward Mystic Seaport.

Downtown Mystic does it to me each time. I don't know if it's the sea air or the historic clapboard houses that line the streets into the village, but there's something magical, as if you're entering a little storybook town.

On Main Street, I sigh happily at the sight of the shops. The colonial storefronts boast pastel awnings and window boxes, as bright and cheerful as a Lily Pulitzer dress. We slow as we approach the Mystic River Bascule Bridge and Aunt Dot rolls down her window to squint down at the boats. "Oh my, that's a classic," she proclaims, pointing down at a wooden runabout, sporting a little American flag off the back. The sun bounces off the water and I take a grateful breath. We pass Mystic Draw-bridge Ice Cream, Bartleby's Café, and Bank Square Books.

When we turn onto Godfrey Street and pull into my parents' driveway just outside the village, it looks like everyone has arrived. The kids come tearing out and launch themselves at me.

"Aunty Mags!" Owen is the first to reach me, and he wraps his skinny little arms tight around my neck.

"Look at you, little bugger!" Only he isn't so little anymore. He's like an overgrown puppy, all limbs, and I inhale his punky little-boy smell when I kiss his head.

"What'd you bring us?" Randall stands behind him, a serious look on his impish face.

"What do you mean? I brought myself! And Aunt Dot!" I say brightly.

Randall scowls doubtfully past me at Aunt Dot, who's clutching her giant purse like either her or the purse might be in danger.

"Oh," he says gravely. But he allows me to pull him in for a big hug, and he squeals in laughter when I tickle him. Then he's off in a flash.

"Finally. Where have you been?" Jane is standing in the walkway with baby Lucy strapped to her chest in a carrier. Her arms are crossed, in front of Lucy, which gives them both a look of disapproval. "You're lucky. Mom's still at the hairdresser, so you didn't ruin the surprise."

"Hi to you, too," I mumble, kissing Lucy's plush cheek.

"So, what are we giving her?" Jane peeks nosily into the gift bag.

"I got her a wrap. I figured she could wear it on cool summer nights."

"A wrap. Huh."

"What?"

Jane wrinkles her nose. "Material?"

"Pashmina."

"Color?"

"Lilac."

She reaches inside the gift bag. "Ooh. Not bad." She tries to pull it out and I smack her hand. Jane will no doubt be trying it on herself, at some point, should she escape the kids for an evening out.

Jane is dressed in pink capris and a white tunic. Her long curly hair is pulled back in a ponytail, and I'm surprised to notice she's wearing dangly earrings—something she rarely does as mother of three small children with lightning-speed fingers.

"You look great," I tell her, following her up the steps. "Are you working out?"

She beams. "Thanks, and no. I call it the Tunic Mirage."

"Ah. Expanding the wardrobe, I see." Since having kids, Jane has had a tendency to stick to what we've fondly dubbed as "the uniform," our code word for her stay-at-home-mom-of-toddlers fashion. It consists of stretchy gray yoga pants, whose purpose is twofold. Yoga pants give the impression that you have either just come from working out or are about to go work out. And the gray hides all manners of stains. (Black highlights vomit, she once confided.)

"Well, look who's here! Come over here, and let me get a look at you, now." That's the thing about my dad. No matter how long it's been or how old I am, Dad always greets me at the door as if I'm still his little girl. And I kind of turn into her each time.

"Hi, Daddy!" He pulls me into a tight hug and the scent of Old Spice wraps itself reassuringly around me.

My parents' shingled cape house is modest. It's not like the stately brick colonial with the white columns that Erika grew up in, situated on a green knoll along the Mystic River. Ours is nestled in a tight neighborhood alongside similarly appointed homes with front stoops and back porches. Dad finally retired from his career as an engineer for the Naval Submarine Base in New London, just a year after mom wrapped up her job as a nurse in a local pediatrician's office. She says he putters around the house now, and drives her crazy. But their marriage is the kind I hope to have someday—snug and familiar, like a pair of worn lambswool slippers.

Jane returns with a tray of cups, and Lucy, who is still strapped to her chest. "I think Dad could use some help with the coffeemaker."

Dad is wrestling with the stainless steel cappuccino maker that was part of my mom's retirement present from the doctor's office. "No, no, I've got this." We watch as he pushes one illuminated button after the other in rapid succession. But it's Lucy's thrashing that distracts me more.

"Does Lucy like that thing?" I ask Jane, inspecting the sling contraption that Lucy is squished into against her chest.

"It's a Balboa. Haven't you heard of it?"

Well, considering I don't have any babies or any friends with babies, yet, no. "Of course I have. It just make her look so . . ."

"What?"

Slumpy, I think to myself. Lucy's chubby legs dangle out one side and her face peers from a narrow opening on the other, which is lined with a pool of drool. "Adorable," I tell Jane, directing her back to the coffeemaker.

Finally, the coffee is flowing, the food is out, and we've

packed all the guests onto the back porch. Mom's car has just pulled in, but after three false alarms of rushing everyone into hiding, no one is taking this final call too seriously.

But this time the front door opens, and I can see the soft outline of my mother through the screen. "Hello? Don?" Her voice is high and uncertain. There's no getting around the fact that about fifteen cars are parked at a variety of angles in front of her house.

"Out here, honey," my dad hollers back. "Just weeding the flower pots." Never mind the fact that Dad never gardens, or that there are never any weeds in Mom's pristine pots. He's giving it his all.

There's a patter of footsteps. Mom's face gamely appears at the sliding door and we lurch forward in one singsong mob. "*Happy Birthday!*"

She throws her hands up. "My goodness! I had no idea!" Whether she did or not, she's crying, and Jane and I move in to hug her first. "Oh, heavens!" She turns to the group behind us and wags her finger accusingly at Dad. "You! Did you do all this?"

"Guilty," he admits, laughing. And when they embrace, for some reason I want to cry, too.

I spend the afternoon being thrust from one guest to the next, politely answering questions about work and the Red Sox. Which means I have to also listen as my parents' friends tell me about their own kids, who, more often than not, are either married, about to get married, or just popped out their first baby.

"What about you?" Mrs. Banks from next door asks me, while I'm serving birthday cake. "Are you married, Maggie?"

Her eyes are wide and hopeful as she thrusts her paper plate in my direction. I resist the urge to nod at the hungry line behind her. It's backing up.

"I'm in a relationship with a great guy," I say, balancing an unwieldy piece of vanilla cake on the knife.

She frowns. "Engaged?"

I shake my head. "But I'm *happy*," I tell her, unsure of whom I'm trying to reassure more. My nosy cousin Ellen is right behind her, listening in. "Maggie is our picky one," she jokes. Cousin Ellen is, herself, very married. To the tune of five children, all under the age of seven. Despite her oh-so-cheery exterior, Ellen's mood is as sharp as her blond bob that prickles her overblushed cheeks as she speaks. "Picky, picky, picky."

Jane and I have never been big fans of Cousin Ellen. Since childhood she has smugly held it over us that she has always been first. First to drive. First to go to college. First to marry. The Christmas that I announced that I was going to Boston to teach, she was also the first to start a debate at the dinner table. All through the meal she peppered me with questions as to what I thought about women who defied their role in the home and maintained singlehood, putting career above a more traditional lifestyle, which ultimately absolved them of eternal happiness. She regarded me sadly and told Wilson, her eldest, to "give poor Cousin Maggie the last piece of pumpkin pie," because I wasn't used to eating home-cooked meals alone in my urban apartment. I'd been too furious to take a bite.

After which, Jane had dragged me into the foyer and grabbed my chin. "Look at that shit!" Jane nodded over her shoulder as Ellen's boys fought on the kitchen floor, her baby howled in its applesauce-splattered high chair, and her husband scurried off to watch football in the den. "Ignore her, Mags. She'd give her lactating left boob to be the one who is single in the city!"

I try to remember this as Ellen thrusts her empty plate under my nose now. "That's me," I say in a singsong voice. "Picky, picky, picky."

My sarcasm is lost on Mrs. Banks, who's still holding up the dessert line as she studies me with concern. "Well, don't be too picky, dear. If you wait too long, no one will be left."

Cousin Ellen nods sharply. "Except for the gays."

I dump a monstrous piece of cake on Ellen's paper plate.

◆ ◆ ◆

It's almost twilight by the time Mom finds me outside on the porch. Her cheeks are flushed. "Oh, honey, what a day. It's too much."

"You deserve it," I tell her as she settles onto the swinging chair next to me.

"We don't have big gatherings anymore, at least not like we used to when you girls were little. I miss them."

"I remember." It seemed like every summer weekend was spent at a neighborhood barbecue. I'd watch my mom at her dressing table as she put on her colorful Bakelite bracelets and selected a swingy summer dress. Later, we kids would race our bikes up and down the street and dart through neighbors' yards, while the grownups clinked their glasses and citronella wafted across the grass.

As if reading my mind, she adds, "Of course now there's

a new generation to keep up with." She nods at Randall and Owen, who at that moment burst through the door and onto the front porch with us.

Owen climbs onto my lap. "Come to my house for a play-date?" he asks. I nuzzle his head, and suddenly I don't want to be anywhere else. "I would love to come to your house," I tell him. "But I think tonight I'm staying over at Grandma's."

Mom's face brightens. "Really? You can stay? Because all I need to do is put some fresh sheets on your bed. And there's so much food left over, your dad and I can't possibly eat it all by ourselves. Plus all that cake." She leaps up. "Or we could order out for dinner, if you want!" Her face falls. "Wait. What about Aunt Dotty?"

"Mom. Sit." Earlier I'd cornered Cousin Ellen's unsuspecting husband in the dining room with a piece of cake and convinced him to drive Dotty home to Providence. I only wish I could see Ellen's face when Dotty piled into the back of the minivan between the kids. "I already arranged that; Ellen's taking her home."

Mom claps her hands. "We get to keep you overnight!" Her enthusiasm fills me with no small dose of guilt.

Normally I come home for only short visits, often racing back to the city that same day, as if I'm in fear of missing out on something. But tonight it actually feels nice to be away from all that congestion and outside on the porch swing with my mother. Here I don't have to worry about plans for the night. Or what to wear, or how I'm going to afford it. I might drive over to the pier and watch the boats in the harbor. Even just sitting home in my pj's with a slice from Mystic Pizza sounds about perfect.

"Sit here and relax," I tell my mom, pulling her back down onto the seat beside me. "I can make my own bed."

She squeezes my arm hard. "I know, honey. You can do anything you want."

◆　◆　◆

Despite the fact we've been eating all day long, and my parents' fridge is bursting with leftover party food, when the last guest finally clears out, I realize I am starving. I'm not alone.

"Whaddya think? Should we call in a sub?" Dad is hovering beside me as I scour the takeout menu by the kitchen phone.

"But there's so much food!" Mom reminds us both loudly from the living room. "We can't let those finger sandwiches go to waste."

Dad sighs. "We won't, dear. You know how I love cucumber sandwiches." He turns back to me. "Meatball sub, extra cheese," he mouths, pointing to the phone.

I place our order and grab my keys. First, I want to drive downtown. "Back soon," I call.

The sun is low in the sky when I walk along Mystic River park, and aside from a few dog walkers and joggers, I've got the pier to myself. The air is heady with salt, and I tip my face to the last of the evening sun before it slips below the waterline. Out on the water there are a few small boats in the distance, the whir of their engines the background noise to my childhood. I step onto the pier and make my way down to the end, where the water laps against the pier pilings. I've missed this.

Before moving away and becoming what my dad playfully dubs as a "city slicker," I always imagined myself living in a cozy place just like this. Where is that girl who would sit for hours

on the pier with her sketch pad and charcoal pencils? Still rem-
iniscing, I take one last deep breath and turn back for the street.
My heart stops.

Cameron Wilder is walking toward me across the green.
He's wearing a baseball hat, so I can't see his expression beneath
the shaded rim. But it's him, I am sure. The leggy stride, the
squared shoulders. He glances up at the sky, and I know. I would
recognize that mouth anywhere, the way the corners turn up
playfully, as if he's about to laugh. He's not alone. Cameron is
with a young woman. And he's pushing a baby stroller.

I freeze.

The woman flips her long hair over her shoulder and smiles
at something he's just said. Instinctively I make a sharp left off
the pier, fumbling in my pocket for my car keys.

But out of the corner of my eye I see him stop and turn in
my direction. "Maggie?"

There's no getting away now.

We meet in the middle of the green. I'm more than a little relieved when I realize that the girl he's with is none other than his
older sister, Anna. But there's an awkward beat before he lets go
of the stroller and gives me a loose hug. "Wow," he says. "It's you."

"It's me." I pull away and smile back at him, aware of the
strangeness that's filled the space between us. Anna saves us.

"Maggie, so good to see you!" We exchange pleasantries, but
I feel Cameron studying me.

"And who's this little one?" I ask, bending to peek into the
stroller.

A tiny cherubic face gazes up at me, her eyes wide and blue.
She has the longest eyelashes I have ever seen. "This is Emory,"
Cam says, reaching in to touch her cheek. I had heard that Anna

had gotten married and had a baby. "She's beautiful," I tell her. "Jane has three kids of her own, too."

Anna laughs. "Three? Wow. She must be busy."

"That she is," I agree, feeling silly that we're all standing around talking about Jane. Emory begins to fuss, and Anna takes the handles of the stroller.

"Be sure to say hi to your sister for me, okay?" Then she looks at Cam. "I'll take Emory for a little stroll along the water," she tells him, leaving us alone.

Up close Cam looks remarkably the same, though there is a haze to his blue-gray eyes that wasn't there before. And a few more crinkles around his eyes when he smiles. "So how long are you visiting for?" I ask.

"Actually, I moved back here. A couple months ago." He looks directly at me for the first time and I feel a little release in my tummy, the same way I used to when we'd sit shoulder to shoulder on the hood of his Jeep.

Cameron moved back to Mystic? The last I'd heard he was still out in California, having finished graduate school.

"How about you?" he asks.

"I'm only visiting for the weekend. It's my mom's birthday," I say. It's been a long time since we've seen each other, but that balmy August night we parted ways in my driveway surges back. I wonder if he's remembering it, too. He'd tried to kiss me goodbye and I'd turned my cheek. Something I've always regretted. When he doesn't say anything I add, "I'm living up in Boston, now. I teach at a private school."

"That's great." I'm not sure if he's talking about Boston or the teaching part, but he doesn't expand either way. Suddenly I'm aware of my baggy sweats and my droopy ponytail. This is not the way I wanted to look if we met up again. And this is definitely not going as I'd always imagined it would. I have the sudden urge to flee to my car. But something holds me rooted to the ground in front of him.

Until he beats me to it. "Well, I'd better get going." He nods toward his sister and the baby, who are waiting at the edge of the parking lot.

"Yeah, me, too." Unsure of how to say goodbye (I am not going in for another awkward half-hug), I lift one hand.

Cameron looks at my hand, then back at me. The night in my driveway flashes once more. And before I realize what he's doing he clasps it in his own, our fingers entwining. My cheeks flush at the familiar warmth of his grip but I force myself to meet his gaze. I squeeze back. "See you around, Mags." And just as quickly he lets go and turns down the pier.

"See you," I manage. But he's already gone.

Breathless, I hurry to my car. It's only when I'm pulling away that I peek back in my rearview mirror. Cameron is standing beside Anna, bent over the baby stroller. She's the one watching as I drive off. I press my hand to my cheek.

When I get home with the subs I'm not hungry anymore. My parents are in the kitchen, at the table, drinking tea. "Everything okay?" My mother has radar.

I hand the paper takeout bag to my dad. "I just ran into Cameron Wilder."

Mom's expression is one of feigned surprise. "Really?"

I take a deep breath, trying to slow my heart rate. "I had no idea he moved back to Mystic."

My mother stares into her teacup.

"So how is Cameron?" Dad asks brightly. All through high

school and college, Dad refused to take any of the local boys I dated seriously, referring to them dismissively as "the car wash kid" or the "lifeguard guy." But he'd liked Cameron from the start.

I shrug, still flustered by our awkward reunion. "He's fine, I guess. He was down at the pier with his sister, Anna. And her baby." I pause. "Emory, I think her name is."

Mom looks up, an expression of uncertainty on her face. "That's not Anna's baby," she says, finally.

"What do you mean?"

Mom and Dad exchange a look before she answers me. "That baby is Cameron's."

Four

"Miss Griffin, are you okay?"

Molly Ferguson is standing opposite my desk, peering at me through her Tina Fey–style pink glasses. I lift my head from the keyboard of my laptop and rub my eyes.

"Were you sleeping, Miss Griffin?"

"Me? Of course not," I stammer, blowing a wayward clump of hair out of my eyes and jerking upright. I have never fallen asleep in class. Not as a student, and certainly never as a teacher.

"Um, I think you have a keyboard imprint on your face."

"What?" I stand, and grab the small mirror I keep in my desk drawer to confirm that there are no leftover pieces of lunch stuck between my teeth should a parent surprise me. Sure enough, there is a row of red squares marching across my left cheek where I must've rested my face on my laptop. "Oh, God. I mean, gosh."

For the last two nights, I'm lucky if I got a combined seven hours of sleep. I've been waking from fitful dreams about weddings. And Mystic. And, despite my consternation, Cameron Wilder. Who (even though Erika insisted he was just a pang from my past that was sure to fade during a rather late-night

discussion upon my return to Boston) has managed to infil-
trate not only my waking but also my sleeping hours. Even on
laptops.

"It's okay," Molly whispers, as I struggle to compose myself now. "Once Danny Phillips fell asleep during my movie
theater birthday party, and he drooled on himself. We took
a picture." She examines my face carefully. "Doesn't look like
you drooled."

Soothing reassurance from a nine-year-old.

"I wasn't sleeping," I insist, though I can tell she isn't buying
it. "I was just listening to my computer. It was making this weird
humming sound."

"Uh-huh." She doesn't blink. "Here's my essay. The timer
went off five minutes ago. Just so you know."

"The timer!" I fly out from behind my desk. "Boys and girls,
pencils down!" Half the class is reading silently, and they look
up at me over their books as though I've kept them waiting.
Which I apparently have. The other half is still scribbling madly
in their mastery test workbooks, pretending they didn't hear
me. I was supposed to end the writing prompt five minutes ago.
I glance at the clock; make it ten.

"Isn't this supposed to be a timed test?" Wrenn Bailey is
studying me like I'm interviewing for a job, and poorly at that.
Wrenn is one of those students who feels the need to give me
constant feedback, and he keeps regular tabs on my management skills, forever reminding me that it's past lunchtime. That
the missing math books I'm looking for are on my desk, exactly
where I left them. And that his father does long division a different way. Now he crosses his arms, awaiting my reply.

"Yes, Wrenn. That is correct. I noticed that many of you were a little behind, and therefore decided to add some extra time so that you could all finish."

He blinks. "Then what's the point of it being a timed prompt?"

I try not to glare at him as I whisk the prompt off his desk, which I already know, while void of any personality or hint of creative expression, will be grammatically flawless. Wrenn is a rule follower. He approaches my assignments, like most things, with suspicious calculation. In his world there is only one right answer, and only one acceptable way to arrive at it. Poetry baffles him. Music causes him to twitch. He will probably make a fine IRS auditor some day.

Then I remember Timmy Lafferty. Timmy is hunched over his closed journal, still wiping the sleep from his eyes. "Will you come speak to me for a moment?" He trudges over, eyes darting back to his desk as if he'd rather be there.

"Are you feeling okay today?"

He clears his throat. "Yes."

I motion for him to come closer. "I read your narrative last night," I whisper. "The one about the sorcerer and the magic owl?" Timmy is the kind of kid who trots quietly along in the middle of the pack. One of those shy gems that you might otherwise overlook, until you give him some creative license, like with the writing assignment the kids handed in yesterday.

His eyes widen. "Was it any good?"

I shake my head. "No. Not good. It was great!"

Timmy smiles so wide I could count each of his orthodontic brackets.

"I think you should enter this in the writer's workshop contest. Have you thought about that?"

Timmy's lips zip closed again. "I don't know."

The writer's workshop is an annual writing celebration hosted by Darby's board of directors. Local authors come in to work with small groups of specially selected students. It's my favorite school event of the year.

"I think you'd really enjoy meeting other authors like yourself," I say.

He smiles just a little at that. "Okay. I'll ask my mom."

Timmy is the exact kind of kid the workshop is made for—talented kids who need a boost of confidence. There's a scuffle in the back row, and I'm suddenly reminded of those who don't need a dose of confidence. "Horatio. Can I help you with something?"

Horatio is rifling through a backpack that I know for a fact is not his. This one is a tattered blue L.L.Bean. His is a monogrammed leather messenger bag that I, myself, would frankly kill for.

Behind Horatio, Brad King chews his bottom lip nervously.

"Nope. I'm good." Horatio continues to rummage through Brad's bag.

I go to his desk and place my hand on the bag gently. This gesture would cause any one of my other twenty students to surrender the bag wordlessly. But Horatio grips it tighter.

"Yo. Let go my bag."

Nice slang touch for Plymouth County. "This is not your bag," I remind him.

"So?" Horatio glares sideways at me from beneath his floppy bangs that are cut to look hip, but in my opinion only serve to make him look more sneaky. There is a collective intake of breath behind me. This is the utmost test of any teacher. Forget parents or curriculum or state standardized testing. Classroom management is number one. If a student picks at the threads of its fabric, you have to mend it. Fast.

I try again in a calm but firm tone. "Horatio. Let. Go. Of. The. Bag." I stare back at him, feeling my chest begin to pound. "Now."

Horatio thrusts the bag in my direction, and pauses for a menacing beat. Then, as if on cue, his face crumples. "Ow! You hurt me!"

The class gasps. Brad King looks at me in horror.

"What?" How could this have happened? I look down at his hand and try to examine it.

"Ow! Don't touch me!" Horatio clutches his finger protectively against his chest and leaps from his seat as if he's been struck by a bolt of lightning.

"Horatio, please. Show me your finger. Did you get it stuck in the bag somehow?"

"I'm bleeding!" He holds up his right index finger, which is covered in red. My knees buckle. I do not do blood.

"Anna Beth, get the nurse!" I cry.

I reach for Horatio's hand, trying to stave off the tide of nausea that is sweeping over me. The boy is bleeding. And he's screaming that I did it. "Let me look," I plead.

But Horatio reels away from me. "No! Don't hurt me again!"

I can sense the other kids starting to panic. There is no way I hurt him. Is there? The whole class is on its feet as Horatio jerks and spins, clutching his bloody hand. He won't let me near him, but maybe that's for the best. I think I'm about to faint. As I envision Horatio being whisked away in an ambulance another thought strikes me: my teaching career is over.

Behind me Wrenn Bailey makes a strangled sound. What now? I spin around. Is he laughing?

Suddenly I notice other kids also straining to contain their amusement.

"Class, be quiet!" I shush them. Can't they see this is a crisis?

But as wrong as this whole scenario is, something else isn't right. I turn back to Horatio, who is now clutching his left hand to his chest. And then to Brad King's desk, where his snack of carrot sticks sits beside a little container of something red.

"Brad, is that . . . ?

Brad nods. "Ketchup."

"Ha! Got you!" Horatio pumps his stained hand in triumph.

Now my temper is the only thing pounding. If I were any less of a professional I would yank his finger off for real. "Horatio!" I hiss. "In the hallway!"

Horatio bends over in laughter and staggers to the door, where he turns and takes a dramatic bow to the room. Though a few nervous giggles escape the class, one look from me and no one dares applaud.

In the hall we are met by a flushed-faced Anna Beth and the school nurse, followed by Dean Hartman, who happens to be coming up the hall from the other direction.

"Where's the injured student?" Mrs. Raines, the school nurse asks.

Unable to speak, I point at Horatio.

She frowns and does a complete inspection of both hands, while Horatio gamely cooperates. "What is this?" Mrs. Raines asks.

"Ketchup," I say between my teeth.

Horatio pops his red finger in his mouth and licks it clean.

"What's going on?" John Hartman pulls up alongside us, his usual good-morning smile faltering.

"Horatio has played a prank on the class," I inform him. "He pretended to be bleeding and covered his finger in ketchup."

Horatio doesn't miss a beat. "It was just a joke," he says. "Miss Griffin is always so grumpy in the morning, I was just trying to lighten the mood."

Mrs. Raines shakes her head in disgust. "Well. I'll leave this to your teacher." I can't tell if she's disgusted by my inability to control my student or by what Horatio did.

John looks from Horatio to me. "Would you like me to speak to Horatio?" he asks, calmly.

Speak to Horatio? I'd like him to take Horatio outside and pull him up the flagpole by his underpants. I nod brusquely.

"This was not an innocent prank," I say. "Horatio accused me of injuring him. And he scared the entire class." I refuse to admit in front of him that he scared me, too.

"I see. Well, why don't we have a talk, Horatio?" John motions for Horatio to follow, and they head down the hall.

"That was so not funny. Horatio's going to really get it," Anna Beth whispers.

I'd forgotten she was still there. I motion her back inside, where the kids pop back to attention and pretend to be writing in their journals. "Okay, class. Casualty averted. Take out your science logs, and meet me at the crayfish tank."

As I watch the group settle down I agree with half of what Anna Beth said. Horatio *should* get it, this time. But the sad truth is, I know he probably won't.

◆ ◆ ◆

At lunch, I stop by the office to check my staff mailbox. Sharon comes in behind me. Have you two heard the news?" Mrs. Coates asks us both.

The news is a yellow piece of paper in every box announcing a budget cut from the board of directors. "What does this mean?" Sharon asks, holding it up.

Mrs. Coates glances nervously at Dean Hartman's closed door. "We don't know for sure yet," she whispers. "But it looks like they're cutting a teaching position. Or two."

Sharon and I exchange a look. "It's not art again, is it?" I ask. Every budget year, it seems that the art and music programs are first to end up on the chopping block.

"Enrollment is down," Mrs. Coates says. "It could be any of us."

I hold my breath. Staff cuts are made by longevity. The kindergarten teacher, Melinda, is our most recent hire. But I'm next after her.

Sharon looks at me. "Don't worry! They say this every year to stir up donations."

Mrs. Coates shakes her head. "I hate budget season," she whispers.

Five

"*ongratulations! You are the highest bidder.*" The six best words a girl can hear after staying up late on a school night to monitor an auction on eBay. The bid in question cost me one hundred fifty dollars, a hit my bank account can't really afford with rent due this week. But—I scored a sleek pair of patent Manolo Blahniks, the soles barely scuffed. A girl on a private-school income has to make it work. I don't think of them as pre-owned. Certainly not used. Rather, I like to refer to them as new-to-me! Best of all, they'll arrive just in time for the Darby Day School spring gala, which is this Saturday.

"I won them!" I shriek to Erika, from my alcove.

"Congrats," she calls back. I find her kneeling on the living room floor, looking through a box of old pictures. She holds up two five-by-seven photos from high school. "What do you think? Should I include this graduation shot, or this one of the party afterward?" Erika is determined to make a photo board for the wedding reception that charts her and Trent's early lives and culminates in their union. She's spent hours organizing piles. So far her pile is significantly larger than Trent's.

Across the carpet her entire childhood is spread out, and

mine right along with it. Birthday parties, Girl Scout camp. Her dog, Blue. I reach for the two pictures she's holding up.

"God, look how young we were."

The first is a group shot of us in our caps and gowns. There're Jenny Potter and Alice Holmes on either side of us. And right in the center are Erika and me. Erika's hair is long and blond, and neatly curled bangs peek out from beneath her graduation cap. I'm beside her, my dark hair permed beyond recognition into incongruous ringlets that are both ridiculous and impressive for someone with such stick-straight hair. "Why did I ever do that to my hair?"

Erika smiles. "It took like three boxes of perm treatment from the pharmacy. Remember? My mother's kitchen stunk for days."

I wrinkle my nose at the pungent memory. Erika had her hair done in the salon, but had insisted one particularly uneventful rainy Saturday afternoon that she could do the same thing for me. My mother had warned me that my hair was too fine, and that the chemicals would be too harsh. But we knew better. Erika's mom, who was all about beauty and less about rules, did not think to check with my mom first. Nor did she question the mini-parlor we set up in her pink-tiled kitchen. She sat at the table drinking red wine and chatting about school friends as she watched us, never thinking to intervene after the first two treatments produced barely a kink in my stubbornly straight locks. By the third, I was a brunette version of Goldilocks. Unfortunately my hair was fried. It all broke off just below my ears about a week after graduation, leaving me with no choice but a sheered bob cut just in time for freshman orientation at college.

"I like the party picture better," Erika says. "We look tan in that one." As though our darker complexions overshadowed the giant red plastic cups of beer in our hands.

"Not sure that's one for the wedding board," I say, pointing this fact out.

"But I'm scanning them all in black-and-white," she insists.

"In which case you only lose your tan. The giant plastic beer cup will still look like a giant plastic beer cup."

"Huh." She shrugs. "I'll find another."

Lured by memory lane, I set aside my laptop and join her on the rug. There are pictures of middle school, where we are awkward and angular. "Ech," she says, glancing over my shoulder. "The ugly years." Though, as usual, Erika looks adorable. Her ski-slope nose and giant white smile pop out more than any tiny blemish she may have had, while my own face is dotted with early acne and my teeth obliterated by the glare of silver braces. Erika's slight frame looked petite, while my own is entirely geometric in its angles. It seemed like years before I developed even the hint of curves, though Jane assured me thirteen would be my year. Up until then, Erika and I used to sneak into Jane's room and rummage around her underwear drawer to sneak a peek at her bras. Giggling, we'd hold one up against our shirts and dance around her bedroom. It was an object of mystery and allure, a representation of things we had to look forward to.

"Find one where we look cute," Erika tells me, handing me a pile from that painful and innocent era.

"Please. You always looked cute."

"Did not," she insists, though there is a small knowing smile on her face. She can't help it.

I hand her another photo. "Evidence A. The Middle School Pep Rally. Who is the girl with the blond ponytail and the pom-poms?" Erika squeals when I hand her the photo.

"I begged you to join the squad," she reminds me, as though that was the only thing standing between me and certain popularity.

"Not my thing."

"You saved yourself for the spelling bee. And the science fair." She holds up a picture of me with the eighth-grade science trophy. And no small amount of silver reflecting from my uncertain smile.

"Okay, okay," I say, plucking the photo from her grip. We both go quiet, looking through the pile of memories between us. A wave of nostalgia pours over me, along with a pang of the old uncertainty and awkwardness I used to feel.

"I was so jealous of you," Erika whispers suddenly.

I look up. "What?"

Her large blue eyes are bright. "Oh, come on, don't pretend you don't know."

"I honestly don't."

She smiles softly. "You were always so sure of yourself, Mags. You're the one who got the good grades. Who went to the good college. You were always the voice of reason to my crazy ideas."

I shake my head, listening in disbelief. "Erika, you're just as smart as me." What Erika may have lacked in a couple of IQ points she more than compensated for in ambition. And social prowess. "Look at you! You went to law school. You're an attorney in a Boston firm, for God's sake. And about to marry someone who thinks the world of you."

Erika nods her blond head solemnly. "I know. And I want all that. It's just that sometimes things seem to be moving faster than I thought they would." She sits back and sighs. "Trent's mother is hinting about grandchildren again."

I have heard this with my own two ears. Trent is Trent Everett Mitchell III. His father, Trent II, is always referring to family whenever I see him at events. The family business. The seaside family "cottage" in Wellfleet. The family foundation that Trent's grandmother started to bring art into the lives of inner-city kids. The Mitchell family name is an old New England one, in both their history and their holdings.

Erika smiles sadly. "Sometimes I just wish we could slow down and hold on to a moment, you know?"

I do know.

But I also know this hesitation is more about Erika pulling overtime at her firm. The jerky male partners continually dump photocopying assignments on her desk or call her in on weekends when there's a big case to research, while they play golf. But even with all that, I have no doubt she'll work her way up to an associate someday, even if, for the moment, it means she copies transcripts for client meetings instead of leading them.

I take a deep breath. "I'm worried, too. I'm worried that you guys are all moving on with your lives. And here I am, looking for yet another studio apartment. And maybe a new job."

She looks at me sympathetically. "That school would be crazy to let you go. But even if they did, we have all summer to find you another one." I love that she said "we."

She pauses. "As far as the apartment goes, have you and Evan talked about maybe moving in together?"

I shake my head. It is something I've wondered about. But it's his first year on the new show, and he's been so stressed with the irregular hours. Instead of feeling closer, lately I almost feel as if we've been drifting apart. "I want to. But then I think it's too soon."

"Talk to him about it. Who knows, maybe he's thinking the same thing."

"Maybe." I don't add that I have no idea what he's thinking lately, with our opposite schedules.

"He may surprise you." She reaches for another photo and holds it up. "Look at this one. Senior party at the Seaport."

I grab the picture. "What were we, sophomores?"

"I know I drove you crazy back then, dragging you to all those parties."

"I wouldn't have gotten into them without you," I tell her.

"And you were the one who made me take honors art in high school, even though it was the only honors class I could get into."

We look at each other for a beat before tears prick our eyes.

"We've made a lot of memories at home and here. No matter what happens this year, we're going to be all right," Erika says, scraping the pictures quickly into a pile. She holds up her pinky finger between us, the very gesture we have made together since third grade. "Promise?"

"Promise," I say. I lock my pinky finger around hers.

Later, Erika says good night and takes the box of photos to her room. She doesn't know that there's one last picture I've held onto. Before bed, I prop it up against a pile of books on my bedside table. Cam and I are sitting at a campfire the night of our high school graduation party.

Behind us the Mystic River glows orange beneath the sunset. I'm grinning at the camera, probably having been ordered to do so by Erika. But Cam's not. Young and earnest, his gaze is as intense as his smile. I've never noticed it before: he's staring right at me.

Even though it's getting late, I pick up the phone. Jane picks up on the first rings. "Did you know that Cameron Wilder moved back to Mystic? And that he has a baby?"

Jane yawns. "Slow down. What are you talking about?"

"Well, Mom certainly did. Of all the trivial local news Mom douses me with each time I call home, don't you think this little tidbit is something she might have remembered to tell me?"

"Well, I had no idea, I swear." Jane is quick to thrust her innocence into the conversation. "Maybe Mom didn't want to upset you."

"Upset me? Why would she think this would upset me?" Jane scoffs.

"Fine. Maybe I sound upset, but I'm really just surprised."

"Well, whatever you choose to call it, why does it matter where Cameron lives or what he's doing? I mean, we've all gone our own ways, right?"

I hate when Jane forgets what it's like for the rest of us on the other side of the picket fence. "It's different for you, Jane. You're married, living in the suburbs, with a family."

"Isn't Cameron allowed to do the same?"

"That's the thing. There is no 'family,' just him and his daughter. The mother isn't in the picture." News that, when my mother finally told me, simultaneously intrigued and saddened me.

I guess I never let go of the hope that one day Cameron and I would run into each other again. It didn't matter how. Our gazes would collide across the picnic tables at Abbot's. Or we'd bump into each other at Mystic Market: there'd be a bottle of wine tucked under my arm—he'd have just picked up a wedge of good Brie. It would just make sense, of course, that we'd then have to share them by the harbor and reminisce about old times. Never once did it occur to me that our greatest obstacle would be an unwieldy pink baby stroller parked between us.

Jane sighs into the phone. "That's rough, but isn't it a good thing that he's brought his baby back home and is making a new life?"

"It's not that."

"Then what exactly?"

And though Jane's response to my bewilderment is no different than Erika's or my mother's, I'm finally beginning to realize just why all of it bothers me so much. It's not just that Cameron has a baby. It's that if I ever did imagine him having a baby, I always thought he'd have a baby with me.

An hour after turning out my light, I sit up in bed. Before I can change my mind, I'm dialing his old phone number.

But as soon as it rings, I'm seized by a thought: what if I wake up his parents? Followed by a worse thought: What if the phone wakes up baby Emory? But it's too late.

"Hello?" Cam's voice is throaty with sleep, but at once both comforting and familiar.

"Cam? It's me. Maggie."

There's a pause. I rush to fill the silence, suddenly feeling the need to explain myself. "Did I wake you?" I picture him glancing at the clock and a rush of embarrassment fills me. "I'm sorry to call so late. Look, why don't I call back in the morning?"

I'm about to hang up when Cam clears his throat. "Hang on a second."

So I do, my heart in my throat. I shouldn't have called. Not at this hour. Not at all.

"Griff." He's the only one who's ever called me that.

"Yeah?"

"I'd hoped it was you."

Six

Friday morning is a particularly steamy one for this early in June, and the crustacean tank positively reeks. The kids are rowdy and distracted. And I've got to figure out what to wear to the annual Darby Gala tomorrow night. But, even though a week has passed, my mind still wanders back to Mystic every time I recall my phone call with Cam.

As soon as Cam said he'd been hoping it was me, all my qualms were stilled. I did not consider that I might be infringing on Cam's privacy. Nor did I consider the years between us that had led us in such drastically different directions. Instead, we were right back at the Sea View Snack Bar in Mystic sitting on the hood of his Jeep Wrangler with a tray of fried clams.

"It was a shock to bump into you at the pier," Cam said. It seemed both an explanation and an apology for his strained silence of that first afternoon.

"For me, too. Which is why I called," I admitted.

Talking to Cam had always been easy. I was relieved to find it was still the same. "So what's new? Tell me everything," he said.

"I'm teaching," I told him.

"That doesn't surprise me. You were such a natural all those summers at camp," he said, then added, "Lucky kids. I bet they love you."

"Here's something you'll love: I have a tank full of crayfish in my classroom."

He laughed. "No way! That's right up my alley. Marine biology in the flesh."

He asked me how I liked Boston, and teased me relentlessly about "converting" to the Red Sox. He'd always been a die-hard Yankee fan.

I asked him if he'd surfed in California, like he used to in Narragansett Bay. Many of our college summer mornings I'd rise before the sun did and drive with him up the coast, a canister of coffee and a tide chart the only things between us. I could easily picture Cam living out on the West Coast. His easy nature around people, his tousled hair on a windy day at the beach as he assessed the surf. It fit.

"So how'd you end up back at home?" I asked, finally.

Cam hesitated. "Yeah, I guess you would wonder about that: I went out west to get my master's in marine biology. And I came home with a baby."

Despite our shared laugh, there was nothing light about it. I listened quietly as Cam filled in the missing pieces to the picture of the boy I used to know.

"I met Lauren in grad school." If calling him could have been blamed on the buzz of summer memories, then hearing him say her name sobered me right up. "We sort of fell in together at the university: same friends, same major, same classes. We surfed on weekends, camped in the San Gabriel Mountains. Things were really good. We even talked about a future."

"Did one of you have a change of heart?" I wasn't sure how

else to ask how a mother could let both her baby and the father of her only child walk out of her life. Or maybe she'd walked out on theirs. It was the question I needed answered to understand Cam's new life.

"It happened over Christmas break, our last year in grad school. We'd both applied for internships up in Alaska, and we were waiting to hear back. Our futures were on the same track and we were almost done with the program. So when Lauren came to me one morning and told me she was pregnant, I figured we could handle it."

I thought about this. Cam loved kids. It sounded like he loved Lauren. He'd do the right thing, without missing a beat.

"What changed?"

"Up until then, Lauren never sat still; she was always the first one up for a beach run in the morning, the first to hit the books or throw together a last-minute dinner party with friends. But suddenly she was sick all the time. And exhausted. It was excruciating for her to finish out that last semester and take exams."

I recalled feeling like I was barely getting through my own grad studies at BC, as it was. "It must've been tough on you guys."

"It was more than that. Lauren ended up getting the Alaska internship. But I didn't."

"Oh, Cam."

"Shortly after, I got an offer at UCLA. It wasn't Alaska, but it included family housing and it was offered to both of us. That made the decision for us."

It was an impossible situation. "What other choice did you have?"

Cam sighed into the phone. "You know, she never questioned it once. She actually congratulated me. But I remember finding her Alaska acceptance letter in the recycling bin a few days later. At first I didn't know what it was. She'd torn it to so many pieces, Maggie. Hundreds of tiny white pieces. Just scattered. Like wishes." His voice dropped away.

I closed my eyes, feeling suddenly sorry for the girl I'd been silently reproaching.

"We graduated, she gave birth to Emory, and soon after our friends took off to follow their careers. Yet there we were stuck in faculty housing, struggling to live off our stipends, with a colicky newborn. After one particularly rough night with Emory, I remember Lauren standing at the kitchen sink while I was getting ready for work. She was just staring out the window, and she said that she felt like her life was over, while mine was just beginning."

"I'm so sorry, Cam." My mind wandered to Jane's own struggles after having Lucy, and that had been in the best of circumstances.

Cam let out a long breath, and I pictured him running his hand through his hair, something he used to do when worrying. "Emory was only eight weeks old when Lauren told me she was going to visit her parents for the weekend. Alone. She said she was exhausted, and she asked if I could handle the baby for the weekend. I was a little surprised, but she'd been so down, and I figured it'd do her some good." He paused. "Two days later she called. From Alaska."

I couldn't think of a single thing to say. So it was true. She'd been the one to leave.

"But we're good now. Emory and I came back here, and I've got my business going. Most important, I've got my girl."

My eyes filled. "That you do," I told him emphatically. In the background, I heard a little chirp. A sweet, gurgly "Ah, ah, ah" filled my ear. I pictured Cam bending over Emory's crib.

"Hold on," he told me. "I've got to get her bottle." As I listened, I got the sense that I was peering into the privacy of their late-night ritual. Now there were three of us on the line.

I let Cam go, telling him that I'd better be getting to bed. Knowing that Emory needed him, even though I wanted nothing more than to keep talking.

"Listen, Mags," he'd said before we hung up, "it was good catching up with you tonight."

"You, too," I said, sorry that I had to let him go. Suddenly sorry that I was hours away in Boston. But when I replaced the phone on my bedside table, I knew that our larger conversation was just beginning.

◆ ◆ ◆

Now, standing in the overheated teacher's lounge, Mystic seems a thousand miles away. Especially when I see that there's already a long line at the photocopier. I grab a water from the fridge and sit down. Sharon comes in and plops down next to me. "Have you decided what you're wearing to the Gala tomorrow night?"

My mind ticks through my apartment closet. These events are always a bit of a tightrope. Many of the parents get roaring drunk, and compete shamelessly to outbid one another at the auction, making for plenty of Monday-morning faculty room gossip. But for us teachers it's a work function.

"Probably a boring little black dress," I say, wondering what my eBay Blahniks would look best with. "What about you?"

She sighs and pats her belly. "Thanks to this baby, nothing

with the word 'little' in front of it." Sharon leans closer. "So, are you bringing Evan?"

I wink. "Maybe."

I've purposely remained vague about Evan at school. The faculty room lunch table is somewhat sacred ground. It is a place where veteran teachers announce first grandchildren with the same enthusiasm they soon after announce retirements. Where younger teachers debut engagement rings. And where more than a few have disclosed divorce or loss.

Throughout my time here, we have debated everything from the merits of best teaching practices, to politics, to what everyone *really* thinks about the PTA president. Everything is fodder for examination. Which is why, as a single girl of a certain age, I'm prudent about what to lay on the table. I'm no fool; I know that the social committee members have been studying me for some time. I have felt the weight of their sympathetic glances when two of the new hirees brandished engagement rings this spring. The veteran teachers are my "other mothers": well-meaning alpha leaders whose expectations are both sweet and hugely suffocating. Which is why I have kept Evan largely to myself when within these school walls, rather than risk inciting the social chairperson to whip out the bridal shower decorations.

"He's a sport for subjecting himself to this crew," Sharon whispers, just before I elbow her gently. Janice Lavender, the librarian, has tilted a curious ear in our direction.

◆ ◆ ◆

By Saturday evening, when our cab pulls up at the Plaza, none of this is concerning me. The night is warm, my dress is sleek, and we've already had a glass of champagne at my place. Evan leaps out and holds the door. Walking into the Plaza, I feel very much like we're in some kind of storybook ball. As we step through the double doors into the Oval Room, Evan stops to look up at the muted mural of sky and cloud on the ceiling.

"I know," I whisper, taking his hand, and leading him across the dance floor. "I felt the same way at my first Darby Gala."

Evan lets out a low whistle. "Makes you wonder if the school would've made more money by just donating whatever it cost to reserve this place."

"Wait until you see the auction list." One of the school secretaries had whispered that it included a weekend stay at Sting's London flat and a ten-day stint on a yacht in St. Barts.

We get drinks and mingle. My colleagues and friends surround us, their inquisitiveness heightened by the pre-dinner cocktails. But Evan handles it all good-naturedly, and the late nights without him these past few weeks begin to slip away.

"You guys aren't at my table," Sharon groans in my ear.

I scan the seating to see which parents we're assigned to sit by. On the one hand, we are professionals handling the most valuable asset in these peoples' lives: their kids. Hour for hour, we log more time with their own children than they do. We hear personal anecdotes, sometimes involving shower curtains or curse words, that they probably would prefer we did not. We hold their children's hands, whether it be through a divorce or a deceased hamster. We cheer for them to write that first sentence as hard as we do to stand up to a bully in the hallway. Most of us love these kids with a genuineness that would cause us to place ourselves between their child and imminent danger without a second thought; we've seen it evidenced on the news too much in recent years. But even among the most reasonable parents and most competent teachers, there's nothing like a social function, fraught with alcohol and high heels, to bring all the cream to the top, whether it be whipped or spoiled.

While I look longingly over at Sharon and her husband seated in the southern sphere of the room, Evan wastes no time in introducing himself around our table. There are the Curtises, seated to the left of us; I teach their son, Will, who is a bright, sweet kid. Next to them is David Artrek, with a suspiciously young date, whose son is a fourth-grade piano prodigy. Across from us are the Merrills, who both work in Boston's theater district, he as a playwright, and she as a producer. It's a lively bunch, and they seem to have started early on the drink orders. I'm grateful that Marion Tolles, our art teacher, is also seated with us. She winks at me when David Artrek's date asks our server for a chocolate milk.

"So, what kind of work are you in?" Glen Curtis asks Evan.

"I'm working on a new crime show for NBC. Maybe you've heard of it? *First Watch*."

"An actor," David says, appraising Evan over the top of his wineglass. His chocolate-milk-drinking date pipes up, "Like, seriously?"

David Artrek frowns but recovers quickly. "I think I just read something about that show in the *Globe*," he says.

David's date has still not recovered, however. "Wait. You mean the one with Angela Dune?" she shrieks.

"Yes, we work together," Evan says, with a smile. "Angie's great."

She elbows David. "He calls her Angie. Did you hear that, David?" A fact that I, too, make mental note of.

I listen intently as Evan responds to the onslaught of questions that follow. The Merrills want to know about the show's director. And Marion has questions about his character. They're still firing away when the salad course is removed, and despite the fact his plate has not been touched, Evan answers each question politely, which only endears him to me more. Later, I slip my hand on Evan's knee and give it a squeeze. "Am I doing okay?" he whispers.

I kiss his cheek, not caring anymore what parents may say. "You are great. Period."

Sated with dinner and drinks, the guests spill onto the ballroom floor for dancing. I notice that the clipboards on the silent auction tables are filling up, and I'm happy. I only wish I had that kind of cash to bid.

Evan returns from the bar with two gin and tonics. "Sorry that took so long. I had to check on an auction item," he says.

"You're my guest, you don't need to bid on anything. Besides, these things go for crazy amounts."

"Yeah, I'm sorry to say I couldn't quite swing the Bali getaway."

I laugh. "What's that one up to?"

Evan smirks, pulling me onto the dance floor. "Not much. Just eleven grand."

We dance for a few songs until the music fades, and a parent I recognize as the head of the fund-raising committee, Bitsy Whitmore, approaches the podium in the front of the room. She sweeps her hair back and raises a glass of champagne.

"Ladies and gentlemen, please join us for my favorite portion of our evening. The live auction of classroom items is about to begin!"

This portion of the night makes my stomach churn. As enticing as the silent auction prizes are, it's always the crafty classroom items that garner the highest bids. It's amazing what parents will pay for something that their children made. Enhanced greatly by the added competition with fellow parent bidders. And martinis.

Sharon finds us standing in the back of the crowd. "This should be good. My bookshelf isn't even finished."

"What do you mean? Your bookshelf looks great," I tell her.

"Well, they better not turn it around to the backside. We forgot to paint it!"

I chuckle. Poor Sharon. The larger her belly grows, the smaller her ability to focus seems to become. "No one will notice."

She gives me a look. "Did you forget what happened last week?"

I cringe. Last week Sharon sent the much-anticipated end-of-year reading assessments home with the wrong students. Scores, and all. Needless to say, that did not go unnoticed. "Look at it this way. At least the bookshelf isn't filled with classified information."

◆　◆　◆

The crowd presses tightly around the stage to get a better look. This year the second graders built birdhouses, which dazzle in a palette of rainbow colors. The third graders decorated a set of Adirondack chairs, which are clearly hand-painted. Complete with swirls, brushstrokes, and fingerprints, the overall effect is both amateur and adorable.

I have to say, biased or not, our fourth-graders' Harry Potter–themed bookshelves look pretty impressive. The largest items on the stage, they wow in both size and color. Like Sharon, I'm dismayed to see a small bald spot in the corner of my shelf that somehow got overlooked. But I'm glad that I took the extra time to help the kids outline the characters in black permanent marker to make them stand out. Even from where I'm standing, Hedwig the Owl practically pops!

John Hartman finds us in the crowd. "Well done, ladies. Everything looks great this year. Should bring in some interesting bids."

We all clap as the kindergarten mural of five-year-old-sized handprints goes for twenty-five hundred dollars. The next two classes sell quickly, the bids falling just short of the kindergarten's amount. I wink at Sharon. In spite of ourselves, each team of teachers revels in the rivalry and hopes that their students' work goes for the highest bid of the night. It's one of the few times we get competitive. We can't let the kindergarten win again.

"Which brings us to fourth grade," the auctioneer announces.

Parents glance over at us and Sharon and I force bright smiles.

"This year the classrooms have designed bookcases. Hand-painted and made with love, these fanciful childhood designs are both inspiring and practical. Just picture these in your children's bedrooms. Because, remember, folks, childhood memories have no price!" He's really laying it on thick.

The auctioneer claps his hands. "Let's begin!"

The opening bid for Sharon's shelf is five hundred dollars. She lets out a low breath. "That's being optimistic."

But quickly it's up to seven hundred fifty, then eight. By the time it's reached one thousand, our heads are swiveling back and forth between the two final bidders. A paddle flashes to our right, and I get a glimpse of our tablemate, David Artrek. But the sleek woman to our left is not to be outdone.

"Who is that?" I whisper. She's minimalist chic in a white tunic dress, her black hair pulled in a low ponytail. A thick gold armband is her only adornment.

"That's Leslie Cryden, one of my students' moms. She works in the valuations department at Christie's."

We share a chuckle. Kid-art it may be, but Leslie Cryden will be hard-pressed to put a low price on this piece. By the looks of it she's not giving up without a fight.

Again and again she raises her paddle as the bidding wages on. Until, despite the pouty look on David's date's face, he is outbid. "Sold, for two thousand one hundred dollars!" the auctioneer cries.

Leslie Cryden is already storming the stage steps.

Sharon leans in. "Glad that's over. But we still didn't beat kindergarten."

"I never realized how cutthroat this cultivated crew could be," Evan jokes.

"Makes me long for a real drink," Sharon says, wistfully eyeing my glass.

"Let me get you another club soda," Evan offers.

I glance at Sharon's husband, who is staring distractedly off in the distance. Does he have Baby-Brain, too? "Don't be gone too long. My bookshelf is coming next," I remind Evan.

"Don't be discouraged, folks," the auctioneer booms. "If you had your heart set on that last bookshelf, there is still one left!" The spotlight moves from the auctioneer to my bookshelf, which suddenly takes on a garish greenish hue under the beam of the stage bulbs. The bald spot glows. "Fresh from Miss Griffin's fourth-grade classroom!"

The spotlight swivels to me, and I tuck my drink behind my back and force a smile in the blinding glare.

"Since that last one was such a success, let's start the bidding high on this one. Who has one thousand for this lovely piece of artwork?"

There is a beat of silence and for a second I fear no one will bid at all. That's too high! Quickly I glance over my shoulder for Evan. *Did he have to get Sharon a drink now?*

Finally, someone raises their paddle. The auctioneer looks as relieved as I feel. "Right here! One thousand! Who has one thousand one hundred?" And like a sudden wave approaching shore, the paddles rise.

"One thousand two hundred. One thousand three hundred!" In seconds we are up to two thousand dollars. Sharon squeezes my hand.

The auctioneer is on fire. "Come on, folks, this is not just a shelf. It's a work of art! A childhood keepsake. Don't let it get away!"

Soon we've passed Sharon's bidding amount. "Two thousand two hundred dollars!" I crane my neck to see who is holding the paddle at the front. To my dismay it is Ainsley Perry.

"Impressive," Sharon whispers. "I didn't think she liked anything about fourth grade."

"It's a fight," I whisper back. "There's nothing she likes better."

Soon the paddles have dropped away, and two bidders remain. Ainsley Perry, and someone standing off to the side of the stage.

"Two thousand, eight hundred dollars!" the auctioneer announces.

"Your class did it! You beat kindergarten!" Sharon shrieks in my ear. But I'm too distracted watching the volley that continues.

Mrs. Perry raises her paddle again, smirking triumphantly. "Three thousand dollars!" she barks. The crowd exhales. Beside her, Mr. Perry shakes his head.

All heads turn to the remaining bidder in the corner. Sharon clears her throat. "I'm dying of thirst."

There is a pause. "Last call. Three thousand dollars. Do we have three thousand one hundred? Anyone?"

Ainsley Perry smiles and lowers her paddle. The women next to her begin to offer congratulations.

"Four thousand dollars!" a voice cuts through the murmurs. I gasp. *I know that voice.*

"You're kidding me." Sharon is tugging on my arm. "Is that??"

"Evan."

The crowd shifts and there in the corner I make out his tall frame. Evan stands poised on the edge of the crowd, one hand casually in his pocket and the other holding up his paddle.

My thoughts skitter in my cocktail-altered state. *It's too much money! Evan doesn't need a Harry Potter bookcase. Just how much is he getting paid for his new show? I have to stop him. We have to beat the Perrys!*

As Ainsley Perry goes to raise her paddle, Mr. Perry puts his hand on her arm. Ainsley Perry flashes her paddle, but this time Mr. Perry plucks it from her hand before she can raise it overhead. She spins around to face him, a wild look in her eye. For a beat, I feel sorry for her.

The auctioneer points at Evan. "Going once, going twice . . ."

The crowd parts as Mrs. Perry stalks through it, leaving the stage area.

"Sold! For four thousand dollars." The ballroom thunders in applause.

My bookshelf is the highest bid of the night. And for the first time in three years we have managed to unseat the kindergarten team. But even they are applauding like crazy!

Across the room, Evan turns my way. He shrugs, as if wondering what the big deal is. But I'm already closing the gap between us on my wobbly heels. "What were you thinking?" I cry, grabbing his hands in my own.

A crowd of my colleagues has gathered around us, including John Hartman, who claps him vigorously on the back. But Evan's eyes are only for me. "Now all the kids can have the bookshelf. You can put it in your classroom."

I shake my head in disbelief. The fact that every student gets to enjoy it is a gesture beyond the huge donation to my school.

"Do you know who you outbid?" I whisper, tucking my hand into his.

Evan cocks his head. "Oh, you mean the Perrys?" He winks, and lowers his voice. "Just so you know, I would've kept going."

"You're crazy!" I cry, throwing my arms around his neck.

He holds me tight. "Since the day I met you."

Seven

Monday morning, I wake up to the patter of rain on the apartment windows. My alarm never went off, and I'm late for work. When I get outside, the light rainfall has changed over to sheets of driving rain that match the steel-gray sky. My umbrella is, of course, in the car, parked up at the far end of the street. I'm already running late as I race down the sidewalk, with my coat tugged up over my head. By the time I flop into the driver's seat, my carefully blow-dried hair looks like I just stepped out of the shower.

When I finally arrive at school the first bell has already rung and the kids are lining up outside my locked classroom door. Despite the nasty morning outside, I can't help but smile at their comments.

"The lights are out!"

"Miss Griffin's not here."

"Who will feed the crayfish?"

"Maybe she's sick?"

"Maybe she's dead," Andrew Willets says.

"I'm not dead, Andrew," I say, sailing up behind them, key in hand. Andrew ducks his chin, but I smile at him. "At least not yet. Good morning, boys and girls. Come in."

Mrs. Coates is making the announcements over the PA "And, now, we'd like to announce the winner of this year's writer's workshop essay contest," Mrs. Coates says over the loudspeaker. "Here is Dean Hartman with the results."

I hurry the children to their seats and seek out Timmy Lafferty. His gaze remains fixed on his book, but his eyes are the size of small plates. My heartbeat upticks at least fifty percent.

"In third place," John Hartman announces, "is a fifth-grader from Mrs. Brigg's class. Jennifer Crier." My students sigh audibly, but we clap.

"In second place, from one of our fourth-grade classes . . ."

The kids perk up. "Hey, Timmy! Maybe it's you!" Johnny Goldman says. Tim flushes deeply.

"Shhh," I remind them, secretly hoping that Johnny is right.

"From Mrs. Olson's class . . ." This time I sigh, too.

"It's okay, boys and girls, " I say. "We don't enter to win. We enter for the experience and the accomplishment."

Tory Whitcomb scowls. Deep down, I'm with her.

"Which brings me to our first place winner." There is a loud crackle over the PA system.

Timmy's hands are shaking as he grips his book. And that's when it hits me. What if he doesn't win? What if I picked this shy kid out of the class, convinced his mother to send him to the writer's workshop, praised him doggedly—and he loses? Would he still be glad he wrote "Four Frogs and a Magician"? Or, ten years from now, would he find that story in a cardboard box in his mother's attic and curse his fourth-grade teacher for post-contest stress disorder? My temples throb at the very thought.

"This year's fiction workshop award goes to . . ." Dean Hartman pauses. For the only time all year I could actually hear a pin drop in my classroom.

"Another student from the fourth grade . . ."

I steal a glance at Timmy. He's sheet-white.

"From Miss Griffin's class . . ." The kids suck in one collective breath. "Timothy Lafferty!"

The class roars. I can't hear anything else that Dean Hartman is saying. All I know is that Timmy Lafferty is being mobbed. The kids have leaped out of their seats and are pounding him on the back and giving high fives. I don't stop them. Tim's freckled face is flushed red. He's smiling so wide I could count every tooth. That is, if I could see through my tears. I take advantage of the chaos to pull myself together before wading through the throng to Timmy's desk. "Congratulations, Timmy." He glances shyly up at me, grinning. "I'm really proud of you, kiddo."

♦ ♦ ♦

My good day only lasts so long. After the final bell, just as I'm putting on my coat to walk out the door, Mrs. Coates pokes her head in my room. "Do you have a moment? The dean needs you."

I'm supposed to meet Evan for a key lime martini and shrimp tacos at one of our favorite bistros, a few blocks over. It's the one night this week that he has time off, and I will not miss it.

John meets me in the doorway of his office. I peer inside, where two people are already seated, backs to me. "I'm sorry to disturb you," he whispers. "It's the Perrys."

Inside Ainsley Perry fixes me with a flat look and extends a limp hand. I actually have to take another step forward to shake it with my own, which at this point is sweating. Her husband barely glances up from his iPhone.

"Shall we get started?" John asks.

I glance desperately at the ancient air-conditioning unit in John's window, which is inexplicably turned off. Are these people cold-blooded? I mop my brow.

John addresses the Perrys. "As you know, we are here to discuss an incident that took place last week."

Mrs. Perry ignores this. "This harmless incident is borne of Horatio's boredom in Miss Griffin's class. Horatio is a gifted child and Miss Griffin is not meeting his needs. I am here to advocate for my son's gift-ed-ness." She clips each syllable sharply.

John politely starts waffling through the deep pile of papers in Horatio's student folder. Horatio does not demonstrate gift-ed-ness. Not nearly. Though I'd happily argue Horatio's other 'nesses—meanness, tardiness, sneakiness . . .

John folds his hands. "I wouldn't qualify this act as harmless, Mrs. Perry. As you can imagine, Miss Griffin was rather upset about this incident. Horatio not only frightened her with his use of fake blood . . ."

"Ketchup," Mr. Perry interjects, not looking up from his iPhone.

John glances at him. "Horatio also made an accusation that Miss Griffin physically harmed him." Now it's John's turn to clear his throat. "Which we do not take lightly. What Horatio did was disruptive. It interrupted the class, the office, and brought the school nurse to the classroom. Seeing what appears to be a bloody accident can be traumatic for other children."

"Did you receive complaints from other parents?" Mrs. Perry asks, arching one overplucked eyebrow.

John pauses. "Not as of yet." He looks to me.

I have to shake my head.

"So your claim about other children being traumatized is invalid."

"Mrs. Perry—"

"And the fact that Miss Griffin is unable to keep my son engaged in meaningful activity so that he has to resort to such creative means of entertaining himself only proves my initial point."

Creative means?

The Perrys have stolen the ball and are storming the end zone. John pauses a beat, but races to intercept. "I think that 'disruptive' would be a more accurate description of Horatio's behavior on the day in question," John says.

"A subjective term," Mrs. Perry says dismissively.

"I see a pattern that I can no longer ignore," John says firmly.

Here it is. I hold my breath.

"We are failing to hold Horatio accountable."

Mrs. Perry gasps.

"Allowing Horatio to continually get away with this sort of behavior is only encouraging him to repeat it. And that is the only disservice I see here."

Touchdown!

"I recommend that Horatio write a letter of apology to Miss Griffin and to the class, to be delivered tomorrow morning. Given his fondness of ketchup, he will also miss recess this week and will instead help the cafeteria staff wipe down the tables after lunch."

"He will do no such thing," Mrs. Perry declares. "It's the last week of school!"

Mr. Perry, whom I'd completely forgotten about until now,

stands. "For the record, I disagree with this decision. But I have a meeting to get to."

"But Richard, are we going to stand for this?" Mrs. Perry glares at Mr. Perry, but he's already halfway through the door. Her eyes flash. "This conversation is not over."

With that she snatches her purse and stalks after her husband. I watch from the office window as they veer down the sidewalk outside and wordlessly pivot in opposite directions, she to a silver Jag, he to a red Audi TT. Neither offers so much as a wave goodbye to the other. And there, I see, lies a big part of Horatio's problems.

"There's something else I want to talk to you about," John says, returning to his seat. I glance at the wall clock. "You're aware of the board of directors' budget cuts for next year?"

I flash back to the yellow notice in my teacher mailbox. "Yes. I heard that they might be cutting some of the arts programs? I think it's terrible."

John shakes his head. "We're hoping to avoid that. However, with the decline in enrollment, and the small class size of this year's third grade, I'm afraid the population doesn't justify our current staffing."

This year's third graders are supposed to be my fourth graders next year. I stand up.

"As you know, if cuts have to be made, our policy is that we start with the most recently hired."

My mind races. The most recent hire was our kindergarten teacher, Melinda, I remind myself. Which would mean she would be the first to be let go. Which also means I would have to step down to fill kindergarten. I sigh inwardly. There is nothing a teacher likes less than being forced to move to a different grade level. I'll have to learn a whole new curriculum. The kids won't be able to tie their shoes, let alone read the novels I love to teach. But at least I'll still have a position. "So you'll be needing me to move to kindergarten?"

John sighs. "I'm sorry, Maggie. But it looks like the board is considering making two full-time cuts this year. Which means not only Melinda's position, but yours, too."

I sit back down. John is saying something about hiring policy and student enrollment, but I cannot make sense of it. All I can think about is my desk, with the African violet and the hand-painted sign: *Welcome to Miss Griffin's class!*

"Nothing has been decided yet," John says, emphatically. "So let's sit tight for now. But I wanted you to be aware so that you're prepared for whatever the outcome may be."

"There aren't any other places to make cuts? Field trips? Curriculum training?"

John shakes his head solemnly. "We've already pared it down in every place possible. I want to assure you of that."

I stare past John to his bookshelves. There are several framed photos of his family. One in particular stands out: John, his two sons in matching khaki pants and pale-blue button-downs, and his wife in a seersucker dress, stand together in front of the ocean. The late day sun on their hair is as golden as the sand beneath their bare feet. Suddenly I want to go home. I want to go home to Mystic.

I stand up. "Thank you. Is there anything else?"

John looks confused. "No. That's all." His expression softens in a paternal, off-the-record kind of way. "Maggie, if it comes to cutting positions, you know I'll write you a strong reference and make some calls—whatever you need."

"Thank you." I look at the clock. It's after five.

Outside, the rain has stopped and the air is balmy for a late-spring day. I will not miss my date with Evan. I text him that I'm running late and break into a jog through the Friday sidewalk traffic, dodging irritated clots of people. When I finally rush through the restaurant doors, the air-conditioning is a jolt against my sweaty skin. The bar is crowded with happy-hour patrons. But Evan is not one of them. Desperate, I scan the tables.

I pull out my phone. "Sorry I missed you, Mag. I got called back to set. Ask the bartender for your drink—it's waiting for you. Cheers."

As promised, the bartender has my key lime martini. I slump onto the only free stool between two businessmen. Cheers, indeed.

◆   ◆   ◆

The second I walk into our apartment, I know my bad day is not yet over.

Erika is sitting on the couch, surrounded by her pink wedding folders. Sobbing.

"What's wrong?" I ask, dumping my bag on the carpet.

"They canceled the wedding!"

"Who did? Trent?" My mind spins trying to make sense of what she's saying.

She picks up a brochure and thrusts it under my nose. "They've got black mold!"

The Century Club is an upscale venue in the heart of the city, where Erika and Trent are having their reception. She's only dragged me there about a dozen times to walk the ballroom and hem and haw over color schemes. And table arrangements. And the location for the cake.

"When did this happen?"

She points at the answering machine across the room, as if identifying the perpetrator. "Just now!"

I push the pile of used tissues off the couch and sit beside her. "Did they offer to make other arrangements? Or help you relocate to a new venue?"

She shakes her head angrily. "No. The contract says that in the event of any problem with the property, they'll give us a refund. But that's it." Her voice breaks and she falls into another chorus of sobs.

"Oh, Erika." Listening to her cry, I decide to keep my own bad news to myself for now.

"Everything's a mess. There's not a place in the city that can do it on this short notice."

"And there's no help at all from the club?" Given all the boasting Trent's father seemed to do about their family lineage, you'd think he'd have more pull.

"The best they offered was a date change. For the fall." She says the word like it's monsoon season.

I try to put a positive spin on this. "Actually, a lot of brides choose to get married in the fall. You've got the leaves changing color and the weather is still nice. Not nearly as hot as July. What does Trent say?"

At this, Erika hops off the couch, her eyes flashing. "Trent suggested we change the date. Can you believe it?"

I can, actually. And given the circumstances, I have to agree. "Maybe you should consider it. After all, the invitations haven't been sent out yet."

"I have chosen a *summer* dress. I have chosen *summer* colors." She smacks her forehead dramatically. "Even the menu is *summer.*"

"What did the planner say to do?" I try to remember the woman's name—but I can't recall anything beyond her sharp black bob and red lipstick. I thought it silly that Erika had to get on a waiting list just to retain her, but surely she was used to dealing with these sorts of crises.

Erika scoffs. "Maribelle quit."

"What? Isn't she supposed to be one of the best planners in the metro area?"

"Well, I sort of let her go."

"Erika, why? You need her now more than ever!"

Erika sniffs. "Because she also suggested a date change. Which I will not do."

I flop on the couch. "Who are you going to hire?"

"No one. It's too late. Besides, we don't need anyone. We have impeccable taste. We can do this."

"Wait. *We?*"

Her voice begins to waver. "If only we can find another place to do it."

I hand her the tissue box. "Don't worry. There's got to be another venue." My mind races, thinking of the reception sites we'd toured.

"The Lenox?"

"Booked."

"Copley?"

"That was Peyton's."

"Remember you guys loved the idea of the Boston Library?"

Erika shakes her head. "Trent's mom already called. She's

been on the phone all day. So has mine. They're both freaking out."

There is a knock at the door, and no sooner have I unlocked it than Peyton bursts in with an oversize Tiffany-blue box. She rushes past me to Erika and the two embrace.

"You poor baby!" Peyton sets the box on the table and with one hand removes a carry-out carton of two coffees, and with the other, a bottle of wine.

"Caffeine or alcohol?"

Predictably, Erika points to the bottle. Well, I could've told her that. Peyton looks at me meaningfully.

"What?"

"Wineglasses." She looks impatient.

"Oh, right." I turn for the kitchen but Peyton brushes past me.

"I've got it. I need a bottle opener, too." Her efficiency in my own place wears on me. She returns with two wineglasses and hands one to Erika. Am I invisible? Peyton pops the cork matter-of-factly and pours. She watches as Erika takes a big gulp, like a nurse administering cough syrup. "Better?"

Erika nods gratefully.

"I've brought the binder."

"Oh, thank God." Erika looks relieved.

"What binder?"

They both stare back at me. "Peyton's wedding binder," Erika says. As if this is something everyone should already know.

"Oh." I watch as Peyton reaches into the bottom of her magic blue box and plucks a large embossed book from its depths. "How much stuff did you bring?" I joke, peering over her shoulder. But no one laughs.

"Okay, so here's the section on venues." Peyton flips methodically to a tabbed section. "Do you still want outdoor or can we look indoors?"

Erika thinks. "Start outdoors. But I don't think we're going to have any luck."

"Nonsense."

I watch in silence as Peyton sifts through glossy folders of brochures with one hand and flips open her laptop with the other. It's no wonder she's climbed to the top of her firm so quickly. Just her confidence is intimidating. Maybe I should put her on the task of finding me a new job.

"Let's begin with a thirty-mile radius of Boston."

I can't help but let out a laugh.

"What?" Peyton asks.

"Nothing. It's just that you two sound like you're launching an FBI search." I put on a mock voice of authority. "Thirty-mile radius of downtown. The suspect must have a liquor license. And an outdoor patio that can seat three hundred!" I can barely get the last part out, but neither one of them cracks so much as a smile.

"Maggie. This is serious." Peyton places a sympathetic hand on Erika's back.

"Just trying to lighten the mood." I trudge into the kitchen and make myself a cup of tea.

Two hours later, the radius has extended to seventy-five miles and beyond. The patio requirement has been scratched. Peyton's bottle of wine is empty.

"Well, we have a few options," I say, trying to sound hopeful. With all of Erika's first-, second-, and third-tier choices reserved, we've only been able to find two places that were available, an Italian hall in the South End and a loft space outside

Back Bay that had been renovated into a trendy gallery with a rooftop deck.

Erika covers her face in her hands. "Vinny's Trattoria is not an option."

"Nor is the loft," Peyton says sadly. "Four flights of stairs. No elevator." We all sigh.

"I don't know, Erika," Peyton says wearily. They were now working on their cold coffees. "Maybe you should consider changing the date. At least you get exactly what you want. And it's only a few months later."

If I have any hope of going to bed tonight and not being late for school again in the morning, it's my turn to talk some sense into Erika. "What about the Cape house?"

Erika shakes her head. "Trent's mother offered it when we got engaged, but even with tents we can only manage one hundred. Save-the-dates for one hundred sixty already went out."

And then it hits me. "Wait a minute. If you're going to move it outside of Boston altogether, why not just keep moving south?"

Peyton is shaking her head "no" already. "Like where? Providence?" She purses her lips.

"Hear me out. What about a Connecticut wedding? At home?"

"In Mystic?"

Peyton is still shaking her head, but Erika is listening.

"Think about it," I go on. "Not just Connecticut countryside, but seaside. You've got the historic village with all its clapboard houses. And the marinas full of sailboats. You can take pictures at sunset at one of the piers—just imagine it!"

Erika nods. "It would let me keep the summer date."

I'm getting excited just talking about it, myself. "There're plenty of hotels and cute B-and-Bs in the area. And beaches."

"And tourists," Peyton groans.

Erika's nose wrinkles.

"True," I concede. "But also fresh seafood. And salt air. And gorgeous weather."

"I don't know—that sounds like starting over. New venue. New decorations. New caterer." Peyton is ticking the list off her fingers.

"Not exactly starting over," I remind them. "The dress is done. The band will travel. I'm sure that Boston florists leave the city to handle destination weddings all the time. The rest we will help you with."

Erika closes her eyes and leans back against the couch cushions. We sit in silence, awaiting her answer.

"My mother always wanted me to get married close to home," she says, finally.

"Exactly!"

"But it would have to be at our yacht club," she says, sitting up straighter.

"We'll call them first thing tomorrow," I promise.

"And we'd need to get a local photographer. Someone who knows all the best spots for sunset pictures," she adds.

"Of course."

Peyton's head is snapping left and right between us. "Are you sure?" she asks. "Mystic is so far from Boston."

I throw her a look. "It's not like we're trekking to Manitoba. Besides, half of the guests are from that area anyway. It's her hometown."

Finally Peyton concedes with a shrug. "I guess we could do a nautical theme."

"We can go to Mystic this weekend!" Erika says. "My mom

can set something up with the club, and we'll make a girls' weekend out of it." It's the happiest she's looked all night, and neither Peyton nor I are going to argue with this.

"I could use a weekend away," Peyton says. She looks to me for backup.

"Perfect. School ends this week, so I'm free." Potentially indefinitely so, I think with a sense of dread.

Erika stands, a sea of white tissues cascading off her lap like the skirt of a bridal gown. She dabs her nose one last time and looks at us. "I can't thank you guys enough for your help tonight. You have no idea what this means to me."

It's been a long day. My Darby worries have faded somewhat, dim with sleep deprivation and wedding planning. Right now we all need to call it a night. "Get some sleep," I tell Erika. "Everything will work out. We'll make sure of it."

The relief on her face is palpable. Before she shuts her bedroom door, Erika holds up her pinky finger, and I raise mine back. "Promise?"

I nod.

"What's with that little thing you two always do with your pinkies?" Peyton whispers.

"Nothing," I say. But seeing Erika flash it, I feel the same way I did when I was ten years old. It's still everything.

Eight

With Erika's wedding safely relocated to Mystic, and just two days left until the end of the school year, I decide it's time to share the news of my possibly imminent unemployment.

"They haven't decided anything yet," Evan says sympathetically, when I tell him the next morning on the phone. "The dean likes you. I'm sure he'll find a way to keep your job."

Erika's take is empowerment. "Think of this as an opportunity. You love to teach, but that private school has never paid you what you're worth. This is your chance to aim for the job you deserve."

Peyton is quick to tie it all up with a corporate bow. "Absolutely. Narrow your target region, garner multiple offers, and you'll be the one in control." She points a manicured finger at me. "Don't be afraid to negotiate."

Clearly, Peyton has never worked in the public sector, and I resist the urge to correct her about the nonnegotiable reality of district salary scales and state policy.

My mother flies the flag of maternal despair. "Oh, honey. This is terrible. How could the dean *do this* to you? Just think—all those lovely poems you had the children write for Mother's Day? And those adorable skits they created for the class play? All for nothing! They're throwing their best teacher overboard!" Perfect. Perhaps I should take matters into my own hands and jump before they do. But, just in case I am considering that possibility, she adds a final directive. "I'm sure everything will be just fine! Come home as soon as you can. I'll bake scones."

Jane goes political. "If the board needs to clean house, they should dump the baggage who just show up for a paycheck. Forget seniority. You should start a petition. Or consult the union. Or something. Jesus—I've got to go—Randall just peed on the rug again."

After the onslaught of input, it takes some effort to sort through the pileup of everyone's feelings to find my own. But when I eventually do, I realize that as much as I love Darby, there is a small flutter inside my chest when I think of starting over fresh. Erika nailed it. Darby was a wonderful place to get my feet wet. But I've always meant to teach in the public school system. The pay would be better and the benefits, too. Sure, the class sizes would be larger. And there would likely be more underprivileged or special needs children to accommodate, beyond Darby's sole "Scholarship Butterfly" that the board of directors loves to boast about each fall. But that is exactly what appeals to me. There would be some diversity. And that is something I suddenly feel hungry for.

With the last days of school upon us, I try to keep these thoughts at the forefront as I navigate the halls of Darby, only to be stopped by both parents and teachers offering me pitying looks and, often, unsolicited job tips. Gossip has spread. The art teacher's Catholic church runs a lovely school in Wellesley. (I'm not Catholic.) Andy Goldman, a third-grade teacher, sends his kids to a progressive Jewish day school. (Nor am I Jewish.) One of my classroom parents has a sister who also teaches fourth grade and is going on maternity leave. (In Chicago!) By the week's end, I am full up on advice and mostly just impatient for some kind of decision from the board. Not knowing has suddenly become the hardest part.

Aside from Sharon, the kids are the ones I will miss most. When I get teary-eyed at each final task: the final spelling test, the final read-aloud book, and ultimately, the final day, I try to remind myself that I still don't know for sure that I'll be saying goodbye. And our year together would be over with the arrival of summer anyway.

But on that last day, when the last bell rings, I can't help it: the tears are threatening. The class rises in one amoebous mob and heads for the door. There are hugs and handshakes and high fives. There are promises to send postcards over the summer, which cause my eyes to sting just a little. I've almost made it without breaking down when Anna Beth taps my arm. "Here, Miss Griffin. This is for you." She hugs me hard in the doorway and presses a handmade pink card in my palm, before dashing down the hallway. A stray tear escapes.

Timmy Lafferty is the last to exit the classroom. I catch him in the doorway as he tries to duck out. "Did you really think you could escape without a goodbye hug?" The boy blushes, but he lets me give him a quick squeeze.

"I'm writing another story," he says shyly.

"I can't wait to read it," I tell him.

Timmy hesitates in the door. "You're my favorite teacher,

Miss Griffin. I'll miss you." With that, he bolts down the hall for his bus.

And then I need a box of Kleenex.

◆ ◆ ◆

Sharon finds me in the parking lot as I'm attempting to stuff the last box into my car. She peers into the trunk of my Volkswagen. "Wow, you packed a lot." She narrows her eyes. "You didn't hear a final decision from the board yet, did you?"

I shake my head. "No. This is just extra stuff I need to clean out anyway." I don't add that I started to pack up my desk, and then stopped myself. One small part of me still held out hope that I'd be coming back in the fall. "But this," I say, reaching for a small box on top, "is for you." I hand her the little African violet that I have somehow managed to keep alive for the whole school year.

"Mags, I can't take that. Didn't one of your kids give this to you on the first day?"

"Yeah, Beth Matthews." A tear rolls down my cheek.

Sharon squeezes my hand. "Oh, sweetie. I can't believe the board left you hanging like this. But whatever happens, you are going to be okay. You know that, right?"

We hug goodbye, and promise to meet for lunch sometime over the summer.

"Don't have that baby until you get home from the Vineyard!" I tell her, wagging my finger.

"Are you kidding? It may be the last trip I ever take. This kid better stay put until August!"

I walk her to her car and watch as she attempts to slide her belly behind the wheel. "I have to say, I'm sort of jealous," she admits, sliding her seat back. "At least you get to wear a real bathing suit on the beach, and not some skirted maternity frock that makes you look like a beached whale in a tutu. Did you decide what you're going to do with your summer yet?"

"I suppose I should start sending out job applications just in case. But first I'm thinking about going home to Mystic. Erika needs some stuff done for the wedding, and I think it might be good to get away."

"Good," Sharon says. "Don't let her boss you around too much. Weddings are meant to be fun."

I narrow my eyes. "Have you *never* been a bridesmaid?"

"Pay attention at the wedding," she teases. "Who knows? Next summer it could be your own!"

◆ ◆ ◆

Evan has chosen a little Thai place in Central Square for dinner. "No more pencils, no more books!" he'd said in a playful message that morning. Although it's only been a couple of days since I've seen him, so much has happened that he's missing out by default. There's a lot I want to talk about with him. As I tell the hostess I'm meeting someone for dinner, it feels like that *someone* is about a hundred miles away.

But he's not. Evan's sitting at a table for two, by the window. He stands as soon as he sees me, a grin spreading across his handsome face.

"Look at you." He plants a soft kiss on my lips, and suddenly that distance closes by at least twenty miles.

"I've missed you." I notice that he's wearing the blue checkered shirt I gave him for his birthday back in April, and the margin closes some more.

"I went ahead and ordered you a glass of Riesling. Goes great with spicy food, okay?" Before I can answer he hands me a menu. "Take a look at the curries. I'm thinking maybe the red one?"

"Oh. Okay, thanks." Evan's efficiency always unhinges me for a few seconds, as I'm someone who likes to ease into things. But I can use some wine. We place our orders, for the red curry, a coconut soup, and dumplings as an appetizer.

"So, school is out and the world is your oyster. What are your plans, Maggie Griffin?" My grip on my wineglass tightens. I have no plans. What I do have is a trunkful of teaching supplies, an apartment lined with cardboard boxes that need to be filled, and an apartment search I have thus far been avoiding despite the fact that my days as a Back Bay tenant are ticking down.

The server brings our dumplings and I watch as Evan digs in. "I don't know," I admit. "We're all heading to Mystic for the weekend to check out Erika's new wedding venue. Beyond that, I really don't have any big plans." I take another gulp of Riesling. Summer vacation is the most eagerly anticipated time of year by teachers everywhere. It spells freedom and flip-flops and sand between your toes. And I finally understand why that sensation is so delicious: it's because it's fleeting. Up until now, every summer vacation has had an end date. A date when we must fold up the beach chairs and exchange our summer reading for textbooks. But not this year. This year my summer stretches out into the uncertain wide open, with no expiration. I don't know yet if Darby will be taking me back. I don't know where I will be living after August. Basically, beyond Erika's wedding and my mother's insistence that I come home to Mystic, I don't know what to do with my summer.

Sharon was wrong. Instead of feeling liberated, my lack of

plans begins to swathe me like a dark shroud. What I really would like is a weekend away with Evan. Preferably to a place void of school-age children, brides-to-be, and inquiring family members. A weekend in Cape Cod would be a good start.

"I was thinking we should get away for a weekend," I say.

"I should have some time off in July."

I stuff a dumpling in my mouth. July seems about as close as Siberia.

Evan studies me. "Since you're going to be in Mystic with the girls this weekend, why don't you stay awhile? Your mom has been asking you to. And you said, yourself, that you really need a break."

True. But I was thinking of getting away with *him*.

"Besides," he's quick to add, "I got my new script for the next episode, and I'm going to be tied up for the next couple of weeks."

I groan. "Nights, too?"

Evan shrugs apologetically. "Sorry, Mags. It looks that way."

I'm disappointed, but he's right, I really could use a week away. There are beautiful ocean beaches just a few miles from Mystic. And since the private schools get out a couple weeks earlier than the public ones, downtown Mystic wouldn't be crowded with throngs of tourists just yet. But I can't help but feel like Evan isn't missing our time together as much as I have been. Couldn't he at least ask me to hang around town? Or wrangle one measly night for us to get away together? Summer is finally here, and yet we have not one trip planned together. I stab another dumpling then dump it back on my plate. I've lost my appetite.

"Maybe I will stay in Mystic for a while," I mumble. I look up at him to gauge his response.

But Evan is already onto something else. He sets his fork down and looks right at me. "I've been thinking."

Those three words cause me to put my own fork down. "About?"

There are too many *somethings* he could be leading into. Erika would say, *Getting engaged?* Jane would say, *Breaking up?* Yet, as his girlfriend, I have to wonder at the fact that I have absolutely no idea what Evan is about to drop on me.

"You've been worrying about finding a new place after Erika moves out," he says, finally.

I let out a breath. An apartment! "Well, technically, we're paid through the month of August, but yes, I need to start looking."

Evan smiles uncertainly. "I was wondering, what if we moved in together?"

The restaurant has gotten crowded, and the couple at the table next to us is commenting loudly on their spring rolls. I lean forward to make sure I've heard him correctly.

"You want to move in together? To your place?"

He shrugs. "We could. Or we could look for a slightly bigger place. Somewhere between both of our jobs."

Finally. Something good!

It's something that I'd been thinking quietly about all spring. But what if he thought it was too soon? What if he thought my wanting to move in together was just a knee-jerk reaction to my friends getting married and moving on? What if it was? And so I decided to wait a bit before bringing it up. And yet Evan has, happily, beaten me to it.

"I would love that!" I say, reaching quickly for his hand. Images of a classic brownstone flash in my head. I can just picture us strolling along Newbury Street together on a Sunday morning, grabbing brunch at one of the restaurants. Or cozying up in a bookstore with a cup of coffee before popping into a market to pick up some dinner things that we'll cook together in our sun-filled two-bedroom with a balcony. I lean forward to kiss him.

But instead Evan drops my hand and pulls out his iPhone. "Good. Because I'm thinking that between our two jobs, the Beacon Hill area might make the most sense. I've looked at some listings and I think we could get a good deal—"

"Wait," I interrupt. Evan looks up. "Before we talk leases, can we talk about us?"

Evan frowns. "Do you need more time to think about it?"

I shake my head. "No, no, it's nothing like that. It's just that this is exciting! It's a big step for us. Let's toast! Or something."

"Oh, okay." He lifts his glass and I lift mine. "To us. And our new apartment. Wherever that may be!" We clink glasses. "So, getting back to some of the listings . . ." Evan holds up his phone so that I can see the screen. "I've bookmarked a few for you."

"But we still don't know where I'll be teaching next year, yet," I remind him. "Maybe we should hold off on neighborhoods."

"Most likely you'll be at Darby. I'm sure they'll work something out, right?"

I'm a little surprised by Evan's take on this. In fact, I'm somewhat irritated, both by the efficiency with which he is handling our big decision and by his casual sentiment about my uncertain employment—something I'm not feeling at all casual about, myself. I know he means to be positive, but it comes off as dismissive.

"I haven't heard a final decision from the board. But if they do cut my position, I could end up anywhere in Boston."

Evan thinks about this. "But you do plan to stay in the metro area, right?"

He's missing my point. "School just ended. Why don't we spend tonight savoring our decision and worry about next steps after the weekend?"

Evan holds up both hands. "You're right, I'm sorry."

The server returns and clears our appetizer plates. I take a sip of wine, trying to push away the sense of disappointment that has crept in. Moving in together is good news. This is something to look forward to.

"So, what's going on with the show?" I ask, switching the subject.

He looks relieved. "They've added more scenes for Jack," he tells me. It still strikes me as funny to talk about his character as if he's a real person.

"That's great. So, is Jack becoming the lead male role?" I like to tease him about this.

"Nah, but the writers are thinking of ways for him to grow as a character," he says, in his usual self-deprecating way. "I've been meaning to tell you, they've decided to make Angie's character a love interest. You know, to add a little spice."

I nod, willing my expression to stay neutral. Beyond the red curry we just ordered, I don't recall Evan mentioning anything about *spice*.

"So, does that mean your two characters are an item?" A fictional match, I remind myself.

Evan shrugs. "Looks like it." He looks at me apologetically. "But you know this is just part of the job, right?"

"Pure acting," I say, to show that I agree. I get it. I'm cool with the fact that a model from last year's *Sports Illustrated* swimsuit issue will be dating my boyfriend on television.

Evan looks relieved. "Exactly. It's purely fictional."

"So, when will *that* become part of the storyline?" I won't call it a relationship. Because it's not.

"Soon." He looks down at his lap. "Uh, I just got the script today, and it looks like we have our first love scene next week."

We have a love scene. As if this love scene belongs to Angie and him, not to those oh-so-fictional characters we were just talking about.

"Is that so," I say, this time working extra hard to keep my expression as impartial as I hope my tone is. But I can tell he's studying my reaction, and I know this is my chance to reassure him that I'm not going to let this become an issue. *God, I would suck at acting.*

"Well, I can't say the thought of you making out with another woman is the best news I've had all day. But like you said, it's just work. Right?"

Evan looks relieved. "Exactly. There are about twenty other people on the set, with lights and cameras zooming in on every angle. Believe me, it's about as embarrassing as it gets."

Every angle, I think. Which leads me to the next question blaring between my ears. "What exactly does this love scene entail?"

Evan looks pained, so much so, that I actually feel for him. "The first one is just some kissing. That sort of thing."

"And the next?"

He folds his hands neatly on the table in front of him. "They have sex."

Outside, the light has faded. The taillights of cars flash in the growing darkness of Mass Ave. Sort of like the cloud settling over our table. "But, it's not like you guys will actually be . . . ?"

"Naked?"

I wince.

"No, no," he laughs, sitting back in his seat like this is actually funny. "Nothing like it. There's all kinds of coverage the cameras don't show. There're cover-ups. Oh, and tape."

I take another gulp of wine.

Evan reaches across the table for my hand and squeezes it. "Can I just say how much I appreciate that you're okay with all this?" He's so grateful that I can't possibly ask what I want to ask. Like, how much tape are we talking? And, what exactly is being taped? The combined image of tape and Angie Dune brings something far more bondage than coverage to mind. Instead I force a smile.

"What a relief," Evan says.

The server arrives. Between the steam of our coconut Thai soup bowls something else rises in the air. Jealousy? Fear?

"Would you like another glass of Riesling?" the server asks me.

I glance self-consciously at Evan's still-full glass. "Yes, please," I say. What I really want to tell her is, "Make it a shot."

Nine

I t's a girls' weekend!" At least, that's how Erika's trying to sell it. Saturday morning finds the three of us heading down the Mass Pike, Erika and Peyton in Trent's BMW and me following. I've decided to go home for a couple weeks, after all. I can apply for jobs online anywhere. The only pressing thing for me to do in Boston is pack up the boxes in our apartment. The real estate agent called and said she has several showings of our apartment this week, and rather than dealing with cleanups and rushing out the door, I'd rather not be there at all.

So far only Peyton is genuinely excited about this trip. Erika is still worrying about the venue change. Which means that this is a working weekend, and my real "break" won't begin until they head back to Boston on Sunday.

"What's first on the agenda?" Peyton asks excitedly, when we stop off to grab iced coffees somewhere north of Providence.

"The yacht club," Erika says. "We've got to meet with the club planner to talk food and setup. And all the colors have to be changed."

"What happened to celadon and gold?" Peyton asks. "You

love those." Erika and I exchange a look. Those were Peyton's wedding colors.

"I don't know. Nautical seems more appropriate, now that we're seaside. Don't you think?" Erika asks.

As the two debate the pros of blue and white stripes with a splash of lobster red, my thoughts wander. The farther away from Boston we drive, the more my thoughts drift back home to Cam.

And in no time we're sailing off Exit 89 and pulling into the village. As I trail them down Main Street, Peyton points to Mystic Pizza. I imagine she's asking Erika if that's the same one from the movie.

At the stop sign in front of the pizza place, Erika smiles back at me in the rearview mirror. I'm right. Every time we've brought out-of-town friends home, it was usually the first question we were asked. As teenagers we watched the movie nonstop, partly because we were suckers for all things Julia Roberts. But mostly because of the picture-perfect ending. The autumn leaves. The seashore. Small-town life. And despite all of it, Julia Roberts ended up with the ridiculously cute (if short) guy. These days Erika claims to have tired of the movie. But I still fall for it every time.

Always flawless, Erika's mother is waiting for us at the club in a pastel suit, attired as if she's presiding over the White House Easter egg hunt. Mrs. Crane twists her pearl choker as we approach. "Hello, hello, girls! Come. The planner is waiting!"

It's been years since I was last at the Mystic Yacht Club, but stepping inside it may as well have been yesterday. Erika used to bring me to their summer clambake and the annual holiday party at Christmas. Nothing has changed. There's a solidity to the building that brings you back in time with the town's whaling history—even though the red pine floors tilt slightly toward the doorways, which are all just a little bit crooked. Yet there is modern grandeur, too, in the mahogany paneled walls, the crystal chandelier, and most prominently in the large picture windows overlooking the stately white porches. We pass the large bar, where I first sipped a Long Island Iced Tea when we were teenagers, and past the ominous oil paintings of long-dead whaling captains whose eyes seem to trail us.

Erika loops her arm in mine and squeezes it. "You were right. It's the perfect spot."

We're introduced to Deirdre, the club event planner. "Ladies, if you'll follow me into the ballroom, we can begin the tastings. We have a new chef from New York. I'm excited to share his menu ideas."

Mrs. Crane does a double take. "What happened to Pierre?"

Deirdre smiles over her shoulder. "Pierre left us last month. But I'm sure that you'll find Chef Ari to be a wonderful addition. He's worked in some of Manhattan's finest spots."

Mrs. Crane purses her lip ever so slightly. "Of course."

Chef Ari joins us to explain the dishes that are brought out. There's grilled shrimp with pesto, Vietnamese summer rolls, and *salmorejo* in tall shot glasses, followed by Dover sole with mango chutney and filet mignon stuffed with crabmeat. All of it to die for.

Mrs. Crane is less certain. She sniffs a spiced speared shrimp suspiciously and sets it back down on her plate. "What about something more traditional? Perhaps a chicken dish."

"Mom, I'm sure the seafood and beef are more than enough," Erika protests.

But the chef is not fazed. "Of course, ma'am. We do a lovely Balinese ginger chicken. Or perhaps you'd prefer a *makhani* sauce?"

"Trent loves spicy dishes," Erika says.

"That sounds so . . . exotic." Despite her privileged lifestyle, Mrs. Crane's palate, along with her social politics, are decidedly stuck back in the early 1980s.

"I went for a traditional menu at my wedding, myself," Peyton whispers to her. But I notice Peyton spears one more shrimp with her toothpick before the chef can whisk it away.

From there we move on to the safer territory of wine tasting, which is by now much needed: Erika selects a champagne for the first toast and wine for the dinner course, plus a rich Muscat liqueur for dessert. It isn't long until the ballroom floor is starting to feel sloped beyond its historic charm. At least it leaves Mrs. Crane in a bubblier mood. She's finally let go of her pearl necklace.

At last we're in the land of confections. Erika selects a three-tier Swiss dot vanilla cake, to which the chef nods his curt approval.

"Fondant?" her mother asks hopefully.

"Buttercream." To me she whispers, "We're going to eat it, not look at it."

As the others follow the pastry chef into the rear of the club kitchen to sample frostings, Erika turns and squeezes my hands in her own. "So, what do you think?" We take a moment to look around the ballroom, envisioning her big day. "I want to put the bride and groom table by the bay window. Of course, the dancing will take place along the wall of French doors, so we can open them onto the porch." The faint scent of salt water floats in, and I can already imagine throwing those doors open midway through the evening.

"It's perfect," I tell her.

And I mean it. But as I follow her back into the kitchen, I can't help but feel a little twinge of envy. Growing up, I tried not to compare my family to Erika's, but sometimes it was hard not to. If life were a plane, we were comfortably seated in the economy section, and she was in first class. But despite the fact that Erika's winter breaks took place out west in Vail, and mine just ten minutes west off Interstate 95 at Ski Southington, I've never felt like I missed out. Sure she flew to Grand Cayman each spring, while the only flying I experienced was watching the birds leave their nests outside my bedroom window. And while I didn't dare mention these differences to my parents for fear of sounding ungrateful—or worse, jealous—I know my mother noticed my feelings. "Was your party okay?" she asked, hesitantly, when I graduated from eighth grade. Erika's parents had hosted an extravagant affair here at the club. The girls wore mostly white dresses and the boys showed up in jackets. I went, too. But it was after my own family celebration of grocery-store ice cream cake with my grandparents on our back porch.

I would never trade the loving childhood that my family gave me. But today, when the pastry chef places a spoonful of lemon buttercream frosting to Erika's lips, I do feel a little scratch of the green-eyed-monster rising up in my throat. It's not the yacht club we're in. Or the expensive wedding she's about to throw. It's the chapter that Erika's life is suddenly in. She's found her partner, she's got the job she studied hard for. And soon she'll be moving into married life with kids on the horizon, just as surely as she'll be moving out of our tiny apartment and across town to her first home. This summer everything I recognize seems to be changing.

Outside, the day is bright and clear. "What do you think of ending the day with a little shopping?" Mrs. Crane suggests in the club parking lot.

Peyton is already on it, stalking the nearby shop windows around the corner. "I need shoes," she says. I could use a pair of sandals for summer. My teacher wardrobe is largely based on comfort and ease, and today I have the urge to buy a pair of shoes that are anything but.

"Come on, there's a cute shoe store this way," I tell them. The day is still young, and maybe a little retail therapy will get me out of my funk.

We're halfway up the sidewalk when I see it. A navy-blue Jeep with California plates, parked in front of the post office. The sticker across the back window confirms it: University of California. Cameron's Jeep. I step off the curb toward it without thinking.

Erika grabs my hand. "Careful, you're gonna get run over." Then she follows my gaze to the Jeep. "What's wrong?"

"That's his car," I say, glancing ahead at Peyton and Mrs. Crane, who have passed us. "Cameron's."

Erika lets out a breath. "Oh, boy. Does he know you're in town again?"

"No."

Erika points discreetly to the post office door. "Well now's your chance."

Sure enough, there's Cameron coming out of the post office, wearing his old high school baseball hat and faded jeans. He's carrying a car seat. I see a flash of pink blanket as he swivels in the direction of his car.

"Look. He's got the baby."

I freeze.

"Go on," Erika says, elbowing me gently. "You might as well say hi."

I nod. But I can't bring myself to move. Cameron opens the Jeep door and tosses a package in the front seat.

"Quick, before he leaves," Erika says. If I jog up the street right now I could probably catch him.

"Are you girls coming?" Now Mrs. Crane has circled back to see what the holdup is, and with the whole crew of us staring up Main Street, I suddenly feel like a voyeur. There's no way I'm running after him now.

"Maggie is ogling her old boyfriend," Erika says, teasingly.

"What?" Mrs. Crane squints. "Oh. The Wilder boy. Yes, I heard he's back in town. Poor thing."

I don't know if the poor thing she's referring to is Cameron or his baby, but I feel a protective wave suddenly rise within me. Cameron doesn't need the likes of us in all our wedding-planning pastels spying on him from the front door of the shoe boutique.

"Come on," I say. "Peyton's gonna get all the good shoes."

Erika raises her eyebrows as we follow her mother, but I shake my head. The moment has passed. When we finally exit the store, three shopping bags between us and one pair of cream wedges for me later, I can't help but glance up the street. Cameron's Jeep is gone. Even though I figured it would be, I still feel a surge of disappointment.

"Where to next?" Mrs. Crane asks. "There are a few new shops down the road." Predictably, Peyton falls into step behind her. Erika lingers in the rear with me once more.

"He's gone, huh?"

I shrug.

"Why don't you give him a call later? When you have a little privacy." She nods at the two figures bustling ahead of us.

"What would I say?"

"Well, you'd better think fast." She points directly up the sidewalk.

It can't be. Headed our way, on our side of the street, is Cameron.

"Maggie?"

He stops just in front of me, the car seat in his arms the only thing between us. Erika has skittered ahead, leaving me behind.

"It's me!" It's all I can think of.

"Wow, twice in a matter of weeks. I thought you'd gone back to Boston for the rest of the summer."

"I did."

Cam nods, waiting for me to continue.

"But I'm back."

Cam breaks into a slow smile. "I can see that."

"I thought you'd left."

He cocks his head curiously. "Left?"

"You moved your Jeep. I mean, I saw you go by earlier. I wanted to say hi, but—"

He points up the street to where the Jeep is now parked. "I forgot to get stamps. Had to come back."

"Stamps. Huh." I wince. Who would ever believe that I was once an English major? Thankfully we are rescued from our ineloquent interaction by a little cooing sound. I kneel down mostly to break the awkward silence, but as soon as I'm level with Emory's piercing blue eyes, I don't want to look away. Her bow lips curl into a smile.

"Remember Emory? I don't think I introduced you properly last time." Cam looks bashful.

"Of course I remember. She's beautiful, Cam."

As if she is determined to make me eat my words, Emory's face suddenly goes beet-red and she arches in her car seat. A small wail erupts from her mouth.

"Oh, oh. I think she's had enough."

I stand up straighter. "Of me? Oh, no. I'm sorry."

"No, no," Cam laughs. "Of running errands. It's almost her nap time. Here. Do you mind holding her a sec?" To my horror, he passes the car seat to me. No sooner do I accept the handle than I lurch forward—tiny Emory is a lot heavier in this con-traption than she appears. The bumpy pass-off silences Emory's crying for a beat.

"Got her?" Cam asks.

"No problem," I say, straightening. And just like that, Emory lets out another long shrill wail.

"She's okay," Cam assures me, bending to reach inside her carrier. He fiddles with her straps, and in one deft move she is free. Cam cradles her head and lifts her from her little prison. Emory blinks at us, stunned.

"Hi, baby girl. Is that better?" he asks her.

She answers with another loud wail.

Cameron tucks her quickly against his chest, and motions to the car seat. "Could you please grab her pacifier? It's pink." There is nothing that sends grown men and women into motion like the squall of a baby. Especially in public.

Emory's shrill cry goes up another octave as I dig through

the little blanket in search of her pacifier. I know the magic of this miracle-inducing plastic sucker from watching Jane pop it into the mouths of her own kids. So where is it?

"It's not here," I cry, trying to raise my voice high enough to be heard over Emory's wails, but not loud enough to startle her further. Though I doubt she could be more perturbed.

"Try the diaper bag," Cam says. He is bouncing up and down in place, swaying back and forth, in an attempt to quell her.

I'm leaning against Cam now, as I fumble through the diaper bag hanging from his shoulder. I'm well acquainted with these bags from my niece and nephews. They have about four hundred pockets. As if a mother (or father) has either the time or the wherewithal to search through all those compartments for a miniature plastic soothing device. Finally, I locate it.

"Got it," I cry, holding it up for her to see. "Look, Emory!"

And at that moment, with me thrusting the pink pacifier triumphantly into the air and Emory still wailing over Cam's shoulder in the middle of the sidewalk, Erika, Peyton, and Mrs. Crane exit the boutique. I freeze.

Cam reaches for the pacifier and pops it into Emory's mouth. Instant silence.

"Are you ladies done shopping already?" I manage to ask in a nearly normal voice.

But they aren't listening to me. All three sets of eyes rest firmly on Cam, who turns Emory around to face us as he cradles her in his arms. Her face is a less frantic shade of red, her long eyelashes wet with tears. She works the pacifier rapidly in her tiny mouth, taking us all in.

"Cameron, you remember Mrs. Crane and Erika?" I say.

"Nice to see you all." Cam leans forward and offers the tips of his fingers, beneath Emory's round bottom, for an awkward handshake.

Mrs. Crane reaches forward and grips them warmly. I send her a million invisible thank-yous.

"Nice to see you," she says fondly.

Peyton is staring at Emory's flushed cheeks with a look of concern. I can't help but wonder how much she wants one of these little creatures now.

"This is my daughter, Emory," Cam tells them, proudly.

Mrs. Crane is the only one who looks genuinely delighted. She leans close to Emory. "Hello, little one." And just like that—*pop*—the pacifier flips out of Emory's pursed mouth. Before any of us can react, it hits the paved sidewalk with a tiny plastic *thwack*. Right on cue, Emory emits one of her deafening wails.

"Oh, dear." Mrs. Crane steps back and we all fumble for the pacifier. Erika retrieves it first. She shoves it at Cam, who holds it in his open palm between the five of us like a broken treasure. Five-second rule?

"Uh, I'm sure I have another. Somewhere," Cam says, not looking very sure at all. He hoists Emory back onto his shoulder, repeating the little jig he'd done earlier, and searches one-handed through the diaper bag. Erika winces. I'm pretty sure Peyton has taken several steps back.

"Let me." I take the bag from his shoulder and tug it open. All four of us women peer inside, like a group of hens pecking for the sole worm.

"Is this one okay?" Peyton plucks a yellow pacifier from a side pocket.

"Yes!" Cameron and I cry together. She drops it uncertainly in my outstretched hand and instead of passing it to Cameron I pop it directly into Emory's mouth. Her eyes flash open and she regards me coolly through her tears. *Cluck, cluck, cluck* goes her little mouth. We let out a communal sigh.

"Thanks." Cameron laughs uncomfortably. "I'm afraid we're overdue for a nap."

We nod as a unit, though Mrs. Crane is the only one who probably gets it. And even she looks like she'd rather be anywhere else right now. "Well, it was very nice to see you," she says quickly. "And Emma."

Cameron doesn't correct her.

The group says a quick goodbye and heads up the street toward the cars. I linger with Cam for a moment, feeling . . . what? That during this awkward little scrape we shared some kind of parental triumph?

"I'd better get Emory home," he says. It occurs to me then that this success I'm feeling proud of is just one of thousands that he probably experiences each day, no one more or less special than any other.

I hoist the diaper bag back over his shoulder for him. "Can I help you put her back in her car seat?" For some reason, I don't want to leave just yet.

"Oh, right." He looks at the car seat still on the sidewalk. "So much *stuff* for such little people," he laughs. It's a standard parent joke, and one that I realize he's now in on. "That would be great, thanks."

I lift up the straps and hold them to the sides, as I've helped Jane do with each of her kids. Cameron gently lowers baby Emory into her plush floral cocoon, and when she makes contact with the seat there is a loaded pause as she contemplates how to respond to this. We both hold our breath. Emory looks at him, then me, her big blue eyes intense and alert. But then she settles.

"Phew. Sometimes that doesn't go so well. She likes to be held," Cam says.

I watch Cam tuck her chubby little arms through the straps, and then I click the center buckle over her round belly. Our hands brush as we work together, and he looks up at me.

"You're pretty good at this," he says.

I smile. "Yeah. Well, Jane has three kids. I've been on aunt duty for a while now."

He hoists the car seat, Emory between us once more. "Thanks, Mags. It was really good seeing you."

"You, too."

We hesitate a moment longer, until Emory makes a small noise behind her pacifier. "Better run," he says. And then he leans forward and plants a quick kiss on me. It's platonic, firmly placed in the center of my cheek. But in that one swoop, I smell Cameron: pine and fresh-cut grass. Like the summer camp we worked at. Like his house, in the pine grove by the Mystic River. He smells like the sweet memory of all those college summers.

When I open my eyes, he is already moving away from me. And down the street.

"Wait," I call. Cam turns.

"I'm home for a while. Maybe we could get together? Or something?"

He looks surprised. But then he says, "Yeah. Yeah, I'd like that."

This is not my style. I am not the girl who shouts after old boyfriends in the street. Certainly not to ask them to get together. Certainly not when I have a boyfriend. But this doesn't feel wrong. In fact, it's the first thing all day that's felt right.

"Call my cell. It's listed under my business name," Cam calls back to me.

"Which is?"

"Saltwater Construction." His smile almost levels me right there in the middle of Main Street.

Ten

Erika holds the bottle of Veuve Clicquot against her chest. "Cheers to my girls," she announces. "For coming to Mystic and rescuing my wedding day!" We're huddled on the four-poster bed in Erika's childhood bedroom, across which is spread an array of preteen slumber-party food: a box of cupcakes from the market, a bag of popcorn, and carrot sticks for Erika. Tonight is about comfort: in lieu of champagne glasses we sip from old mismatched Stonington High Bears coffee mugs, and except for Peyton, who's breaking in a new pair of patent red sandals, we're dressed in our pj's and socks. We clink our mugs ceremoniously. "And to Maggie, who was right about coming home," Erika adds.

It's a funny thing. Since moving to Boston, Erika and I have both returned to Mystic to visit, but oddly enough, never together. Gone were the long college vacations that once drew us back home at the same times. Which makes it special now; it's as if we're back in high school again, and planning what to do with the intoxicating freedom of a teenage weekend. "It's good to be back, isn't it?" I say. But even though she feels the nostalgic novelty, too, it's not the same.

Unlike my room back at home, whose dusty-pink walls are still covered in posters, Erika's room has been professionally re-decorated. Her mother has repainted the walls in ivory, and the taffeta drapes are a rich burnt copper. It looks like something out of a southern mansion, with its sconce lighting and rich embroidered accents. I hate it: I wish that Erika's pom-poms were still hanging over her bed and that our high school photos lined her bookshelves in neon frames.

"What do you think the guys are doing at home?" Peyton asks.

Erika rolls over onto her tummy. "Trent said he was going out with guys from work."

They turn to me, expectantly. "What about Evan?"

"Working late on set," I say. "Again." I've told them about his new scenes with Angie Dune. That's the thing with friends: you don't have to hold back on your gut response. And you know they won't, either. "Are you kidding me?" Erika practically shouted. "Are you going to go down there and watch?"

"I've never been to his set," I reminded her. "Wouldn't it be a little obvious to suddenly show up for that particular scene? Besides, Evan isn't supposed to bring friends by to gawk. You know how sensitive he is about keeping things professional. It's his first show."

My friends find it strange that Evan has never invited me to visit his set. But it's his first big break, and it's important to him not to get distracted.

"If that were Trent, I'd find a way on set," Erika had said, confirming the sense of initial dread that I'd felt when Evan told me about their new love scenes. I'm still not crazy about it, but what really bothers me has more to do with the fact that

Angie Dune sees more of my boyfriend than I do in any given week.

"Once you get settled into a new place and he wraps up this season, you guys will be able to spend more time together," Erika reassures me now, flopping back on a pile of pillows.

"Speaking of new places, have you found anything yet?" Peyton asks.

I shake my head. "There was a cute one-bedroom that I could actually afford on the West End, but when I called, it had already been scooped up."

"So are you going to look for another roommate?" Peyton asks.

I smile. "Actually, I already have one. Evan wants us to move in together."

Erika shrieks. "I knew it! That would be so great. Now you can get a bigger place."

"Were you surprised when he asked?" Peyton wants to know.

I smile. "Not really. I was more relieved."

Peyton looks at me funny, and I know what she's thinking. Why not *thrilled*?

"Now I won't have to worry about you!" Erika says matter-of-factly. "I didn't like the thought of you living alone in the city."

I don't add that I didn't, either. "Evan's going to keep an eye out, and the plan is to start looking at places together when I get back. In fact, I'm thinking I might head back to town next week."

"Which brings me to someone we ran into in *this* town." Peyton, having moved on already, props herself up intently on her elbows. "So, what's the scoop on this Cameron?"

I shrug. "I ran into him a few weeks ago when I was home for my mom's birthday party. But other than that, I haven't talked to him since senior year in college. It's weird bumping into someone you were once so close to."

Erika can't help but chime in. "He was the boy-next-door summer romance that ended like they all do. He went out west, Mags came to Boston. Now he's a dad, and she's got Evan. End of story."

"Thanks for the plot summary," I say, elbowing her playfully. But I notice that Erika seems eager to switch the subject. She's never been a big fan of Cameron, something I could never put my finger on.

"Whatever he was, he's pretty cute," Peyton says. Her eyes are growing glassy, which means she's reached that in-between stage of a light buzz and sheer joy. Which is not too far off from total wretchedness, bent over a toilet bowl.

"Cute or not, he's on a whole different page from where his life used to be," Erika reminds us. "He's got a kid now. What woman is going to want to walk in and take all that on?"

Her words hit me in the stomach.

"At least he's stepping up and doing the right thing," Peyton says.

Erika isn't as admiring. "What choice does he have? The mother left." Then, "What kind of woman up and leaves her own kid, anyway?"

"We don't know the whole story," I say, sifting carefully through the details Cameron shared with me on the phone that night I called him. I'm not sure if it's more out of respect for his confidence, or out of my own desire to keep it to myself, but I haven't disclosed all the details to them yet. "From what Cameron said, they were a grad school couple about to head out on environmental internships, and Emory came as a huge surprise during their final semester. Apparently Lauren stuck around in the beginning, but ultimately she couldn't handle it." The girls are studying me carefully, and I'm sure Erika is wondering when this news was made privy to me. And why I haven't shared it with her sooner.

"Well, I can't imagine it. But I also can't imagine leaving your baby."

"Maybe she suffered from depression, or something. Postpartum is a pretty prevalent thing, you guys," Peyton says. Then, when we look at her strangely, "What? So I've done a little reading."

"My sister had postpartum," I say. When it happened, it didn't seem as close to home as it does now. I was fresh out of college and moving to Boston for my first job. I felt for Jane, but I can't say I ever really understood it.

"I'd forgotten about that." Erika sits up, suddenly more interested.

"Remember? After Randall was born. It was really hard on her: she could barely get out of bed. And she had Owen to look after, too."

Peyton's expression softens. "I feel like the more people I know who've had children, the more I'm hearing about it. It's out there and it's happening, but it's not something anyone talks about at the time."

I appreciate Peyton's sensitivity. "Well, it's not really something you want to talk about. Everyone's so excited to meet the baby, no one wants to hear that the mom is crying on the toilet while her husband hovers outside the bathroom door with a bawling infant who needs to nurse."

"Was it really that bad for Jane?" she wants to know.

"For a little while it was. But Jane saw a therapist, and my mom stepped in to help. It didn't last more than a couple of months, and she's in a great place now."

"Since we're talking about babies," Peyton interjects, sitting up taller, "there's something I want to share with you girls."

Erika's the first to ask. "Oh my God. Are you pregnant?"

Peyton bites her lip, something she does only when she's nervous, which is rarely. "Not yet." She breaks into a huge smile, and I can't help but smile, too. "But we're trying."

We take turns with congratulations and hugs. It's a mixed emotion: the thrill tangled up with the acknowledgment that our lives are changing, and we're all heading in different directions. Again.

"I'm ready," Peyton says. Her voice is rich with determination, and I can see it in her eyes. "Chad and I have been talking about it for a while. I'm in a good place at work, and we're all moved in to our new home. If there's such a thing as a good time, this seems like it." She looks around at us, gauging our response.

Erika's words are generous and immediate. "You're going to be a great mom."

"What do you want, boy or girl?" I want to know.

"Healthy," Peyton says without missing a beat. Then she ducks her chin bashfully. "Full disclosure: I do have visions of a pink-and-brown gingham for the nursery."

"Ha!" I laugh. "I knew it."

"But this is just between us," Peyton says, wagging her finger. "Chad would kill me if he knew I'd told you guys this early on. So, zip your lips." She turns to Erika. "And you, young lady, have some work to do. My baby's going to need a playmate."

Erika smiles obligingly. "Where's the bottle?" she asks, hopping off the bed. "With all this baby and wedding talk, I need another drink."

I groan in agreement and hold up my mug.

"Count me in," Peyton says.

Erika holds up a hand. "Hang on. Should you drink if you're trying?"

Peyton rolls her eyes. "Do you see Chad in this bed?"

"Please. Give the girl a drink, or she's going to start talking baby names," I warn.

A look of delight flashes across Peyton's face. "Well, since you mention it . . . Emma if it's a girl, and Devon if it's a boy."

I cover my ears. "Make her stop."

"Although Reese is a good unisex choice."

"That's it!" Erika grabs the nearest pillow and whacks Peyton. After a cry of faux outrage and a quick adjustment of her ponytail, she jumps up and grabs a pillow of her own.

There's a moment of stillness, and then we all fall into it like ten-year-olds at a slumber party.

Later, as we lie on Erika's bed catching our breath and absorbing the events of the night, I can't help but think about the bottom line that Erika was getting at earlier. Cameron isn't a hero. He's just a young guy with a child who has had to grow up fast. Who has long outgrown the college memories of an old girlfriend the likes of me.

◆ ◆ ◆

It's almost midnight when I finally tiptoe into my house. Mom has taped ads for several local job openings for me on the fridge, not because she thinks my job will be cut, but just in case *I decide* I don't want to return to Darby. *Second-grade teacher. Lit-*

eracy teacher. And a UConn Master of Fine Arts flyer, for good measure. The fridge contents are much less interesting than when we were kids. Mom's salad fixings, Dad's Cadbury bars. But standing in the kitchen doorway, I suddenly know what I want. And it's not in the fridge.

On the den laptop I type in *Saltwater Construction.* The site is impressive, from the crisp graphic design to the video tours of past projects. I scroll through Cameron's work: residential renovations and a historic lighthouse preservation. Instantly, I feel a stab of shame for having lamented his foray into carpentry and leaving marine biology. The guy has talent.

I look at the clock. It's twelve thirty. Cameron won't be walking in the door from a Saturday night with friends. He'll be long asleep. Or, more likely, waking throughout the night to feed Emory. My phone vibrates on the desk beside me. There are three new texts from Evan. It occurs to me that since coming home, I haven't gotten in touch with him once. I close the laptop and head upstairs to bed.

Eleven

The next morning I awake in my childhood bed. Sunlight streams through the gingham curtains and I roll over, pulling the pillow over my eyes.

My parents are down in the kitchen. "You came in late last night," my mother remarks. I don't remind her that I am no longer sixteen. "Here, I made your favorite."

She plunks a plate of blueberry pancakes at my usual seat at the kitchen table. All I really want is to make a small fruit smoothie and then go for a run.

"So what's the plan, Stan?" The Paul Simon reference is an old favorite that my dad has used on us for as long as I can remember, but this time I have to force the smile. He sits beside me and digs in to his own plate, which is swimming in a thick puddle of syrup.

"No plans," I say.

"How's the wedding coming along?" My mother's eyes are bright at the mention of it.

"Erika decided on the yacht club, and the menu is pretty much set. It looks like it's going to work out after all."

My mother nods approvingly, pointing the spatula as she talks. "I think it's wonderful she's having it here in Mystic. So much nicer for a summer wedding. Her mother must be relieved."

My father shakes his head. "Such a lot of money for one day," he says ruefully. He knows this, of course, having married off Jane already.

"So what are you and the girls doing today?" Mom asks.

"The girls are going back to Boston this morning, and I think I'm going to head out for a run."

"Already?" my mother asks, turning from the stovetop. "But they just got home."

My mom seems to be under the impression that we are all home for summer vacation, as if we're all still in college. Which makes me wary of staying home too long—I don't want her to think that just because my circumstances are up in the air at the moment that I'll be moving back home. "Mom, they have work tomorrow."

Her eyes flash hopefully and she points to the fridge. "Did you see what I saved there for you?"

It's no use. I shove a forkful of pancakes in my mouth. "I did, thanks. But what's with the MFA program at UConn? I live in Boston. And I'm a teacher."

She lifts one shoulder and smiles. "I know, but you've always loved to paint. I still have your art portfolio upstairs in the hall closet. And if things change at Darby, this might be a window for you to open."

"Can't hurt to think about it," my dad says, swirling the last of his pancake around the plate. "You're only young once. Before you get tied down to a mortgage and a family, you should consider your options."

I love that my parents' belief in me is as unwavering today as it was when I won second place in the school art show with a watercolor of a cardinal. I can't think of any friends whose parents are as doggedly supportive; if Erika had ever wondered aloud about going to grad school to study art, her father would've had a heart attack. In her house, business was the only way to get ahead, and getting ahead was what it was about. It makes me realize how lucky I am. But we're well past the years of trying out for talent shows or taking a semester to study abroad. At this point in my life, practicality isn't something I can afford to shake a stick at.

I thank my mom anyway, and tuck the brochure into my purse in the mudroom before grabbing my sneakers. Even if I have to be a grown-up, I love the fact that someone else still hears the voice of my childhood.

Our street is quiet on Sunday mornings, despite the snug houses tucked in side by side. I jog to the bottom of our hill and turn left toward town. River Road is a popular running route that loops outside of the village and along the Mystic River. Across the way to my right is the Seaport, its long wooden pier dotted by boats. The brackish river water is pungent in the morning air. Rocky outcroppings rise among the wooded hillside on my left. I jog past the dirt pull-off for the Peace Sanctuary Lookout, a spot I climbed regularly as a kid. Just beyond it the woods give way to sloping green lawns, and private homes dot that side of the road.

My favorite, the historic Edwin Bate House, looms ahead on my left. Mystic is famous for its seafaring past, so historic homes are prevalent. But this one has always been special. As little girls, Jane and I fondly dubbed it "the wedding cake house" because of its romantic white Greek Revival portico. I slow as I pass, noting for the first time that the stately white façade has been stripped of paint. Workers have erected scaffolding on the northern side of the house, where clapboard siding has been removed. I wonder who owns it now.

After two miles, I turn around and head back toward town. The sound of power tools breaks the morning stillness, and this time I stop at the bottom of the driveway of the Edwin Bate house for a better look. Now its stripped front gives the old captain's home an air of vulnerability beyond its age. Stained insulation sags from gaps in the clapboards. A worker on a high scaffold tears off a strip of siding, and a wave of protectiveness rises inside me as it falls into a pile of debris with a splintering clatter. The house has been empty for several years, but now my curiosity propels me up the driveway.

I'm met with the burning smell of a power saw cutting through fresh pine. The stately national historic registry placard inscribed *Captain Edwin Bate* has been removed from the front entrance, and for a beat I imagine the house like a lost pet without its ID tags. The workers don't seem to notice me as I head up the stone walkway. I pause at the front door, which someone has left ajar. "Hello? Is anyone inside?"

It's been years since I've been in this entryway, the farthest I've ventured into the house, when we trick-or-treated as kids. The high ceilings of the foyer are painted a pale blue, and the doorways leading into the main rooms off the giant entryway are tented in plastic. But the grandeur of the house rings through, despite the sawdust and debris of construction.

I'm half-tempted to keep going, but outside there is a sudden crash. I step back out, glancing nervously at the scaffold.

Dust rises from a newly dropped pile of siding. As I stand there looking at it, one of the guys hauling it away catches sight of me. "Can I help you?" he shouts.

I shouldn't be here. So, I offer him a quick wave and head down the front steps. I slip between two big vehicles in the driveway, glancing quickly at the logo on the door of one of the trucks as I jog by. *Saltwater Construction*, the words encircling a bold compass rose. I halt, a fresh plume of curiosity rising.

The worker is still watching me from the front yard. "Hey," I shout back to him, feeling bolder now. "Where's Cameron Wilder?"

"Not here," he shouts back.

I raise my hand once more before breaking into a run toward home, muttering to myself, "And neither was I."

◆ ◆ ◆

Before the day is over, Jane calls. I'm out on the back porch, with a book, an iced tea, and a bottle of dark pink nail polish.

"So, I hear you're home! What's new? How's summer going?" Jane's voice is suspiciously melodic, and her house is suspiciously quiet in the background.

I lean back into the lounge cushions and admire my still-wet Watermelon Juice pedicure. "Well, considering school ended forty-eight hours ago, so far so good." I pause. "What's up, Jane?"

She lowers her voice to a desperate whisper, all pretense of polite inquiry abandoned. "You have to come over."

I sit up. "What's wrong? Is it one of the kids?"

"No. It's me. And my sanity. Toby's firm is going on their

annual summer golf trip to Newport. And I'm going with him."
She says the last part as if she's running away.

"Next weekend?"

"Tomorrow. I need your help."

I put the brush back in the nail polish. "You can't be serious."

"As a heart attack, Maggie. Think full cardiac arrest."

This is not like Jane. Sure, she has lured me home in the
past to help out with the kids so that she and Toby could snag a
brief getaway or a night out. But that was with a polite week of
advance notice. Tailed closely by adulation, good-natured cajol-
ing, and subsequent bribery. She *cannot* expect me to sacrifice
my first days of summer. "Jane. No way. School just ended. I
haven't even had time to locate my flip-flops. And you want me
to babysit the kids for how many days?"

"Yes. Yes, that is exactly what I want. And it's only three days."

"What's going on?" I have my own problems to deal with
this summer, and as much as I love my nephews and niece,
I've got an apartment to find and a job hanging in the balance.
Babysitting three kids for three days is hardly the retreat I came
home for.

"What's going *on*?" Jane echoes me in a tone somewhere
roughly between exhaustion and hysteria. "How much time do
you have?"

Never enough, I think to myself. "Just tell me."

"Randall has boycotted potty training. As in, he's launched a
total potty prohibition. He will not go. At all. Anywhere. Until
he cannot hold it anymore, at which point he whips off his
pull-up diaper, usually in public, and aims. Today he stripped
down and peed all over the library rug. Right in the middle of
Mommy and Me story time."

I can see where this would be upsetting. But I am not sold. "I'm sorry to hear that."

"And then there's Lucy. Who is teething. She's been up crying all night and all day. And now she wants to nurse twenty-four–seven."

"Jane, that sounds awful, it really does, but my plate is kind of full at the moment, you know?"

"Wait, there's more. Owen. My sweet-tempered, sleep-through-the-night-since-three-months-old, lovable, easy Owen, has suddenly decided that there are trolls under his bed. And he will not enter his room day or night without me. Or get into his bed. For anything. Which includes sleeping."

"So where does he sleep?" I ask, scrambling to keep up with the nightmarish images that pop up as fast as Jane can narrate them.

"Oh, you know. Somewhere in *my* bed. Depending on where Lucy and her teething rings are sprawled. Or where Randall has not peed in the last two hours. Usually in the spot where Toby no longer sleeps, since he's moved out onto the living room couch."

I let out a long breath. "Jane."

"Maggie!"

I want to help. But rescuing Jane from her offspring in crisis mode is far beyond my "Aunty Mags" qualifications. "I'm sorry you're going through this. Truly. But if you and Toby are overwhelmed, then how could I possibly manage all this on my own?"

Jane doesn't miss a beat. "Tiny white straitjackets, Maggie. Blow horns. Chocolate bars. Whatever it takes." There is a knocking sound in the background.

"Where are you?" I ask, suddenly cognizant of the fact that

I have not had an uninterrupted and child-free phone call with my sister in the same number of years since her firstborn has been on earth.

"In my office."

I wince. "The toilet?"

"You're catching up."

"Have you talked to Mom about this?" I'm buying time. And attempting to assemble some footmen.

"I don't want to bother her."

So, you're bothering me. In the aftershock weekend since twenty-three nine-year-olds exited my classroom. The very classroom that I may not be returning to. In a city where I have to find a new place to live. I close my eyes.

"Jane, is there any way Toby can reschedule his trip and help out? This sounds like a family thing."

"No! He offered to stay home, but I won't let him. I *need* this golf trip."

I consider this. "But you don't golf."

"Maggie. Listen very carefully. I don't care if they're going *boar hunting*. This trip is in Newport, where there are beaches and sailboats, and seaside bistros that serve cocktails with names like High Tide Painkiller."

The background knocking sound grows, followed by voices.

"Mommy is *busy*!" Jane hisses. I can picture the kids and the dog hovering outside the bathroom door. Except for Randall, who's likely peeing on an antique carpet.

"Okay, okay. I get it."

There is a high-pitched gasp on the other line. "So, you'll come then?"

"After the picture you've just painted? What choice do I

have?" Already a headache is creeping across my forehead. There goes my weekend apartment hunting with Evan. And the intoxicating beauty of the unplanned, unfettered, first weekend of summer nothingness I'd been chasing since last September. "But you owe me big."

Jane is instantly restored. "Mags, you're the best! Thank God. Thank *you*." The background knocking has grown to pounding, and I can hear the bathroom lock click open. I collapse back into the recess of the lounge chair cushions.

Jane's singsong voice is robust and jovial as she returns to her little charges. "My darlings! Mommy's back. Guess *who's* coming to visit?"

Twelve

M y single goal for the weekend is for my sister and brother-in-law to return home to find their three off-spring accounted for, moderately clean, and mostly dressed. Not exactly reaching for the stars, I know. But so far I have managed to do just what I had hoped for. As an unexpected triumph, I also successfully bathed Lucy after she covered her hair in pureed sweet potato at lunch. While the replacement of Mommy with the aunt hasn't necessarily won Lucy over, the boys have fallen in line. Owen slept soundly the first night on his cot beside Jane's bed. I actually enjoyed going to sleep to the soft rumble of his little-boy snores. Randall has only had one "accident," thankfully outside in the yard. And even Lucy's teething troubles seem to have diminished.

Despite my windfall success thus far, Saturday afternoon finds us collapsed across the living room in various states of repose, desperately in need of a new activity. We've exhausted the LEGO bin, the finger paints have finally been scrubbed from the kitchen island, and Samson the dog, having been relieved of his dress-up clothes, stares at me from the safety of his bed like he rather wishes we'd all just vaporize. I don't blame him. While this is hardly the time to get in touch with Cam, suddenly I have the urge to commune with someone who will be as spent as me.

"What do you think about going to the playground?" I ask, clapping my hands together. It's the exact kind of utterance that causes my father to frown during family visits, his eyebrows knitting together. "We never used to *ask* you kids where you wanted to go," he'd say. "We just *told* you. You were lucky to be going at all."

So, in that vein, when Randall shakes his head, *No*, I scoop him up with one hand and snag his sneakers in the other. "It'll be fun!"

With our destination not up for further discussion, we have crossed one hurdle. Actually pulling out of the garage is quite another matter entirely. We pause outside my sister's minivan in disarray. "I'm hungry," Randall groans, holding his stomach as if he hadn't just eaten a grilled cheese sandwich and a box of Goldfish an hour ago. But apparently I've forgotten snacktime. To delay any longer would invite an upset of biblical proportion. I also realize that Owen's wearing fuzzy slippers, which Jane would tell me is an invitation for injury on the playground. And I cannot find Lucy's backup pacifier, which even Randall declares we are *not* leaving the house without.

After nineteen minutes scrambling between the mudroom and the garage, I have assembled a small cargo of goods that would likely ensure survival in the minivan for at least a week. A diaper bag, a toy bag, a snack bag, three sippy cups, a tiny pink sweater, one more cup of coffee, and a pair of knotted sneakers later, we are ready to go. Buckling the kids into their respective car seats should only take another seventy-two minutes. When

I finally slide into the driver's seat and glance in the rearview mirror, Owen looks stricken. "What about Randall?"

I swivel around. Sure enough, Randall's car seat, which I strapped him into not thirty seconds ago, is now empty. Owen points. Beyond the windshield, in the far corner of the garage, attempting to scale a stepladder, is his brother. Not for the first time this weekend I offer a reverential nod to my sister and make a mental note to stop at the liquor store on the way home; I don't know how she does it. I pull out my phone and call Cam.

◆ ◆ ◆

We drive to the playground at Owen's school. It's a gorgeous afternoon, and a towering leafy maple provides just the right amount of shade as Lucy and I sink onto a bench together to watch the boys who have taken off at breakneck speed for the swings. There is only a small handful of other parents and children around. "Take turns, boys!" I call, as Randall scrambles up the front of the slide into Owen, who is coming down. We're only four hours away from their parents' much-anticipated return: all front teeth are still in place, and I plan to keep it that way.

"Boys can be rough," someone says from nearby.

Lucy's head swivels. But I know this voice.

"Cam." My chest flip-flops as I slide over to make room for him on the bench.

Emory is strapped to Cam's chest in a baby carrier, facing out, and as he sits next to us, she and Lucy lock eyes. Over Lucy's cherubic smile is Cam's own, and in the face of all that brightness I can't help but grin back.

"Dare I say, it looks like you have your hands more full than

I do?" he says jokingly. He unstraps the carrier and lifts Emory out, placing her close to Lucy. Her chubby legs kick in excitement. "I certainly didn't expect to see you with two more kids than I have."

I laugh. "I didn't expect to be here with them," I admit. "I'm watching my nephews and Lucy for the weekend while Jane and her husband are in Newport." I lift Lucy up so she can look at them. "But I think I'll stick around a bit."

"You staying for the summer?"

"Not the *whole* summer," I say, emphatically. But it occurs to me that even after a grueling few days planning the wedding with Erika, and now babysitting Jane's kids—things that would normally have me hightailing it back to Boston—oddly enough, I still have no burning desire to pack up. Evan's been so busy at work, all we've managed is a few brief calls. And besides, it's been surprisingly nice being back at home. "Yeah, the school year ended and I figured it'd be good to get out of the city for a little while."

Cam turns and smiles. "Welcome home, Griffin." He's got an attractive couple of days' growth on his chin, and that weekend-rumpled look that I like: relaxed and happy. Very different from the last time I saw him on Main Street, and in a good way. I glance away and turn my attention to Lucy.

"How old is she? Six months?" Cam asks.

"Seven," I say, marveling at his accuracy. Jane complains all the time that Toby can't remember the ages of his own kids.

The babies are entranced by each other, and Emory's leg thumps against Cam's lap as she tries to wiggle closer. Lucy keeps turning her head away, then glancing back coyly, giggling.

"So, how beat are you after a weekend with the kids?" He pauses, then adds, "Tell the truth!"

I laugh. "Totally beat." By the time I tucked the kids into bed both nights, I forgot all about my plans to steal a few hours' peace in front of the TV, collapsing instead into a dreamless fog beside Owen. "How's Emory as a sleeper?"

"She's getting better," Cam says, "though I've aged about ten years in the process." His eyes crinkle when he says it, the same way they used to when we'd joke around together.

"Kids. They're no small job," I say, in agreement.

"Speaking of small . . ." Cam looks at Emory with obvious tenderness. "You can't believe the quantity and scale of the equipment these little people come with. The high chairs, the Pack 'n Play, the swing, the changing table . . ." He lets out a long breath.

I point across the playground at Randall, spinning at vomit-inducing speed on a tire swing. "Just wait until she can get away from you."

Cam shakes his head. "Honestly, I'm so tired, I can't think five minutes past now."

I stand Lucy up on my lap and bounce her on my knees. "I can't wait for a good night's sleep tomorrow night," I admit, thinking wistfully of my childhood bed and an open window. But I feel foolish the second it comes out of my mouth. I've only had to do this for two days, after all.

Cam just smiles knowingly. "Tell me about it."

On the jungle gym, Randall is poised at the edge of a high landing. "Randall, no jumping!" I call, remembering that I'm not only using "no" again, but now yelling it across the expanse of the playground. "Let's make safe choices," I add quickly.

As we watch the boys fling themselves onto the playground equipment, I question my decision to call Cam. Strapped with four little kids between us, it's more like a test in sanity than a chance to meaningfully catch up. And at this rate I am probably only cementing the impression that I have no idea what I'm doing.

"You're doing great," Cam says, as if reading my mind.

"You're lying."

"No, you are. But you may want to take Randall to the restroom."

I look up just in time to see Randall tugging on the waist-band of his pants and assuming the squat position by the slide.

One breakneck stop in the Porta-Potty later, I'm beyond ready for Jane to come home. My phone rings.

"Hello?"

"Maggie? It's John Hartman."

Lucy begins to fuss and I cradle my cell under my chin while jiggling her up and down on my hip.

"I tried calling you at home but couldn't reach you."

"Yes, sorry about that. I'm visiting family for a couple days," I say, knowing that the board must have made a decision for John to be tracking me down. I hold my breath.

"Is now a good time?"

I move away from the playground noise toward a small grove of trees, straining to listen. "Now is great," I lie. "Do you have any news?"

John sighs. "I just heard from the board of directors. I'm sorry, Maggie. They're cutting both positions after all."

I spin around. Randall is perched at the top of the slide. I watch as he flops down on his bottom and launches himself down the chute, my breath escaping my chest with the same whoosh. "I see."

"We looked at every viable option to try to avoid this, but with enrollment down, the board can't justify the expenditure. I really wish it were otherwise, Maggie."

Randall's feet emerge from the tunnel at the bottom of the slide. He lies very still, looking up at the sky.

"I know, John. I appreciate you pulling for me." Tears prick the corners of my eyes.

"I've written you a strong reference, Maggie. You're a natural, and I hate to lose you. If there's anything I can do to help, don't hesitate to ask."

John's sincerity is palpable, and I know this is hard for him, too. But I can't help but wonder that my reference is already in the mail. I think of the cardboard box sitting on my desk at Darby. The sole box I didn't pack in the trunk of my car as a last-ditch attempt at wishful thinking.

"I will," I say, turning back to the bench. "Thank you."

"Everything okay?" Cam asks. The sun is low in the sky, highlighting his earnest expression.

"Yeah," I lie. "Just a friend." There is nothing I can do right now. Not about the box on my desk back in Boston or the teacher applications I will apparently be filling out now with fresh urgency. At the moment all I can think about are the facts that I have nothing for dinner, Lucy's diaper probably needs to be changed, and I'll need to cajole everyone off the playground before I can even contemplate the joy of strapping them back into their car seats. A fresh sense of helplessness washes over me.

Beside me Emory starts to fuss. "I should probably get her home," Cam announces. "It's about dinnertime. And that's a nonnegotiable in our world, huh, Em?"

Suddenly the thought of Cam getting up and leaving is more than I can bear. Without thinking I blurt out, "Wait. Want to grab a couple of slices at Mystic Pizza?"

Cam pauses to adjust Emory on his lap. His blue eyes travel lovingly over her face. "Well, I'm afraid Emory's too young for the pepperoni special," he says, gesturing at her toothless smile.

I nod, embarrassed both by my rash invitation and lack of attention to detail—Cam's most important detail of all. I should just round up the boys and take them home. I should get back to Boston and get my life together.

But then Cam grins at me. "Though I'd love a slice."

◆ ◆ ◆

The boys are wiped out, the playground having exhausted the last fumes of their seemingly bottomless tanks. They slump wordlessly into the vinyl booths at Mystic Pizza while I settle Lucy's car seat on the bench beside me, and, for the first time all weekend, we all sit still.

Across from me, Cam balances Emory and her bottle in one arm and holds up a menu. "What do you think, will two pizzas do it?"

I do a silent count in my head, knowing the boys will easily eat two pieces each. "We could probably get away with a large," I say.

Owen begins to protest. "Nah," Cam says, waving his hand, "let's get two. Then you can bring home leftovers, right, Owen?"

Owen and Randall clap.

"Okay, who can draw their favorite toppings?" I ask, smiling gratefully as the waitress delivers crayons and paper to the booth.

As they get down to business with their paper pizzas and I get Lucy started on a jar of butternut squash baby food, I look up to find Cam watching me. "Look at you. You're quite the natural." Emory, also worn out from fresh air and new faces, is nodding off in the crook of his arm. Glancing down at Lucy, I see she's not far behind.

"It's always a toss of the dice taking her out," I say. "I get so focused on keeping up with the boys that I have to remind my-self to slow things down and stick to her feedings and naps. Or all the wheels fall off the bus."

Cam laughs. "Yeah. I've had too many rides on that bus." He leans closer, admiring Lucy, who sucks noisily on the spoon. "But she looks rather pleased with life. I'd say Aunty Mags has pulled it off."

Pulling off the burp is another matter entirely. Lucy is not an easy burper, but I know from experience it's not something I can skip. This isn't my last clean pair of jeans for no reason.

Cam watches as I lift her over my shoulder, suddenly self-conscious. Despite my gentle flat-handed pats, Lucy won't give up the burp. I pat a little faster and firmer. Still nothing. And she's starting to protest.

"Did you ever try the sitting burp?" Cam asks.

"The what?"

Cam sits Emory up facing out, to demonstrate. "That looks complicated," I say, switching shoulders instead, and resuming my rapid-fire patting. I'm beginning to break out in a sweat.

He shrugs. "Or you can keep thumping. It's got a decent beat." I give him a level look. It's not lost on either of us that he is the expert here, so finally I surrender.

"Face her toward me, and lean her forward just a little." I try my best to mimic Cam's demonstration. On the first pat Lucy emits the loudest belly burp I've ever heard, which sends the boys into a fitful of giggles.

Cam winks. "Well played."

The pizza place is still empty at this early hour. Having settled Lucy, I'm finally able to lean back and let out a long breath. "So, you're the one tearing apart my favorite house in town," I say.

Cam's eyes twinkle. "You know the Bate house?"

"Jane and I used to call it the Wedding Cake House, it was so beautiful. Please tell me the owners aren't changing it."

"Oh, they're changing it," Cam says.

"What do you mean?"

He smiles. "Relax. They're actually restoring the original design. We're even returning the front portico to its former self. Which you've probably never seen, unless you've looked at pictures in the Historical Society."

I shake my head. "My favorite part was that portico; it looked so grand, especially flanked by the formal landscaping."

"Then you'll love the restoration. It's even grander," he says.

"Are they having the side gardens restored, too? Wasn't there a fountain?"

Cameron nods, seeming genuinely surprised at my interest in the house. "You seem to know quite a bit, Griffin. You should come by sometime. Make sure I'm doing it honor."

"I'd love to."

As we talk softly over the kids' heads, the scratch of crayons on the tabletop the only other sounds, I'm struck by an overwhelming sense of peace: this sticky, sleepless, minute-to-minute marathon of a weekend with the kids has actually been the most rewarding few days I can remember.

When the pizzas arrive the boys devour their slices, reviving just enough to pepper Cam with questions. "How do you know my aunt?" Owen asks, studying Cam carefully.

"Your aunt and I have been friends for a long time. We both grew up here in Mystic."

Owen considers this information as Randall interjects with his own questions in quick succession. "What's your baby's name? How old is she? She's smaller than my baby." He points across the table at Lucy. "That's my baby."

Cam answers each question, and even balances Emory in one arm as he helps Randall cut his piece of pizza into small squares with the other.

"Thanks, Cam, but I can do it."

"I've got it," he says, watching as Randall shoves three small squares into his mouth at once. "Easy there, tiger."

Emory has begun squirming in his lap. "I think I need to change her," Cam says, rising. He glances out the window to where his Jeep is parked.

"Outside?"

He shrugs. "Typical single-dad problem—the only changing table is in the women's room."

I hold out my arms. "Let me."

Cam shakes his head. "Thanks, but you're still eating. Besides, it's no big deal, I'm used to this."

I stand up. "Cam, hand her over. Unless you think it'd upset her." I look at Emory's thick-lashed eyes warily. Such tiny people can exert such huge control.

Cam looks relieved. "Thanks, Mags. She won't mind at all," he adds, passing her gently to me. He slides into my seat beside Lucy, who looks at Cam like she might mind, however, and I say a quick prayer for everyone at the table to just keep it together for five more minutes.

Cam rummages through Emory's diaper bag. "It helps if you give her this guy to hold when you change her." He pulls out a fuzzy gray hippo. "And there's one more thing." A look of consternation crosses Cam's face. "You'll probably notice her scar."

"Scar?"

He touches his chest gently. "Shortly after she was born, Emory had to have some surgery." He pauses, glancing over at the boys still working on their pizza, and lowers his voice. "She has a heart condition."

Standing in the middle of the pizza place with Emory tucked against my chest, all I can do is nod. But a thousand urgent questions fill my head.

"She's fine—you don't need to worry about handling her like china or anything," Cam adds quickly. "I just thought you should know. I didn't want it to surprise you."

"Of course. Thanks for telling me," I say, willing my expression to remain neutral, even though fresh panic fills me. What kind of condition would necessitate surgery at infancy? And how bad a scar could a baby have that Cam felt compelled to warn me? But before I can put words to any of these fears, Emory starts to squirm in my arms and Cam quickly hands me her diaper bag.

"You'll be fine," he says, as if reading my mind.

The women's room is dimly lit as I lock the door behind us. I unroll the cloth changing pad covered in little ducks and balance her gently on my hip. Unlike Lucy, Emory does not protest when I lay down her down, but instead puts her chubby fist to her lips and starts sucking on it calmly.

"Hi, baby girl." I unsnap her onesie gently. Emory doesn't take her eyes off me. "Just going to get you changed," I tell her, softly.

When I roll her onesie up to remove her diaper, I see the small pink ridge running up the center of her ribs. My breath catches. "You brave little thing. What have you and your daddy been through?" I change her diaper and roll her onesie back down gently. The scar disappears.

"Okay, all done!" I scoop her up, and press my nose to her little head. Emory smells like shampoo. And something else: like Cam. I kiss her three times, before I bring her back out to her dad.

Back in the booth, the boys are revving up again. Emory is warm and heavy against my chest, and it's with some reluctance that I hand her back. "Was she good for you?" he asks.

"The best."

I can't take my eyes off Cam. There are so many things I want to ask him. About the surgery that made that scar on Emory's perfect little chest. About what it means—if she really is okay. And if he is.

But then the server arrives with the check, and Cam snaps it up. I protest. "Don't be ridiculous," he insists. "It's my treat. Besides, you've got baby food in your hair." He winks playfully as I put a hand to my head, horrified.

"Why didn't you say anything?"

He waves me away. "Because you're enjoying yourself. And I'm enjoying that," he adds.

I glance at him, my cheeks warming.

The server returns with Cam's change. She looks around the booth at all of us as she clears our plates. "You have a beautiful family," she says.

I shake my head. "Oh no, we're not—"

But she's already headed for the kitchen, the plates rattling in her arms.

I glance around the booth, trying to see what she saw. Two toddlers, two babies, two diaper bags, and a car seat between us. "God, can you imagine if all this was ours?"

Cam laughs aloud. "No! No, I cannot."

But in that moment I see the picture we make. Beside me, Lucy coos in her baby carrier. Owen's and Randall's mouths are stained with pizza sauce. Across from me, Cam bends to kiss Emory's cheek. In that moment I am inexplicably happy. Baby food in hair and all.

Thirteen

A wave of heat engulfs the northeast coast, delivering temperatures in the high nineties and a stifling humidity that makes it hard to move. Since Dean Hartman's call, my desire to return to Boston has become more insistent. I need to put my life back in order. As much as I like my mom's home-cooked meals and Dad's bad jokes, I feel helpless being back in Mystic.

But Erika convinces me otherwise. "I'm melting," she groans into the phone. "You can't even walk up Commonwealth without feeling like you're going to get stuck in the pavement."

Evan confirms this. "It's hotter than hell."

"How are you handling it on set?" I ask. Even though they tape in the studio, a good deal of the action scenes are shot outside.

"We had to film until midnight last night, just to avoid the afternoon heat. One of the crewmembers fainted. And the humidity set off Angie's migraines."

"Poor thing," I say, grateful that he can't see me roll my eyes.

"I'd give my left arm to be away from this and out on the coast," he says. "You should stay put. No reason to rush home."

No one's rushing, I think. But deep down I feel the pressure. I need to find a job. And we need to look at apartments. "What's your schedule like?" I ask, anyway.

"I'm on set for the rest of the week," he says apologetically. "So grab some ice cream. Hit the beach with a book." The very things that'd be more enjoyable if Evan were here to share in them. It feels like we haven't seen each other in forever.

"Isn't Erika coming back soon, anyway?" he asks.

Erika just has a few details to wrap up for one of the partners before she can leave. "Yeah, she'll be here soon. But even though you're tied up at work, I was thinking that maybe I should start looking at places. I can narrow down some choices for us."

"Oh, you just reminded me! I've found one that I think will work."

This is news to me. "You've already picked out an apartment? Without me?"

"Relax, Maggie. I got a tip from one of the crewmembers that there was an old brick schoolhouse near Charles Street that his sister was vacating. It's gorgeous. Two bedrooms, hardwood floors, lots of sunlight." He pauses. "The only thing is they don't allow pets."

I bristle. "I can't just abandon Mr. Kringles," I say, trying unsuccessfully to keep the frustration out of my voice.

"But cats make me break out in hives," he says, with a matching level of frustration. "I think I'm allergic."

It's a discussion we've had before. When Evan sleeps over, the only "reaction" he's had has been itchy eyes, at worst. Which has prompted me on several occasions to suggest seeing an allergist. "You don't know that for sure," I remind him. "You said that your grandmother's cat doesn't bother you. Maybe it's just hay fever or something environmental. Can't we get you to a doctor first, like we agreed?"

He doesn't answer right away. "You know how busy I am at work."

"I know, honey," I say, with more empathy this time. "Mr. Kringles has been with me for years. I'd have to convince my parents to take him, and I would miss him. But giving him up is something I'm willing to do if we are *absolutely* certain you're allergic. Okay?"

I can picture his brow wrinkling in consternation. When anything interferes with work, he gets flustered. The man could lose a toe, but wouldn't leave the set to see a podiatrist. It's gone from admirable to somewhat ridiculous.

"Fine. I'll schedule an appointment with an allergist. But in the meantime, I'm wondering if I should just go ahead and sign the lease. I'd hate to lose this place."

"But I haven't seen it yet," I remind him. Sometimes Evan's singular focus overshadows other details. In this case, me.

We end the call with a terse goodbye, Evan agreeing, again, to call an allergist, and me agreeing to look over the listing link he's sending. With the decision to stay in Mystic having been made mostly for me, I find myself wandering around town. I grab an iced coffee at Bartleby's and head over to Bank Square Books to browse. Later, armed with a new summer read, I cross the Bascule Bridge to Mystic River Park and walk along the pier. I'm glad that it's not crowded in town today. I imagine most of the tourists have headed up the coast to the nearby Rhode Island beaches to escape the heat, or hit the air-conditioned recesses of the aquarium and the seaport shops. I find a spot on a bench and people-watch as I sip my coffee.

Growing up in Mystic, summers were like an endless vacation. Sure, there were drawbacks to living in a tourist destination, like the traffic that clogged Main Street—the standing room only in restaurants, and the inevitable bumping elbows and backsides with strangers on the stalled sidewalks. Still, there was something so magical about this season on the Connecticut coast that it transcended all of those boat-shoe-wearing intruders who flooded our little village. From the roaring orange sunsets that fingered the sky to the crisp white sails that slapped taut in the wind, I know how lucky I am to be here, sitting on a bench, watching the boats in the harbor.

Last night Jane and Toby arrived home from Newport looking somewhat less exasperated. Toby's nose was red with sunburn. "I told him to reapply the sunscreen," Jane said, shaking her head, as she dropped her bags and scooped up her kids. But there was a new nonchalance in her tone.

"So how was it?" I asked them, positioning myself strategically in front of the full sink of dishes. The kids were still standing, after all.

Toby high-fived me. "The bomb."

Jane scoffed. "The bomb? Really. That's how you describe a romantic weekend in Newport with your wife?"

I tried to conceal my smile.

Toby looked genuinely confused. "What? C'mon, honey. I shot a seventy-two on the golf course, and I won the office pool." He wrapped an arm around Jane and winked. "Then I took this one out for dinner and won her, too."

Jane rolled her eyes. "Don't believe a thing this man says."

"Well, we all survived just fine here," I told them, perhaps a bit too enthusiastically.

Toby hoisted Randall up onto his shoulders. "How'd the rugs make out?"

"Just one tinkle in the yard," I mouthed.

He high-fived me again. "See? The bomb!"

Now, with my babysitting detail complete, and Erika not due to arrive for several days, summer is mine to contemplate. I stretch out on the bench, debating the merits of going home to work on teaching applications or driving up 95 to one of the beaches, when my phone vibrates. I pluck it out of my purse, hoping for some pictures of the schoolhouse apartment from Evan.

But it's Cam. "Still in town?"

"I am," I reply.

"Remember how we used to climb up to the lookout on River Road?"

"Never forgot it."

"Meet me there at eight?"

Cam's invitation to meet at the Peace Sanctuary lookout sparks my curiousity. But it also sparks visceral memories: in his Jeep with the top down and James Taylor wafting through the speakers. A cooler full of cold beers clinking on the backseat. Climbing the dirt trail up the hillside to the lookout, where we'd lean over the railing to take in the views of Mystic River, we'd see constellations spread across the July sky ceiling overhead. It's one of the defining summer hallmarks in my memories. And I wonder what it means that I suddenly can't wait for eight o' clock to arrive.

◆ ◆ ◆

That night, I tug on a pair of denim shorts and a loose white T-shirt and slip into a pair of sandals. It's an outfit as casual and breezy as the night outside my window, and it's not lost on me that it's something I would never wear in Boston. Evan must still be filming, and right now he seems a million miles away.

Already the peepers are throbbing in the night air as I drive along River Road. Cam's silver Jeep is parked in the small lot by the base of the hill. I wonder for a heartbeat if he left his old high school Wrangler out in California, along with all of the plans he'd made.

Cam hops out and comes over to lean in my open window. He's so close I can smell his aftershave. "You came."

"I said I would." And I wonder if he had second thoughts, like I did. And what that means.

He opens my door for me and steps aside, a simple but chivalrous gesture that reminds me of my father. "Follow me."

The path up the wooded hillside to the lookout is steep. Without street lamps the blanket of growing darkness seems especially thick. I stumble once, over a rock, and Cam reaches back to take my hand.

"You okay?"

"Yes," I say, feeling alternately clumsy and flustered by the brush of our fingers.

We reach the clearing at the top and step up onto the platform of the lookout. Directly below there is the whir of a passing car along the road, and then it grows still again. The river stretches out before us and the lights of the Seaport glimmer across the way. I can make out the narrow silhouette of the

Mayflower II hoisted up on blocks in the boatyard. Cam sets a six-pack of beer on the wooden bench and the bottles clink against one another.

"A sound from our past," I laugh. "I haven't been up here since college."

"I find myself coming up here more and more," he says, opening a beer and passing it to me. The bottle is cold in my hand and the beer even colder in my throat. I'm suddenly thirsty.

"So," I say.

Cam leans back. "Here we are. How many years later—eight?"

I do the math in my head, aware of the warmth of Cam's closeness on the bench. "Something like that," I say. "Where's Emory tonight?"

"I put her to bed before I left. My mom is watching her."

I smile. "One of the advantages of moving back home."

Cam lets out a small laugh. "One, I guess. It can be tight quarters being back in the house with all of us." But he's quick to add, "Honestly, they've pretty much saved me this year. I couldn't have done it without my folks."

"I'm sure. But give yourself some credit, too. You're running a new business. And raising a baby." I don't add, "all by yourself," though I think it.

"It's why I came home." Cam takes a deep sip of his beer. "So, tell me about teaching. I always knew you would."

"How? I was an English major," I remind him.

"I know. But I saw you with those kids at Camp Edgewater. You were a natural."

The sentiment warms me. "Well, I've really loved teaching at

Darby. The salary isn't huge, being a private school. But the kids come in every day prepared to learn, and they're from families who expect the best. It was so different from the urban student teaching stints I had in grad school."

"I'll bet. Those must've been rough."

"They were. Some days you were glad if a kid just came to school, let alone came in with breakfast in his tummy and his homework done. You know what I mean?"

Cam shakes his head.

"But that's all changing now," I admit, turning back to the view. "My position has been cut due to budget changes. In fact, that was the phone call I got at the playground the other day. So, I'm back to square one." I turn to Cam. "You hiring by any chance?"

He smiles at my joke, but concern crosses his expression. "Maggie, I'm so sorry. I didn't realize you'd lost your job. Why didn't you say anything?"

I shrug helplessly. "Deep down I didn't think it'd really happen. I complained about the hassle some of those parents gave me, but I had some really great kids."

Cam listens, quietly. "You'll miss them, huh?"

I nod. "But I've been working on applications for public school positions. I think I need a change, even if I don't feel entirely ready for one."

Cam regards me for a long minute. "Change is scary."

I realize at that very instant how trivial my worries must sound. "Oh, Cam, I shouldn't have—"

But he puts a hand up. "Don't apologize. You're on the cusp of some big transitions, and I don't blame you for being hesitant. Fear is good. It means that whatever it is you're contemplating, matters." Cam pauses. "Any school would be lucky to have you. Are you looking to stay in Boston?"

His question surprises me. Boston is where I've lived and worked since college. It's where all my friends are. "That's the plan. Although, my mom keeps sharing these local employment clippings with me. Not that I ever considered moving back here," I say, then regret it as quickly as it's out. "I mean—" I smack my forehead for emphasis. Two insensitive remarks in less than two minutes.

Cam smiles. "No, no, I get it. There's more opportunity there. Your whole life is there."

Not all of it, I want to say, suddenly. I steal a glance at his strong profile out of the corner of my eye. For the first time since arriving home, I don't feel the usual push and pull of Boston. I don't want to be anywhere else.

"Em and I have been living with my parents for a while, but I'm working on something else."

"Oh?"

Cam smiles. "As soon as I wrap up the Bate house, it's going to be my next project." I want to ask what Cam is working on. I want to know where he'll be. But he interrupts the thought. "So, what part of Boston do you call home?"

"I'm in Back Bay for now."

Cam lets out a lone whistle. "Nice area. Isn't that where Tom Brady lived?"

I'm surprised he knows this. As if reading my mind, he turns to me and smiles. "Hey, just because I'm back home in sleepy Mystic doesn't mean I've never experienced anything else." And even though I know Cam's teasing, I feel a beat of guilt. Just because all of his plans were turned upside down doesn't mean he never had any.

"Well, I won't be staying there much longer. Erika's moving out in August, after the wedding. We were only there thanks to both her salary and her dad's monthly contributions. So I've got to find a new place to live, too."

Cam nods thoughtfully. "You'll figure it out, Griff," he says, finally. "I have no doubt you're on the road to all kinds of wonderful."

I'd wanted to ask Cam about California, and about his graduate research, tonight. But suddenly they seem so far off. There are more pressing matters. *Wonderful* matters.

"Will you tell me about Emory?"

He turns to look at me, and breaks into a slow smile. "I'd love to."

Emory Blanche Wilder, named after her great-grandmother on Cam's mother's side, was born during a winter storm in January, three weeks early. Lauren and Cam had just started their last semester of grad school. Aside from her small size and early arrival, she was perfect. A peachy-complexioned baby girl, with blue eyes and a small patch of golden downy hair on her head. The doctors did not realize right away that anything was wrong with her. It wasn't until her follow-up appointment at the pediatrician's when her parents mentioned to the doctor that her breathing seemed to change during feeding sessions, that anyone realized she had ASD.

"It's a congenital heart condition," Cam explains, "called atrial septal defect. Basically, she has a hole in her heart."

Hearing Cam say it out loud causes me to put a hand to my own. "What does that mean for her?"

"She was born with an opening in her septum. The blood flows between the two upper chambers of her heart."

"Is that why I felt her chest swoosh? Like a river?"

Cam turns, his eyes flashing in the light from across the way. "You felt that?"

I nod in the growing darkness, wondering if I've said something too personal.

He looks away and runs his hand through his hair. "That's exactly how my mom describes it. Like a little river in her chest."

Cam stares out at the river as he tells me their story, but I don't mind that he's not making eye contact. Because the more he shares the less I trust myself not to cry. "So, the first surgery she had at eight weeks old didn't seal the opening as we'd hoped. Usually they wait until babies are older and stronger, because the chance of a successful outcome is stronger, too. But Emory couldn't wait. She wasn't thriving. So now we're looking at having a catheterization done at Yale this summer. If it goes well, that will hopefully be our fix."

I let his words settle on the warm night air around us. "I still can't believe all you've been through together. She's so little."

Cam shakes his head. "Sometimes I can't, either." But then he grins. "She's a tough little nugget. After that first surgery, when she was in recovery and coming out of sedation, we were a wreck. They'd let us in to be with her, and we just couldn't stop staring at her. I think I was holding my breath the whole time. And yet when she woke up, she smiled at both of us."

Us. "So, Emory's mom was still in the picture at that time." It's something I've been wondering about since our first meeting on the pier.

Cam pauses, as if sifting through his thoughts. "It was complicated. We took a leave from school and came back to Connecticut, specifically so that we could go to Yale's cardiac catheterization lab. Lauren and I got though Emory's procedure and recovery, but even afterward it was an awful time. Lauren hadn't planned to have a baby to begin with. And here she was walking away from everything she'd worked for in her life and trying to cope with having a really sick child. It was scary for both of us."

As I listen to Cam, I'm a little taken aback by the credit he is giving Lauren—listing the few things she did right, before doing the most wrong thing a parent could do. Finally, he lets out a long breath.

"But yeah. To answer your question, Lauren left us shortly after. She couldn't handle it."

My mind spins: Had Lauren left because she didn't want to be a parent? Or because she couldn't come to terms with being the parent of a sick child? But as the trill of peepers rises in the woods behind us, I realize it doesn't matter why she left. Cam stayed.

We lean over the railing, side by side. I set my bottle down and reach over. Cam's hand is chilly when I place my fingers across his.

"I'm sorry, Cam. I think it's really admirable the way *you're* handling all this." Even having heard his story, it's still hard for me to wrap my arms around it. I can't help but think of Jane, and my two healthy nephews and niece.

Cam lifts one shoulder. "Emory is my focus, now. Keeping her healthy and happy and making sure that she's gaining weight—that's everything. Until the next procedure. And then we'll do it again."

The heaviness of our conversation seems out of place against the summer night. "Is there any time frame for her next surgery?"

"In a few weeks. It sounds scary, and believe me, when I first thought of doctors working on my child's heart, I was terrified. But they do these catheterizations all the time now. It's a day procedure—she comes home the same night if all goes well."

Cam seems so calm as he shares this. "So, right now, she's doing okay?" I ask.

"Well, her immune system is fragile, so there are precautions we take, and there are medications we have to keep her on— like heparin. I guess you could say that we have more doctor appointments than most babies." His voice softens. "But right now, yes, she's okay."

"How about you?" I ask gently. And I wonder as I ask it if anyone else has asked Cam how he is. I wonder if he's even had time to ask himself.

But Cam doesn't hesitate. "I'm a dad now. I'm *her* dad. I have to be okay."

It's a line that separates Cam and me. No matter how many diapers I've changed for my niece and nephews, or how much I think I've gleaned from Jane about staying up with a sick baby all night or waiting in a doctor's office for test results, these are not vigils I have ever had to keep. I am not a parent, let alone a parent of a sick child. I will not pretend that I can imagine the fear that Cam has felt. And yet my heart pumps, with all its health and vigor, with new wonder for this man standing beside me.

Fourteen

A few mornings later, Erika wakes me up. "I'm on my way," she barks into the phone.

"What?" I roll over and look at the clock. It's barely seven thirty. "Where?"

"I couldn't take the scorching city another second. So last night I packed my bags." She tells me that she's taken two weeks of leave for her wedding—a week more than originally planned. Her boss, Raj, instantly threatened to replace her, but she knows he won't. "I wrapped up his briefings a week early for the Landry case. Besides, he loves me," she says, with no small amount of assuredness. And I believe her.

"So where are you now?" I ask, stifling a yawn. It's too early in the morning to process all this.

"I'm on the Mass Pike." She pauses. "God, Maggie. I can't believe this is the last time I'll drive the Pike as a single woman."

I swing my legs over the side of the bed. "Fascinating point. When do you get here?"

"In about an hour!" she shouts. There is a rushing staticky noise in the background.

"Are you in Trent's car, with the top down, by any chance?" I ask.

"Of course I am. Do you have any idea how much stuff a bride and groom need for their wedding weekend? I couldn't possibly carry all that on the train."

"Right. So, then how will Trent get here?"

Erika is not fazed. "By train."

We make plans to meet for dinner. "I need a shot just to get the strength to pull into my parents' driveway," Erika groans. "My mother is in full wedding-madness mode. How am I going to manage two weeks at home with my parents?"

"Ha, tell me about it. I've already been home for a week."

"So what have you been doing? Since you left town it's like you've fallen off the planet."

I pause a beat. I haven't mentioned Cam or Emory. Or my official unemployment.

"I've been making sure your big day is all set!" I say instead.

"You're the best, Mags."

◆　◆　◆

Twelve hours and two cosmos later, we're seated at Bravo Bravo's on the water as Erika scrolls through her to-do list. "You have no idea," she says before taking a long sip of her icy drink, "how many loose ends there still are to tie up."

I don't add that I have some of my own, too. Erika is in venting mode, and I've learned that it's best to let her get it all out if I expect to get a word in later.

"Did I tell you what happened? I left my veil behind in Boston!"

"Surely Trent can just ship it for you."

Erika looks at me as if I've suggested Trent make her a new veil out of paper napkins and Elmer's Glue.

"I am not trusting my veil to the postal service. Someone will have to personally drive it down."

"Maybe Peyton could just bring the veil when she comes for the wedding?"

Erika shakes her head as if something is crawling in her ear. "And risk it being forgotten? Besides, I need it now so it can be pressed in advance, along with my dress."

I don't ask who will get the dubious honor of driving the veil from Boston. As long as it's not me.

Erika continues down her list. "So, let's see . . . the band has confirmed their reservation at the inn. The florist okayed the freesia that I wanted to add into your bridesmaid bouquets. You're okay with that, right?" Erika glances at me quickly for confirmation, but she's already on to the next item before I can nod my head. "The caterer called for final head counts for the rehearsal dinner clambake." She pauses. "Did you know they ordered two thousand clams? Does that seem like a lot of clams to you? Oh, and Trent's mother flies in from her pre-wedding Canyon Ranch retreat next Sunday. Shouldn't *I* be the one taking a pre-wedding retreat?"

I smile into my cosmo at the fact that Trent's mother comes at the end of the list, after the clams. "Well, it sounds like everything is pretty well under control," I say, hoping we're done with lists for the moment. "When do Trent and the groomsmen arrive?"

There are two weeks until the actual wedding, but Erika has turned the event into a bit of a drawn-out occasion, with golf outings, family dinners, and boat trips leading up to the big day.

For those who come to town early, there will be at least four days of events to attend. I'm already exhausted just thinking about it.

"Didn't Evan tell you?"

I shrug, feigning forgetfulness. I've kept our recent communications brief to avoid being pressed any further about apartments. It's too stressful.

Erika shakes her head in disgust. "They're not coming in until the Thursday before. Trent is wrapping up some big deal at work, and he insists that he get it done before the honeymoon. I had to move the golf event out by a whole day."

I make a mental note of this; if the groomsmen don't arrive until the Thursday before the wedding, that means it'll be twelve days until Evan and I are in the same zip code. Our crab cakes arrive. When I first came home, I was pining for Evan to arrive. But now I can't deny the fact that I'm counting the days I have left alone.

"So what's new with you?" Erika says finally, dabbing the corners of her mouth with her napkin. We're done with dinner, which means the time it'll take to eat the small dessert we've ordered to share (which we both know Erika will only stare longingly at) is my allotment of talk-time.

"Well, it's official. I lost my job."

Erika jerks upright. "Why didn't you tell me? Here I am dribbling on about wedding stuff. How are you feeling"

My feelings are still mixed. The sense of initial freedom has been replaced with the fear that I won't find anything. Almost worse is my other fear that the one job I find will be something I don't like at all. "It's so strange—I suddenly can't imagine not going back to Darby. I'm not going to see those kids again. I'm not going to teach in that classroom, with the birch tree right outside my window, and Sharon just down the hall. I'm going to have to start all over." I shake my head.

For once, Erika doesn't say anything. She reaches across the table and puts her hand on my arm.

"And did I mention that I hung out with Cam?" I laugh at the absurdity of all of this. None of it is funny.

Erika sits back in her chair and smiles sympathetically. "By that, do you mean you happened to see him in town? Or did you actually make plans to see him?"

Here is where it gets murky. "Both."

The server brings our chocolate cake, which both of us stare at blankly for a moment. "Wow. You have been busy." Erika runs a finger across the chocolate frosting and pops it in her mouth. "Let me ask you something. Do you have feelings for Cam again?"

It comes as an instant relief: someone recognizes my distress and she's tossing me the lifesaver. And yet I can't reach for it. Because, outside of sympathy and fond memories, I'm not sure if I have genuine feelings for Cam. And second, what good would it do if I did? Cam's life is full and complicated. And mine—well, right now it's just complicated. "I'm confused," I say finally.

"Does Cam know about Evan?"

Only then does it dawn on me that I can't recall ever having mentioned Evan. Not even once, despite the fact that Cam has shared so many intimacies with me. A fresh guilt fills me. "No," I say in a small voice. Then, when Erika narrows her eyes, "It's not like I've meant to keep Evan a secret or anything. He's just never come up." And right there, I realize the depth of what I've just said.

Erika lets out a long breath. "Okay. There's something I have to tell you. Do you remember that summer a few years ago when I took time off from work and came home?"

It had been a surprise to all of us. Erika never took days off from work—not for illness or vacation. Certainly not for personal matters, her wedding excepted. But that's exactly what she did three summers ago.

Erika had been pulling all-nighters at her firm, right through a case of walking pneumonia, to prove herself during a high-profile divorce case. At the end of the trial, the partners planned to pick an associate for promotion. When the case closed the firm won a landmark settlement for their client. It was a celebration all around, and word in the halls of the firm was that Erika was a shoo-in for the promotion. She tried to play it cool, but we all knew how much she wanted this. Her father, who rarely called except to confirm that we received his monthly rent contribution, was suddenly checking in daily to see if there was any news. Erika dashed out and bought an expensive new suit the night before the firm was set to make their announcement at their annual summer party. I remember watching her get ready that night: she asked me to apply her lipstick because her hands were too shaky.

Which is why the blow was particularly sharp when she was passed over for a younger associate, who not only scored low on the bar exam and came in late every day during that case, but also happened to be the nephew of a partner. Erika hit rock bottom. For the first time, she turned in her vacation time and left Boston and the firm on "indefinite leave."

"I'd never seen you like that," I say, remembering how worried I was. I never told her at the time, afraid I'd only add to her sense of fragility.

"I know. I was so drained all I could do was lay around the house when I got here. But each afternoon my mom dragged me out to the club for some 'fresh air.' While she played tennis, I'd sit on the porch with a book or just stare out at the water.

"One day, Chase Warner showed up with his family for lunch. Remember Chase?"

How could I forget? As good-looking as he was affable, Chase was a hard-to-ignore summer resident. He lived in Providence and attended prep school somewhere in Massachusetts, but each summer he and his family moved into their Connecticut shore house. I only crossed paths with Chase a few times when I tagged along to Erika's country club events. But he was an epic figure in Erika's summers growing up: her first kiss, her perpetual summer crush, and eventually her on-and-off-again boyfriend.

"You never told me you saw him during that summer," I say, leaning forward. I get the sense there's more.

Erika smiles uncomfortably. "Yeah, well. There's a reason I'm only telling you now." She takes a deep breath and shifts in her seat.

"I was miserable being back in Mystic. I was lonely and bored, and I didn't know if I wanted to go back to law. And there he was—fresh out of grad school, tan and fit and friendly, having just returned to celebrate his father's retirement. I wanted to crawl under the porch when I laid eyes on him, but he sat down in the Adirondack chair right next to me. He talked me into having lunch with him that day. And the next."

"And?" I press.

"And for the rest of those two weeks we were inseparable." Erika flushes deeply.

I slump back in my chair, dumbstruck. She and Trent have been together for five years, and that summer was right in the middle of it. "Are you saying what I think you're saying?"

Erika lifts one tanned shoulder, almost sadly.

"My God." A million questions flood my mind, but I'm too flummoxed to put words to any articulately. "But you never . . . why didn't you tell me?"

"I'm sorry, Mags. I tried to, but I always lost my nerve."

"Well, you should've tried harder!"

I stare out at the water, imagining them. Having dinners in town, walking along the pier. Playing tennis at the club. Spending evenings . . . doing *everything*. Just like any other summer romance. Only Erika hadn't been single.

"Does Trent know?"

She shakes her head.

"What happened? Tell me everything."

"It lasted less than two weeks. Eleven days, exactly."

I resist the urge to point out that it's been three years since those eleven days, and surely she could've found a time to tell me.

"I know it reeks of indecency, but it wasn't like that. We had such a history, and I was in such a bad place."

"What was it then?"

She smiles, in spite of herself. "It was lovely."

"Lovely?" Even I don't know that I could use the word to describe what, let's be honest, was an affair.

"And I can't tell you how different and lovely it made me *feel*. We stayed up late talking about books and politics and old friends from the club who we hadn't seen in years. One weekend we took his parents' boat up to Watch Hill and stayed up late eating oysters and drinking wine on the deck, having sex under the stars. It was like we were kids again with the whole summer to ourselves." Her eyes are bright at the memory, even still.

I can feel myself giving in to the images she describes; it does sound magical. Would I have been able to walk away from such temptation if I were going through what she had? Suddenly I'm not sure. "So it filled some kind of void," I say. It's an offering of understanding; if not forgiveness.

She nods, her eyes filling with tears.

"I could never tell Trent. It was my mistake, my journey, however you want to look at it. But it would kill him, Mags. I never saw any reason to do that."

While I can't imagine Erika keeping this from Trent, I also can't picture her telling him. Certainly not now. Trent's an old-fashioned guy, and it would be a hit to his very core. In some ways, perhaps keeping this from him is kinder. It ended. Trent is the one she went back to.

What I still can't get past is the fact she kept it from me. Her lifelong best friend. "You didn't think you could trust me with this? Not one word in all these years?"

Erika's expression clouds. "It wasn't about trust. Believe me, I wanted to tell you. It would've taken some of the burden off if I had. But I was so ashamed, Maggie. I didn't want this to change the way you felt about me. Your moral compass is pointed due north."

"Is not!" I disagree, thinking of my long talk with Cam at the lookout. The way our knees touched on the bench. More important, the way I felt when our knees touched.

"I wouldn't be telling you now, except I don't want you to get stuck like I did."

"Stuck?" Until now, I didn't think we'd kept any secrets from each other. Just as I didn't realize Erika thought me too much of a Pollyanna to share a secret as big as this with. "I'm not stuck," I tell her now, emphatically. I will find a new place and a new job, and Evan and I will work through it together. As for Cameron, he's a friend. Someone I share history with, yes. But we haven't crossed any lines. Maybe if she'd had more meaningful relationships before Trent, and hadn't jumped from guy to guy, she'd understand that.

Instead of getting upset, Erika softens. "By stuck I mean that I got caught up in nostalgia. There I was, run-down from work and having been passed over for a promotion I'd deserved. I needed to escape. So, I let myself believe that being back here in Mystic was real. That Chase and I were back where we were meant to be." She pauses, and swipes at a tear that tumbles down her cheek. "I let the past catch up with me."

"That's not always a bad thing," I say, sticking to my guns. "I think that our pasts are a big part of who we are today."

"Well, in this case it was a bad thing. I didn't just lie to Trent and to you, Maggie. I lied to myself. It was easier to come home and lick my wounds where everything was sunny and familiar and safe. But it wasn't real life."

A plume of defensiveness rises in my chest. Is she comparing what she did with Chase with my being home in Mystic this summer? Because our two stories are nothing alike. "I'm not licking any wounds," I say.

"Maybe not," she says, steering away from the question mark of my present situation. "But you are in a serious relationship with someone else back in Boston. Someone you can build a life with. Isn't that what you want?"

I don't have an answer. "Evan's great," I say, finally. "I'm not trying to replace him, and I'm not running away from anything in Boston. I'm hardly *involved* with Cameron. It's nothing like what you did."

Erika stiffens, and for a beat I feel bad. It's a low blow. But she's the one drawing a line in the sand. Our situations could not be more different, and I can't allow her to suggest otherwise.

"Then what is it like?" Erika asks, her tone cool.

We avoid looking at each other as the server arrives to clear the dessert plates. Even after she's gone, I stare into my lap. Erika plays with her bracelet distractedly.

"It's a friendship revisited, kind of like revisiting home. Yes, it's comfortable like old slippers, it's familiar. But it's innocent." I look at her. "And if something were going on, I would've told you."

Finally she offers the nearest thing to an apology. "I'm sorry I kept that secret from you. And I'm not trying to tell you what to do with your summer, or your life, for that matter. But I'm worried about you, Mags."

"You don't need to be."

"Listen, you're a sentimentalist and you've got a huge heart.

Which is what I love most about you. I just don't want you to fall back into the past, and risk losing what you've invested for your future."

I can feel my ire soften. Even if I disagree with her take on things, and even if it still stings that she kept something so big from me all this time.

I sit up and meet her gaze. "So, what happened with Chase in the end?"

Erika shrugs. "I forced myself to face reality. Mystic wasn't my life any more than Chase was the guy for me. You know the rest. I packed my bags and went home. To Boston."

"I still love my life in Boston," I feel the need to remind her. "And Evan and I have made commitments to each other that I intend to keep. But being back home and hanging out with Cam has been good for me. Just give me some wiggle room on this, okay?"

Erika looks at me sympathetically. "Okay. Just remember one thing."

"What's that?"

"Maggie, home isn't a place. It's not where your old boyfriend is, or your parents still live. It's more than these neighborhoods and beaches that stir up old feelings. You've built a career and friends and a relationship away from here. Wherever you end up, home is inside *you*."

Erika has struck a chord. It's the theme song of our generation, the motto I've read in countless magazine articles and social media posts. *Love yourself before you can love others. Be at home in your own skin.*

But when I think of home, I don't think you can exclude

time, place, and loved ones: the things that have made me who I truly am. I know Erika has a point: home and self should be one and the same. But I still can't help but wonder if she's missing a finer point. What if home is where you feel most like your *real* self?

Fifteen

The next afternoon, I make a point to try to catch Evan during lunch. I'm happy when he picks up and I can imagine Erika sighing with relief somewhere across town. Evan is animated as he tells me about work, but behind his pep I can hear his fatigue. "You're exhausted, aren't you?"

"Yeah," he admits. "And I miss you."

I soften. "Me, too. Erika's here and it's all wedding, wedding, wedding."

"It's less than two weeks away. I can't wait for the break," he says. Which makes me wonder: Is it me or the long weekend that he can't wait for?

We talk until he has to get back to work. He pauses before hanging up. "Mags, I'm sorry I've been so tied up lately. I promise I'll make some time for us when I get down there. Maybe we can slip away for a night, to Rhode Island or something?"

I smile. "That'd be great. What do you have in mind?"

But when he doesn't answer me, I realize I've lost the call. A moment later my phone rings again.

"So which sounds better, a romantic stay at the Ocean House or a night out in Newport?" I ask.

There's a pause. "I'm thinking Ocean House. But Emory's not quite big enough to ride the Watch Hill carousel yet."

I almost drop my phone. "Cam?"

He chuckles. "Yeah. Sorry—obviously you were expecting someone else."

"No. I mean . . . What's up?"

"Well, I hate to bother you like this, but I've got a last-minute client meeting tonight. And I'm sort of in a bind."

"What's the matter?"

"This developer from New Haven just bought a spot along the river and it looks like he's leaning toward my bid. We were supposed to meet this afternoon, but he got stuck in traffic. He wants me to drive over there now."

"Let me guess, you need help with someone little?"

Cam lets out a sigh. "Do I ever. My parents went to Block Island for a couple of days."

"When is your meeting?"

He pauses. "In ten minutes. The guy is on his way now."

"So am I."

◆　　◆　　◆

I haven't been in the Wilder house since I was in college, but when Cam invites me in, I feel like I'm nineteen again. The toile wallpaper in the entryway is the same. As are the damask couches in the living room, and the heavy rose-colored drapes. I stop to look at a high school photo of Cam on the bookshelf. "It wasn't a mullet," he says, coming to stand behind me. An ongoing joke we shared.

"It was almost a mullet," I tell him, laughing. Emory lets out a coo. "See? Even she thinks so."

He motions me to the rear of the house, through the kitchen, which has been updated with cherry cabinets and granite countertops. "The pantry is over there if you get hungry," he says, pointing to a walk-in.

"Thanks. It's beautiful in here."

"Well, the basement is not. So brace yourself."

I follow him down the carpeted steps to the finished basement, the former rec room where we used to hang out and watch TV. The old overstuffed sofas have been replaced with leather and the carpeting switched out for hardwood. The pool table is gone, and the bar area has been turned into a small but cozy corner kitchen.

"What are you talking about? This is great, Cam. Did you do all this?"

Cam piles a stack of dishes in the sink and runs a cloth over the counter.

"I had to make some updates when Emory and I moved back," he says, quickly shoving a pile of mail into a silverware drawer.

It's a bright space with walkout doors to the side yard, much bigger than my Boston apartment.

"Emory and I share the guest room," he says, motioning me to the rear. We stand in the doorway together, surveying Cam's bed, the crib, and the changing table. "It's kind of cramped," he says.

"It's cozy," I tell him.

Cam shows me where the diapers and wipes are, and I watch as he fumbles through their shared dresser looking for pajamas. Each drawer he opens flashes in pinks and greens, and he looks up bashfully. "Typical girl. Totally took over the clothes storage."

"I can do that, really," I say, shooing him out. "You don't want to be late."

He leaves me with two fresh bottles, points out the bouncy seat, and is halfway up the stairs with Emory still in his arms before I catch him.

"Uh, if you want me to watch the baby, I sort of need the baby."

We both laugh. "Right. Sorry, I'm just not used to leaving her with anyone besides my mom." He looks at me bashfully.

"It's okay, Jane is the same way. I've got my cell, you've got yours. We'll be fine, right, baby girl?" I ask Emory as Cam gingerly passes her to me.

Emory looks between us like she isn't so sure. "Go. Quick. Before one of you cries."

Cam leans in to kiss Emory, whose little face is right next to my own, and for a second we're a triangle of faces pressed closely. "Okay, then. Bye."

I hoist her up on my hip. "It's just you and me, baby." She seems to be taking me in through little peeks, though every time I look directly at her she turns her head. Five minutes after Cam has left she starts to cry.

At first it's just a little hiccupy cry, an uncertain whimper about being left with me, a stranger. Lucy used to do this, so I walk her around the basement apartment, humming and talking to her. We make a few laps of the living area and kitchenette, and she seems to settle a bit. But soon she starts crying for real, and we move to the windows, a trick I learned from Jane. Her gaze fixes on the garden and she calms, so we step outside into the side yard. "Let's check out Grandma's yard. It's so pretty out here, huh?"

The sun is lower on the horizon. We walk together through Mrs. Wilder's perennial beds, which are thick and lush with hydrangea and lilies. I kneel down and pick a yellow lily, and Emory's eyes widen. She reaches with a fast hand and grips it tight. "Pretty. Like you, Em."

She brings her clenched fist, flower and all, abruptly to her mouth. Yellow pollen covers her nose and cheek, and she wags her head in surprise. "Uh-oh. Let's not eat that." I wonder for a faint heartbeat if she could be allergic. Or if it's poisonous. Back inside we go, to clean her up.

A half hour later we've washed our face, changed a diaper, given the swing a go, and tried the bouncy seat. To little avail. Emory oscillates between moderate fussing and weepy tears, her gaze sweeping the room, probably wondering when her daddy is going to rescue her from this strange lady. I am starting to wonder the same.

"Daddy's coming back really soon, sweetie. It's okay." I retrieve a fresh bottle from the fridge and place it in the bottle warmer as Cam showed me. Jane breast-fed all her babies and never had such a contraption. When the light goes off I test it on my wrist, fearful of scalding her. But it's only lukewarm. "Perfect," I say, settling Emory on my lap on the couch. But she does not think so. She arches her back away when I offer her the bottle, refusing. I try again, and she begins to cry louder. "Maybe you're not hungry yet." In five minutes we're back out in the garden, Emory jigging on my hip and a sense of dread spreading through my chest. I've never had this much trouble soothing Jane's kids. I remind myself that I've been a fixture in their life since they were born. But, as silly as it is, I can't help but take it somewhat personally.

Despite being outside, Emory is now in full-blown wailing mode. I grab my cell, but realize I don't know whom to call. I'm certainly not going to interrupt Cam's meeting. And Erika is not an option. The thought of my mother flashes briefly, but then I imagine the look of confusion on her face—upon learning that ten years later I am back in the Wilder basement—followed by a disapproving sigh.

Once, when Owen was a baby and Jane was rushing out the door for a doctor's appointment, she had what she called one of her worst-mother-ever moments. It was a cold winter afternoon, and she'd just tucked Owen into his snowsuit. He'd eaten and been changed, but the second she put his snowsuit on, he began howling. She wondered if it was his diaper, so she checked again. She thought maybe he was hot, so she unzipped him. But by then she was late and overwhelmed, and so she impatiently tucked him into his car seat, cranked up the radio, and drove off, praying the ride would calm him down. Halfway down the road when he still hadn't let up, Jane pulled over, sensing something really was wrong. And it was. When she removed his snowsuit to check more carefully she realized one of his little thumbs had been bent back in the sleeve. In her haste, she'd overlooked it. The second she freed his arm, Owen silenced. Then Jane began to sob.

Remembering that, I hurry Emory back inside. I lay her on the changing table in their shared room and undress her quickly. Maybe I put the diaper on too tight. Maybe her toe is tangled in a thread in her sock. Oh God, maybe there's a spider stuck in her pajamas that's bitten her at least twenty times by now. Flustered, I tug the suit off as gently as I can. But everything seems fine.

"What is it, Em? Your diaper is dry. Your pajamas are okay. You're not hungry." I lean over her, desperate and fully cognizant of the fact that I'm pleading with a six-month-old. "What is it?"

And then her eyes lock on mine and Emory stops. I wipe the tears off her plush cheeks with my thumb. "See? It's okay." I keep my gaze on hers, unwilling to break our eye contact. Gingerly, I tuck her chubby legs back into her pajama feet as best I can. I button her up, smiling all the while. And then, suddenly, she smiles back at me.

"There's our girl!" In that moment I am overcome. More than for any parent conference, or student win, or classroom score.

This time when I scoop her up, she settles heavily against my chest. "You tired?" I certainly am. Outside the sky is darkening. I carry her around the room, singing "Silent Night." It's the only soothing song I know all the words to. I grab the bottle from the counter and move to the rocking chair in Cam's dim room.

This time, Emory takes the bottle eagerly. Her crying and her visitor have probably both worn the poor little thing out, but she looks up at me contentedly from the crook of my arm. I rock and she sucks noisily at first, then more softly. Soon her lashes flutter, and her sucking grows intermittent. "That's my girl," I whisper in the growing darkness.

Much later, there is a noise overhead, followed by the fall of footsteps on the stairs. "Maggie? I'm home."

I blink at the silhouette that fills the doorway. "Cam?"

Emory is a warm weight, still in my arms, which have grown stiff and ache. I glance down at her, sleeping soundly.

"Did you fall asleep?" he whispers.

I nod, rising slowly, mindful not to disturb her. "Here, let me help."

Cam steps into the room, but I shake my head. "It's okay. I've got her," I whisper.

I bend over the crib, holding Emory away from my chest

as I lower her to her mattress. She stirs, and I hold my breath, keeping one hand on her tummy as reassurance, as I've seen Jane do. When I'm sure she's settled, I tiptoe out.

Cam is waiting in the kitchen, pouring us each a glass of water. "How'd it go?" he asks.

I stretch and look around. The floor is strewn with blankets and soft toys. The bouncy seat is tipped over. "Great. She fussed a little when you left, but we worked through it."

Cam cocks his head. "Just a little? I forgot to mention, she's teething."

I make a face. "Never would have guessed."

"So she worked you over, huh?" He chuckles softly and hands me a glass.

"No, no, she was great. Just wondering where her daddy was. How'd the meeting go?"

"It went well, I think. I should hear back from him tomorrow. Hey, it's still early. Do you want to hang out for a bit?"

Sitting on the couch in Cam's parents' basement, like we used to as nineteen-year-olds, should feel strange. But the strange thing is how normal it feels. Cam tells me about the house renovation bid and gets up to grab the blueprints, his expression intent as he walks me through the plans. After, I tell him about Emory, coming clean about how I'd almost called him at one point in her crying jag.

"You can call me anytime," he insists, shaking his head. "Now I feel bad. You were so great to help me out tonight."

"No, I'm glad I did. Even with the rough start, I have to tell you, putting her to bed was really sweet." I glance back at the bedroom door, left ajar in case she needs us. And then at Cam. "You go from those moments of feeling so desperate to feeling so . . ."

"Numb?"

I laugh. "I was going to say full. Content. But yes, I suppose numb works."

Cam looks at me appreciatively. "That's just it; they're so little, and yet they can make the whole world screech to a halt in those moments. You did great, Mags. Thanks for helping me get out of a jam." He leans back against the cushions, quiet for a moment. "Being a single parent you find yourself needing help more than you'd like to admit. But it's still hard to ask."

I look over at him, his eyes heavy with fatigue. "You can ask me anytime." And as I climb the stairs on my way out, I find myself feeling surprisingly good. Good about helping Cam out, and even better about how I was able to keep it together with a crying infant. But mostly, how good it felt while she slept in my arms, this helpless little creature, who moments earlier had me feeling so helpless, now snuggled against my chest. It was a feeling I couldn't quite put my finger on, but terribly satisfying.

Cam walks me to the door. "So which did you end up deciding on?"

I pause on the front step, confused. "Which?"

"Romantic night at the Ocean House or wild night in Newport?"

I fiddle with the straps of my purse. "Oh. Yeah, that was for a weekend trip I was sort of planning."

Cam smiles. "I'm just teasing you, Mags. I'm glad you've got someone to make plans with."

While I've never *consciously* kept Evan away from Cam, I still feel as if I've been caught. Or as if I've somehow betrayed him, after the many confidences he's shared with me. But neither of those sentiments stings as hard as his comment: if Cam is glad I have *someone*, then what does that make *us*?

"I probably should've mentioned that earlier," I say, struggling to meet his gaze. "I'm seeing someone back home."

"What's his name?"

I flush. "Evan."

Cam jams his hands in his pockets and looks somewhere past me, out into the night. "Evan's a lucky guy."

◆　◆　◆

As I walk to my car, I can't shake the feeling that I've messed up somehow. I will not glance back to see if he's watching me go, I tell myself. But halfway down the driveway, when I do, the door has been closed. I stop beside Cam's Jeep, wondering if I should go back and knock on the door. What would I possibly say if I did? As I stand there, something bright catches my attention in the backseat—Emory's polka-dot car seat. There are stuffed toys strewn across the seat and a half-filled sippy cup tipped on its side. A bag of diapers gapes open on the floor. The front seat, however, is tidy—all business. Several poster tubes lie neatly across the passenger seat. Probably containing building plans like the ones he just showed me. Then I notice that around one of the tubes is a bright-yellow plastic teething ring.

As I walk away, I wonder how long Cam will get to rest tonight before Emory is up for her next feeding. Or diaper change. So much has changed for him. And I go from feeling like some kind of hero for helping him out tonight to a meek teenage girl, tiptoeing home from Cam's basement once again.

Sixteen

The wedding looms, spiraling in its own countdown, and I feel like a trajectory thrown from its path. I spend my mornings running errands to the florist and the club with Erika, and my afternoons working on teaching applications in my parents' den. Nights, I'm exhausted. One evening, after my father has poured me a beer and invited me to come listen to the peepers in the yard with him, Evan calls.

"What are you doing tomorrow night?" he asks.

I let out a relaxed breath. "Probably the same thing I'm doing right now. Sitting on the deck and going to bed early with my book. Why?"

"What if I could book us a night at Ocean House?"

As much as I've been distracted and busy, it has been hard waiting for Evan to commit to a visit with his hectic schedule. Now the very thought of just the two of us in a world-class resort is overwhelming. "Tomorrow? You can get away for a night? Tell me you're not teasing!"

Evan laughs. "I can only get one night away," he cautions, "but I promise I'll be all yours. No set talk, no wedding talk, no job or apartment talk, promise?"

"I promise!" I practically shout. We make plans for him to drive in tomorrow morning after his final scene is wrapped. That night I can barely sleep, I'm feeling like a child before Christmas morning. This is good; this is exactly what we need.

Erika swings by the next morning to pick me up to go shopping. I'd promised to go with her to the jeweler to get the groomsmen's gifts, a set of Tiffany silver flasks, engraved with the guy's names. "I'm sorry, but I can't go with you. Evan's coming! He reserved us a room at Ocean House."

Erika squeals. "Well, well. Don't let me keep you from the festivities. What time does he come?"

I glance at the kitchen clock. "Around noon. He's picking me up after he wraps. Though it won't be easy getting out of here; Mom and Dad are going to want to talk his ear off." Thankfully, my parents are out for their morning walk before the day gets hot. My mother has already peppered me with no shortage of Evan-related questions this morning, and I'm banking on the hope that a long walk will wear her out so that she doesn't do the same to Evan when he arrives.

Erika gives me a hug. "I'm glad he came through," she tells me. "Don't worry about the groomsmen's gifts, you guys need this time."

Though I do feel a bit bad; the gifts are something Trent really should be doing, and now Erika is doing it alone. "Wait! Don't forget the list." I rummage through my purse for the list I made, having carefully rechecked for the correct spellings of the guys' names. My purse is a mess—sunglasses, water bottle, protein bars. At the bottom is something round and hard. I pull out a plastic green-and-blue ball with little rubber spikes.

"What is that?" Erika asks, plucking it out of my hands.

I recognize it immediately. "Oh, no. It's Emory's teething ball."

Erika makes a face and hands it right back. "What's it doing in your purse?"

I shake my head, wondering the same thing. "I babysat for her the other night. It must've ended up in my bag somehow."

Erika is looking at me with the same curiosity my mother regarded me with.

"What? He had a last-minute client and needed some help," I say.

"Some help, or *your* help?" I know what she's implying.

I toss the teething ring back in my purse and hand her the list of groomsmen. "Have fun," I say, ignoring the question.

"You have fun," she says, walking out the door. "I expect details tomorrow!"

◆ ◆ ◆

But there will be no details to share. By eleven thirty, I'm waiting downstairs with my bag. I've packed a sundress for dinner, two bathing suits, and a couple shorts and shirts. And this time, no book—I plan to be spending my evening sipping wine with Evan.

By noon, my mother is staring out the window with me. "Mom. Please," I say.

"I'm sure it's just traffic," she says, scurrying into the kitchen. "Why don't I make you a sandwich?"

By twelve thirty, the sandwich and I are both waiting at the kitchen counter. Evan hasn't replied to any of my texts. I'm starting to worry.

Then my phone rings. "Babe. I'm sorry I've kept you waiting." Evan's voice sounds strained, and distant.

"It's okay. Where are you now?"

He pauses. "You're not going to like this."

"No. No, tell me you are not in Boston."

"I'm sorry."

"Are you leaving now? Because if you don't hit the road in the next hour, we're going to miss cocktail hour on the porch. And that's something I really could use right now."

"Honey, I'm not going to be leaving at all. Angie came in late today and our scene got pushed back. I have to stay."

I cannot believe what I am hearing. I'm not sure if I'm more furious to learn that my Ocean House night has been canceled or to learn that Angela Dune is the reason for it. "What do you mean she came in late? How could she do that? Can't they just reschedule it? We have plans." I know I'm almost shouting and I know it's not Evan's fault, but right now I could deck him.

"Listen, I know. I'm disappointed, too. I tried to get them to reschedule, but the crew is here and ready to go."

"Angie was supposed to be there and ready to go!" I remind him angrily. "Why was she late anyway?"

Evan sighs. "Maggie. That makes no difference, you know that."

And now I am mad at him, too. "Do not speak to me like I am a child, Evan. Do not. She's the reason you are still there—doesn't that bother you in the least?"

Evan sighs again. "Listen, there's nothing I can do. The shoot is starting now."

"So what time will you get here, then?"

"Maggie, it's going to go all day. I'm afraid we'll have to reschedule the Ocean House for another time."

I know this is not his doing. And I know I'm not behaving like an adult. But I'm tired of always waiting for Evan. For scenes to wrap, for schedules to be posted, for him to get off set. It doesn't matter whose fault it is or isn't: the fact is, if I don't get off the phone, my disappointment will get the best of me, and I don't want to say something I'll regret. "We'll talk later, okay?"

I hang up the phone before he can answer. When I go out to the kitchen, my mother is pretending to read the paper. "Mom, this house is the size of a shoe box. I know you heard. He's not coming. End of story."

My mom looks at me with a softness that makes me feel ten years old again. "I'm sorry, sweetie. I know you were excited to see him." She doesn't add that she was, too, which is generous of her. The whole family's day is now derailed thanks to the whims of Angie Dune.

Mom pats my hand. "Why don't you go find Erika, and see if you can have some fun today, after all?"

◆ ◆ ◆

My phone rings just as I'm pulling into a space on Main Street. I fumble in my bag to grab it. "I just got here," I say. "Are you still in the jewelry store?"

Only, it's not Erika. It's Cam. Calling to invite me to see the Edwin Bate house. "It's done. I want you to come see it before the owners start moving things back in."

I'm more relieved than I should be when he calls. And it has nothing to do with missing a night at the Ocean House, though it does have something to do with Evan. Since mentioning Evan to him the other night, I've felt like I almost closed some kind of door between us. A door that I've realized I want to remain open. And now I stick my toe into the cracked doorway and nudge it just a little bit wider.

The sun is low in the sky when I finally pull in the gravel drive at the Bate house. I can't help but shake my head. "Cameron Wilder. What have you done?" I murmur.

Round boxwoods have been planted in a snug row against the gray stone foundation. Weeping cherry trees flank both corners of the front yard. The old scrolled steel fencing has been torn out and replaced with a white spindle fence. Bright copper caps, too new to be tarnished yet, glimmer atop freshly painted posts. I let myself in through the gate.

My phone dings in my pocket signaling a call from Erika. I turn it off, just as I hear his laugh. "Wow, you're actually on time," Cam says, standing in the front door.

I'm surprised to see that he's freshly showered, hair still wet, in a crisp collared shirt. The crew is gone for the day. "Since when am I not?" I ask wryly.

He taps his chin. "I seem to recall a birthday dinner. And some purple candles."

I stop in front of him on the step. He smells like pine and fresh soap. "What candles? What are you talking about?"

"Remember those handmade candles you used to like so much, from that gift shop in town?"

I nod, a vague memory of lavender and beeswax coming to mind.

"I bought you a set for your birthday. And then grilled you a fancy dinner on my parents' deck. Remember that night?"

That recollection—and Cam's sharp memory—both catch me by surprise. "And I was late!" I say, trying not to laugh.

"I wanted everything to be perfect, so I set the table and lit the candles right before you were supposed to show up. You were over an hour late." He raises his eyebrows.

I wince as the details flood back. "You cooked filet mignon. By the time I got there they were cold."

Cam nods. "Your lavender candles had melted down to a purple puddle on my mother's deck table. She never let me hear the end of that one."

"But the steaks were still good!" I insist, still feeling a stab of guilt all these years later.

"Liar."

I laugh, and Cam grabs my hand and tugs me inside. "Come on. This is even better than cold filet mignon."

My eyes travel upward as we enter the foyer. All the old moldings have been restored. Painted a cool ivory, they pop against the historic blue-gray walls. Cam leads me across the marble floor and up the newly refinished stairs, still covered in construction paper. "I love the smell of fresh paint. There's something so promising about it," I say.

Cam nods. "I think so, too." The hallway at the top is long and dim, and we pass several closed bedrooms until we reach the room at the end, where daylight spills through the cracked door. Cam pushes it open and stands aside for me to enter first.

I step inside. Stately built-in bookshelves line the wall. An antique brick fireplace sits across the room. Flanking it are floor-to-ceiling windows.

I follow Cam into the sun-dappled center of the room. "Look at all the light."

"That's not the best part," Cam says, crossing the honey-hued floors. "Here." He opens a set of French doors and I follow him outside onto the balcony. It overlooks the street below, and just beyond it, the wide gray expanse of the Mystic River. Already, stars appear against the purple twilight sky.

"Oh, Cam. This is just . . ." I can't think of a word. The sky and the water are too much.

"I know. It's why I wanted you to come." We stand a moment looking out.

"I don't remember seeing this in the plans."

"Because it wasn't," Cam says. "The owner had the architect add it in at the last minute. It's a surprise for his wife."

I let out a breath. "She's a lucky woman."

Cam leans out over the railing and looks back at me. "It wasn't easy to squeeze all this in by our deadline. I hope she appreciates it."

"She will." We stand awhile, taking in the view below. "Does it feel good now that it's finished? Or is it sort of sad?"

Cam smiles appreciatively. "Both. This was my biggest project so far. Which came with some big headaches. But I'll miss it."

The road below is still. The nearest neighbors are a few acres beyond a shroud of hemlocks. For now, it's just the saltwater views, the piney smell of construction, and us.

"You gave the house its life back." I take my eyes off the view to look at him. "How old is it again?"

"Two hundred and five years old." Cam smiles. "It stayed in the family for the first hundred and fifty. That's a lot of Bate history."

"I bet a lot of babies were born in this place."

"And probably a few lives passed."

"Good lives."

He turns to look at me, his profile sharp against the darkening sky. "I hope so. I like to think that old houses have souls. Does that sound spooky to you?"

I can't tell if it's the spirit of the aged building, or the imagined family lives that were made in it, but the pull of history warms me. "Not at all. I think it feels reassuring to think of all the lives made here. All the things these walls saw and heard. Sort of puts things in perspective."

Cam opens his mouth to say something, but closes it and looks away.

"What?"

He shakes his head, but his lips press into a smile. "Let's lock up and get out of here."

◆ ◆ ◆

We end up at the Harp and Hound, an Irish pub on Pearl Street with cozy wooden booths. We grab stools at the bar and Cam orders us Moscow Mules. "Cheers to the completion of the Edwin Bate," he says, clinking his copper mug against mine.

"And to the start of many more restorations," I add. We take deep sips and sit in silence.

"Did you know the Daughters of the American Revolution used to meet here?" I ask him.

"At this pub?" He laughs. "Can't imagine how those meetings ended."

"No, in this building," I say, punching him playfully.

"You still do that," Cam muses.

I turn to look at him. "Do what?"

"You fill in silences. With trivia and all kinds of odd facts."

"I can stand silence," I tell him. "I've changed a lot since you last knew me."

"Is that so?" I can tell by his grin that he doesn't believe a word of it.

"I can!" I insist.

He looks at me over the rim of his mug. "Okay, then. Show me your stuff, Griff."

I glance around. There's a couple at a corner table, and an older gentleman at the end of the bar. "You're on."

We both face forward, sipping our Mules. There is no way I am letting him prove me wrong. He's not the only one who's grown up since college.

When the bartender comes to ask us if we'd like a menu, we both shake our heads no thank you and smile at her.

I glance over at him and raise my eyebrows. He returns the look.

A couple minutes go by, and my drink is empty. Cam notices this and shows me his own, which is still half full. I'm about to say *No thanks*, but I catch myself.

After five more minutes, we're both smiling too widely, struggling to contain our laughs. I give him an imploring look, and he shrugs, as if to say, *See? I told you so.*

But when the bartender comes by again, I wave her over. Pointing to my mug, I smile and nod.

"You want another, honey?"

I nod again.

"You okay?" she asks, glancing back and forth at both of us.

We nod in unison. While I watch as she makes me another Mule I start to feel a rush. It's a mix of the alcohol, which I drank too quickly, and the sense of triumph that I'm winning this bet. But I'm too confident, because when she returns with my drink, I blurt out, "Thanks, that looks delicious!"

Cam slaps the bar. "I win!"

"Hey." I spin around. "That didn't count. I was talking to her."

The woman shakes her head and leaves us, and by now we're both leaning against the bar laughing. "Ah, Griffin. You always were my chatty little thing." Which makes me glance away. The endearment and the possessiveness in his words are not lost on either of us.

"So, how is Erika's wedding coming along?" he asks, finally. "Is the town going to be shut down for the big day?"

It's not unlike Cam to make fun of Erika, but I am surprised that he's asking about her wedding, of all things. "You really want to hear about Erika Crane's wedding? Because I know how much you two adored each other in college." It was an unspoken but simmering resentment that I sensed Erika held for Cam all those years ago, something I always attributed to the fact that for the first time in our friendship my attention had shifted away from her. Sharing was not her thing. But somehow we'd all come through unscathed.

He shrugs. "I do, actually. It's nice to think that some of us have found their other half."

I make note of the weight of his comment, as I fill him in. He listens with genuine interest while I tell him about Trent, the upcoming wedding week, and the missing veil. I feel slightly guilty that Erika is fair game for our small talk, especially when Cam adds, "I'm surprised she hasn't sent you back to Boston to get her veil."

"She's changed," I say, in her defense. But for old time's sake, I pretend to look at my watch. "You can ride shotgun when she calls to ask."

Cam snorts. We order a platter of calamari to share and I'm

glad that our night together will last longer. It's so easy talking to him.

My phone dings twice more as we're eating. "Go ahead, take it," Cam says.

"I'm sure it's nobody," I say, feeling a stab of guilt the second the words come out. I haven't talked to Evan since I hung up on him earlier. "So, how's the little one?"

"She's good." He pauses. "We've got an appointment in Providence on Thursday morning."

"Everything okay?"

Cam pauses. "I was going to tell you. They did some blood work at her last checkup and there were a few question marks. It seems that her oxygen levels were a little off, too. So they've decided to move up the catheterization."

This is much more serious than a simple follow-up. "Cam. Here I am going on about the wedding. I'm so sorry . . ."

He shakes his head. "Please, don't be. It's nice to laugh for a change. Besides, if I worried every time some lab work came back with a question mark, I'd be worried all the time." He smiles roughly. "Parenting 101."

"So you're taking her back to Yale?"

"Yeah." Cam shifts uneasily on his stool. "I had to tell Lauren," he says.

Lauren has been mostly absent from my picture of Cam and Emory, and therefore mostly absent from my thoughts. But of course, he had to tell her. She is Emory's mother. Will always be Emory's mother.

"What did she say?"

Cam sighs. "She didn't. She's out in the field doing research, so I left a message at their office in Juneau. I asked her to fly out here for it." He looks at his hands. "It's a routine procedure, and we've known for a while that Emory would have it done this summer. But still."

I know what Cam means. No matter how routine anything is, when it involves a loved one, it's frightening. As much as I tense at the thought of Lauren coming back into Cam's and Emory's life, every little child deserves a mother. Whatever Cam's reasons, I respect them.

"I don't think she'll come," he says, finally. "And I suppose it will be a lot easier if she doesn't. But I can't say I won't be disappointed."

I imagine Cam making the call. Not being able to reach the mother of his sick child, and relaying the facts in a message, as if she were a stranger. And I realize that to a baby Emory's age, that's exactly what Lauren is.

"I want to go with you."

Cam looks genuinely taken aback. "Griff, that's really sweet of you, but you don't have to. We've been down this road before. We'll be fine."

"I know you will. But I still want to come, if it's not an imposition, that is." Despite the fact that I feel a sudden urge to help, to do something, it occurs to me that Cam may prefer to do this on his own. And that my coming may be more of a distraction than a comfort. "If you'd rather, I can visit afterward. Bring you lunch? Keep you company for an hour?" I don't add that if Lauren does end up coming, I will stay out of the way. That I will leave this to the family, because in the end, no matter how absent she may be, Lauren is still family.

Cam takes a long sip of his drink and looks at me squarely. "All right. Company would be nice."

We order another drink. "I drove by Camp Edgewater yesterday," I tell him. "The kids were out in the sea kayaks. Brought back a lot of memories."

Cam laughs, and reminds me of the summer night we "borrowed" two kayaks and went out onto the river together. And how afterward, we forgot to lock them back into the stand. When the director found the boathouse open the next morning he'd confided furiously to Cam that he suspected another counselor, an arrogant kid who was notorious for coming in to work late and screwing around. I was secretly elated when the director pegged him as the culprit.

"But then you messed it all up!" I remind him.

"I couldn't let that kid take the blame," Cam says, even now.

"Why not? The guy was such a jerk. Remember he backed into your Jeep in the parking lot and denied it."

Cam grimaces. "I'd forgotten about that."

"At least you got off easy, Mr. Honesty."

"Easy? I had to wash every boat on that campground. It took me three of my afternoons off."

"But you never ratted me out," I say fondly. "Or used it against me."

"Maybe I should have," he says, leaning in. "Is it too late?"

It's a *moment*. Whether it's the pull of the memory or the drinks, I find myself leaning in toward Cam. But then Cam straightens, excusing himself. "I'll be right back."

Flushed, I hail the bartender for a glass of water. My phone vibrates again in my pocket. There are a page's worth of texts, the latest from Evan: "Where are you?" An earlier one from Erika confuses me: "Evan is the best! You lucky girl." I wonder what she is talking about. And then she calls.

"Maggie, where have you been all this time? Why haven't you been answering?"

Just then Cam returns.

"Sorry, I have to call you back." It's a classic Erika move; she should understand. I turn the phone off altogether and slide it into my purse.

Cam plops himself on the stool beside me. I try to read his expression. Did he call home to check in about Emory? Should I have called Evan to check in with him? Suddenly it feels as if there are more than just the two of us sitting here at the bar.

"You want anything else?" he asks, finally. What I want is to rewind to five minutes ago. But the moment, or whatever it was, has broken.

"Maybe we should call it a night," I say. No sooner are the words out than I'm hoping that he'll disagree. That he'll try to talk me into one last drink. It won't be hard.

But he doesn't. "Good call," Cam says. He hails the server for our tab. "I have to get up early tomorrow."

A breeze has picked up outside. I wrap my arms around my middle, wishing I'd brought a light jacket. "Cold?" he asks, and before I can answer Cam drapes a loose arm around my shoulders.

We walk, sides pressed lightly together, up the sidewalk toward our cars. Halfway across Bascule Bridge, Cam pauses. I turn to him at the exact moment he turns to me, and whether it's because his arm is still draped over my shoulder, or the timing, our noses bump. And our lips brush. I don't know who steps back first, but before we do, it happens—so quickly it could almost escape time and notice—except for the fact that I *know* it happened. We kissed.

We stand for a beat of silence, staring at each other. "I'm sorry," Cam says quickly. Something flickers behind the blue-green in his eyes.

"Don't be. Really, it's—"

"It's what?" Cam is hanging on my every word. But before I can answer, a car pulls up alongside us on the bridge and stops. The window rolls down and the driver leans over.

"Maggie? Is that you?"

I freeze at the sound of Evan's voice.

Seventeen

W hat a wonderful surprise! You made it after all," my mother says in her high-pitched "company" voice. She gestures for Evan to sit on the couch, as my father settles into his armchair across from us.

Evan rises to help my mother with the tray of iced tea she's carried out from the kitchen. "I'm sorry to impose on you both, Mr. and Mrs. Griffin, but I was able to get away from the set last minute, and I was hoping to surprise Maggie. I felt bad that we missed our Ocean House plans."

"Can you still go?" my mother asks, looking hopefully between the two of us.

I'm still in shock, and going to the Ocean House is the last thing on my mind.

"Unfortunately, I canceled the reservation," Evan explains. "I didn't think I'd make it in time, and if we didn't, then they would've charged me."

My father narrows his eyes.

"But I can get a room at the Mystic Inn, for myself," Evan adds.

"Nonsense," my mother insists. "We have plenty of room

here." She hasn't stopped smiling since we walked through the front door. "And please, call me Marie."

My parents met Evan once before, back in the fall, when they came to Boston for a weekend. We'd been dating for only a few months at the time, so I'd kept the introductions brief and had him come by their hotel for brunch the Sunday morning before they went back home. I remember barely touching my eggs Benedict, for fear that if I didn't steer the conversation, they might ask him something embarrassing or make some weighty comment about our relationship that exceeded the few tender months we'd been dating. Like the first time that Jane brought Toby home to meet all of us, and my mother asked Toby if he wanted children. "What?" she'd protested when Jane cornered her in the kitchen after Toby had left. "Your college years go by fast—why waste time dating someone who doesn't have the same vision for your future?"

"My vision, or yours, Mother?" Jane had shouted back at her.

Now, seated politely across from one another in my parents' chintz-filled living room, there is a long beat of silence, but I'm too overwhelmed to fill it before my mother does.

"Maggie, can you believe that Evan drove Erika's veil all the way down from Boston!"

Her eyes land on me, expectantly, and it's all I can do not to turn away from their hopeful glare. "I cannot," I say. Leave it to Erika. "Let me get some snacks. You must be hungry, Evan."

Safe in the kitchen, I pull my phone from my pocket. "Want to guess who's sitting in my parents' living room?"

"I've been trying to reach you all night. Why did you hang up?"

"Erika! You know how mixed up I am right now. How could you pick Evan to drive your veil down here?"

"I didn't, I promise! He mentioned to Trent that he was going to surprise you. It just made sense that if he was already driving to Mystic anyway . . ."

I'm near my boiling point. So, maybe she didn't exactly arrange it. But, despite the fact that she knew how conflicted I was, she sure didn't let a free ride for her veil get away from her, either. "You shouldn't have let him. You should have told me. Or something." I don't know whom I'm most upset with. To be fair, Erika did try to call. And the only thing Evan is guilty of is being sweet—to both of us. Which leaves only me.

"Mags, you've got to calm down. This is a good thing. He came all the way here to make things up to you!"

I slap a block of cheddar cheese on a platter and check the expiration date. It's only a day past. Just like my sanity.

Erika adopts her legal adviser voice. "Listen to me. Seeing Evan face-to-face will wipe away any doubts you're feeling. You'll know he's the one."

"All I know is that my head is about to explode. Want to take a guess where Evan found me?"

"I thought you were at home."

"Erika, you are so late to this party. We're here now. But an hour ago I was at the Harp and Hound with someone. And Evan just happened to spot us walking over the bridge as he drove through town."

She pauses. "Wait. Not with Cam?"

"You've arrived."

"Maggie! What happened?"

At that moment my mother comes bustling in to the kitchen behind me and grabs a box of tissues. "Erika, I have to go. I'll let you imagine all the rest."

My mother is actually humming.

There is a series of loud sneezes from the living room. Mom holds up the box of tissues. "These are for Evan. Your dad's telling him all about the boat show at the Seaport. You should take him."

I follow her to the doorway. Evan is listening politely as my father goes on about the boat show, but I can see from here that both his eyes are swelling up. It's then that I notice Winston perching on the back of the couch behind him. And all of our strained conversations about Mr. Kringles and apartments come wheeling back.

"Oh look, another member of the family wants to meet you," my father says. I watch in horror as my father scoops Winston up and deposits him right on Evan's lap. Evan sneezes again.

"Dad, Evan has allergies!" A flash of alarm crosses his face, and my father leaps up to relieve Evan of Winston. But Evan holds up his hand.

"It's okay," he lies, scratching behind Winston's ears for emphasis. "Now, what were you saying about the Seaport?"

My father launches back into his history lesson, and my mother fusses over my arrangement of the cracker tray, while Evan mops his runny nose. At that moment our eyes meet, and he winks. Despite our missed connections this summer and everything that I just left on the bridge, my heart tingles. I wink back.

◆ ◆ ◆

One hour and two doses of Benadryl later, my parents have finally gone upstairs to bed. I sit beside Evan on the couch and press a tissue to nose. "You are such a sport. I'm sorry about this."

"About what?"

"I guess we can skip the allergy testing." I dab his nose again.

"Don't worry, it looks worse than it is."

"You didn't have to hold the cat in your lap. And pat it all night!"

He smiles. "It's your father's cat."

"And you're his daughter's guest," I say. But it comes out wrong.

Evan tucks a piece of hair behind my ear, his brow furrowed. "Is that who I am? The guest?"

"Of course not. You know what I mean."

This is Evan's first visit to my home. I should be elated. I should be sitting on the pink rug in my childhood room with him, paging through my old photo albums and showing him my junior high art show plaque. The things you do when you want to share the span of your life with someone special.

"So, who was that with you earlier?"

I've wondered when Evan would get around to asking me about Cam; now my mixed sense of guilt and uncertainty simmers to the surface.

"That guy you were walking with," Evan adds. He doesn't mention the arm around me. I wonder what else he may have seen.

"Cameron? He's just an old friend who recently moved back to town." I try to keep my expression even. "With his daughter,"

I add, as though Emory serves as an appropriate barrier to my having been walking on the bridge with Cam's arm wrapped around my shoulder.

Evan nods thoughtfully. "Cameron. Haven't heard you mention him before." Hearing him say Cam's name out loud brands the moment in my mind.

"He's just an old friend," I say again. "I babysat for his daughter recently, and we were just catching up and grabbing a bite to eat," I add.

Evan shrugs. "If you say that's all it is, then that's all it is."

Only, I didn't say *that's all*.

When Evan leans in and presses his lips to mine, it's familiar and warm. Not awkward or confusing. There is no doubt about whether or not this kiss happened or how Evan feels.

"Was it okay that I surprised you like that?" he whispers.

I press my cheek against the soft blue of his Tufts T-shirt, relieved. "I'm so glad you did. And I can't believe you brought Erika's veil."

Evan tips my chin and kisses me again. "It had nothing to with the veil."

I decide right there on my parents' couch that if Evan asks me anything else, I will tell him. I will answer any question he poses. Even if it's why my lips touched Cameron's. But he doesn't.

"So, what do you want to watch?" he asks, as I flick through the TV stations. If only my mind could switch as easily as the channels.

◆   ◆   ◆

Evan has to head back to Boston. We do a whirlwind tour of Mystic, which is thankfully quieter than normal because of a light rainfall. We grab ice cream, drive over to the Seaport, and walk around in the mist. It's not at all the kind of summer day in Mystic I'd described, but Evan doesn't seem to mind. Only once do I wonder about Cam, not having spoken to him since I climbed into Evan's car the night before. If Evan is thinking about it, he doesn't let on. As we walk over the Bascule Bridge to the pier, I grab his hand. I will talk to Cam later. And even though I have no idea what I'll say, I'll worry about that later, too.

Before Evan has to leave, my mother begs me to pop by Jane's house so that I can introduce him. Which turns into an early dinner. Which turns into a Griffin family event.

We arrive early, which I have learned is never a good idea when visiting a family with small children, especially on a rainy day. Even with pizza in tow.

"Everyone, I'd like you to meet Evan." I glance around Jane's kitchen at all the upturned faces. Lucy's tiny face is red and twisted—in the midst of full meltdown in Jane's arms. Randall is seated in the middle of the floor behind a tower of LEGOs, his mouth stained an unnatural shade of purple. The dog is chewing something under the table that looks like a purse. "Evan, this is everyone."

Owen is first to break the silence. "You're not Cameron."

My mother and Jane's faces flash with something akin to confusion, followed by suspicion. Evan looks at the ground, and for a second I think the room will burst into flames.

"This is my friend *Evan*," I say, redirecting Owen to the LEGO tower after a quick hug. Luckily, the usual chaos of Jane's house interrupts the moment anyway.

Lucy is fussing and Jane is in a foul mood today, I can tell, as she plunks Lucy in my mother's arms and stalks across the room to rescue something glass from Randall's grip. Toby is sprawled across the couch in a pair of sweats. He shakes hands with Evan from his prone position, a move that garners steely glares from both Jane and me.

"Sorry, dude. Don't mind me." He points affectionately to Lucy, who is wriggling in my mother's arms in the next room. "It's been a while since I've slept."

"That's rough. How long has she been up for?" Evan asks warily.

Toby shouts out to the kitchen. "Janey, how old is the baby?"

Jane scoffs. "You mean *Lucy*? Who is *seven* months old?"

Toby winks at Evan. "That long."

Grand Central has nothing on Jane's house at dinner hour. There is the usual family banter, where everyone talks over the top of one another, no one listens, and conversations are repeated at least a half-dozen times before we sit down. Jane makes an initial scramble to scoop up toys and kick stray shoes out of the way, before giving up and dumping them all in the dog's bed. Randall announces loudly that Lucy's diaper needs changing.

I steal a peek at Evan to see how he's handling all this. Toby has gotten up long enough to pass out beers to the guys, and the men have hunkered down in the living room to watch the game.

Jane corners me in the kitchen. I notice Lucy isn't the only one who's been changed; Jane's traded her stained yoga pants for crisp jeans.

"Did you just put on makeup?" I ask.

She ignores me. "So, how is Evan's visit going?"

"Okay."

Jane shakes her head. "Just okay? Are we talking about the same guy in the pressed shirt who's entertaining my kids in my living room?"

I glance over. Evan has moved down to the carpet and is building LEGOs with Randall. Toby and my father are still glued to the couch.

My mother, who has busied herself with the salad, is pretending not to listen, but she can't help herself. "Evan surprised Maggie. Isn't that sweet?" She points the salad spoon at Jane. "Did you know Erika forgot her wedding veil in Boston, and Evan drove it home for her? Saved her all that trouble."

Jane drains her glass of wine. "Jesus. I can't even get Toby to drive to the market for milk. And if he does, all he comes home with is a bag of Twizzlers."

"I can't wait to see an episode of Evan's show," my mother continues. I wonder how many of her book club friends she has called since he arrived.

"It doesn't air again until this fall, Mom," I remind her again.

"How long's he here for?" Jane asks, dumping more wine in to her glass. The Newport trip has clearly worn off.

"He has to drive back tonight," I say. "They're filming to-morrow."

My mother actually sighs. "Such a fascinating line of work."

"I don't care what he does for work," Jane scoffs. "The man helps out." She nods toward the living room, where Evan is clearing the men's beer bottles. We watch in silence as he brings them into the kitchen and rinses each one before setting them in the recycling bin.

"Shall I set the food out?' he asks.

"Thanks, that would be great," Jane says sweetly, before abruptly excusing herself to go to the living room. "Dinner-time!" she barks.

There is a rumble as everyone heads for the table. "What's for dinner?" Randall asks, suspiciously.

"Pizza," Evan tells him, bringing the boxes to the table.

Owen brightens. "Cameron took us for pizza!"

I wince, glancing around to see who else has heard. Evan doesn't seem to have noticed. But my mother does. I ignore her flat gaze, and start passing out plates. "We've got cheese and pepperoni."

"Cameron likes pepperoni," Owen continues. "That's what we had at the pizza place."

"Owen, why don't you come sit by me?" I say.

Jane plops down on the other side of me. "So. Slices with my kids and Cameron. When exactly was this?"

I can tell Jane is haggard-tired and mad at the world today. And she especially does not like it when her children's schedule, menu, or social interactions are in any way altered without her knowledge. But surely she is not about to start in with me. "You were on your way home from your lovely weekend getaway," I whisper. "The one I gave up my first weekend of summer to babysit your offspring for?"

Jane nods toward Evan, who is laughing at something Toby said, and lowers her voice. "You've got a guy like this, and you're hanging around with Cameron?"

I ignore this. "We were at the playground and the kids were starving."

This does not dissuade her. "But I left you a homemade cas-serole. *Organic* quinoa casserole."

"The kids had fun, Jane. It was just a playdate." I pass her the salad.

"You mean a *date*."

"Yes, Jane. Because four kids under the age of five makes for a really hot date."

Jane shrugs, stabbing at her salad. "I don't get it, Maggie."

"It was just pizza. It was impromptu."

Jane shoves a slice of cucumber in her mouth and grins wickedly. "Impromptu? Or impassioned?"

I glare at her.

Toby slides into a chair beside Owen and grabs a plate. "So, what've we got?"

Jane smiles at him. "Impassioned pizza."

Toby frowns at his plate.

"We forgot drinks," I say loudly, desperate to switch the subject before my mother joins us. "Who wants water?"

Owen turns to his mother. "They didn't have water at the pizza place. Maggie let us get Coke."

Jane turns an apoplectic shade. "You gave my kids *soda*?"

Toby smirks, probably because he's relieved not to be on the receiving end of this lecture for once.

"Do you have any idea how many dyes and sweeteners are in a bottle of soda? They cause cancer."

"Relax, Jane. They had water, too."

Owen shakes his head. "We drank the Coke."

"So," Evan says, having passed out plates to everyone else. "What can I get you, Maggie?"

I fix him with a grateful smile. "Cheese, please."

"You want a Coke with that?" Jane snips.

My mother is heading our way with a stack of napkins. My father is wandering around looking for a free seat.

There is a moment of silence as everyone digs in, before my father sets his piece down with an expression nothing short of wistful. "This is great. Where is this pie from?" He grabs a box and reads it aloud. "*Mystic Pizza.* I haven't been there in ages. Have any of you?"

Jane shoots a look at me.

My mother finally sits down. "I think I'll have a slice of pepperoni."

"Cameron's favorite," Owen says.

Eighteen

I needed to talk to Cam. About that moment—that kiss—whatever it was those few days ago on the bridge. But there were far more pressing matters.

Thursday morning I arrive as I said I would at Yale-New Haven Children's Hospital. The woman at the cardiac catheterization lab reception counter asks me for identification. "Are you family?"

"Cameron Wilder, the father of your patient Emory Wilder, is expecting me," I tell her. Which is not entirely true. In fact, he may be hoping that I don't show up at all.

The nurse glances at her computer screen. "Are you Lauren Peale?"

My cheeks flush at the mention of her name. I glance down the hall, feeling suddenly out of place.

"No," I say. "I'm Maggie Griffin."

"Family?"

Lauren Peale is family. Lauren Peale, the mother, who may at this very moment be coming up in the next elevator. But I'm already here, and no matter what Cam may think of me right now, I want him to know my word is good.

"Yes," I lie. "I'm family."

Inside the room, Cam is sitting on a hospital bed, bouncing Emory gently on his lap. They don't notice me standing awkwardly in the doorway.

"Good morning."

Cam looks up. "You came."

But he's not the only one in the room. "What a surprise." Mrs. Wilder is sitting in the corner armchair, and she looks at me quizzically. But I'm so relieved that she's not Lauren that I return her look with a smile.

"Just wanted to drop by and wish you all well. I brought you lunch," I stammer, holding up a bag from Mystic Market. "And a little something for Emory." His eyes travel to the pink gift bag in my other hand.

Cam stands, shifting Emory to his hip. She turns to look at me and breaks into a grin. It's all the permission I need to step into the room and tickle her foot. "Hi there, baby girl." She's surprisingly rosy-cheeked and alert. "So, everything went well this morning, then?"

Cam grimaces. "Actually, we're still waiting for our turn in the catheterization lab. There was a change in the schedule."

"It's been a long morning," Mrs. Wilder says, still studying me. "Would you like a seat?" She gestures to a chair beside her own.

"Oh, no, thank you. I'm fine." I hand Cam the gift bag. When he reaches in and pulls out the little stuffed elephant I brought, Emory locks her eyes on it.

Mrs. Wilder stands. "I think I'll get a drink of water."

Cam waits until his mother is well down the hallway. "Thanks for all this, it's really nice of you." Then, "I didn't think you were coming after all."

"Is it okay that I did? I don't want to impose, but we'd talked about it the other night—"

Cam finishes the sentence. "Before your boyfriend came." His tone is void of any sentiment.

A wave of guilt hits me dead center. "Yeah. Before that."

Emory breaks the thick silence that follows with a squeal. She reaches one arm out toward me and instinctively I reach back.

"She wants your necklace," Cam says, glancing at the silver heart pendant my grandmother gave me. I touch it, realizing only now the significance of my having worn it here.

"Can I hold her?"

Cam gently passes her to me. When I show her the pendant, Emory seizes it, a silver heart in her tiny fist. I glance at Cam.

For the first time since I arrived, he smiles. "Careful. She's got a thing for shiny objects."

"You've got good taste," I tell her, and without thinking I press my nose to her head and inhale her baby scent. A wave of worry rises inside me as I do. "I can't believe you've been waiting all morning. How are you feeling?"

He sits on the bed. "We're hanging in there."

There is the sound of nearing footsteps in the hall. We all turn. I'm filled with relief as an older couple carrying flowers walks by.

"Cam, I'm sorry, but I had to tell the nurse that I was family."

He shrugs. "That's okay."

"She asked me if I was Lauren." I watch him carefully, but there is no indication of surprise or offense at my having asked.

"Yes," he says. "I put her name on the register."

When he doesn't offer any more, I do. Fully aware that this is not my business. "So she's coming, then?"

Cam shakes his head sadly. "I don't think so. She finally sent a message that she was working in the Seward Peninsula. She thanked me for the update on Emory, but . . ." He doesn't finish the thought.

At that moment, a young male orderly breezes through the door. "Hello, sunshine! It's almost your turn." He comes up to me and tickles Emory's tummy. Emory emits a small noise of distress and turns in her father's direction.

"Just a few things to go over, first." I hand Emory back and stand to the side, watching as they take her vitals and do a brief checkup. Cam answers each question calmly. No formula since last night. Water until 4:00 a.m. Wet diaper fifteen minutes ago. "So are they ready for her now?" Cam asks.

"Just about."

Mrs. Wilder returns and hovers by the bed. They undress Emory together, and put on what looks to be a tiny hospital gown, but still it swallows her up. She starts to cry. The nurse applies a numbing cream to Emory's upper leg, where I assume the catheter will be placed. Soon after, the cardiologist who will perform the catheterization arrives with an attendee. He introduces himself as Dr. Weil.

"It's okay, Emmy," Cam murmurs. He sways her back and forth, as Dr. Weil goes over the procedure. Emory will be taken to the cardiac catheterization lab and the anesthesiologist will sedate her under general anesthesia. At that point, the catheter will be inserted through a small incision in her groin and advanced into her heart with the help of ultrasound. Additionally, a transesophageal echocardiogram will be done with a probe placed down Emory's esophagus, to take pictures from inside Emory's heart. Measurements will be taken of the heart valves and blood vessels, and the doctors will determine the actual size of the defect. If all goes well, Emory will remain under anesthesia and the device to close the hole between her ventricles will be delivered through a long sheath. Once it is properly placed using X-ray and ultrasound, the catheter will be removed and Emory will be brought to the recovery room. The entire procedure is expected to take two to three hours.

Instinctively, my eyes travel to Cam's. He is reverent; a man about to hand over his only child. But he seems at peace with all that Dr. Weil has just explained.

Suddenly I feel too large and out of place in the room. When Cam shakes the cardiologist's hand, tears spring to my eyes.

"I'll be right outside," I say, though no one is listening.

Out in the hallway I press myself against the cool concrete wall. Moments later Dr. Weil leaves the room. His gait is purposeful as he moves down the hallway toward the bank of elevators. He can't be any older than Toby—I imagine him waking up this morning and drinking coffee at his kitchen counter, still in his pajamas—yet here, now, this otherwise ordinary man is in charge of Cam's little girl's heart.

Moments later, Emory is wheeled out of the room, just a little bundle in the center of the bed. Cam walks alongside, holding onto her the whole way. Emory looks uncertain. I wonder what she makes of all the bright lights and strange faces.

I want to follow them. I want to say something to Cam. But they're already halfway down the hall and I realize I don't know what my place is here.

At the elevators, Mrs. Wilder stops and hugs her son. She remains behind as Cam steps inside with the nurse and orderly. The elevator doors close. I watch as she puts a hand to her forehead. It's a moment before she turns and sees me still standing there.

◆ ◆ ◆

"What do you do in Boston?"

The cafeteria lighting is only half a shade less bright than the glare of the hospital halls, and I feel utterly exposed sitting across from Mrs. Wilder at the narrow café table.

"I'm a teacher at a private school just outside the city. But I was just let go, so . . ."

She glances at the clock, and I can't blame her. She probably wants to call her husband. She's probably worrying about her grandchild.

I stand up. "I should go. Would you please let Cam know that I'm thinking of them?"

Mrs. Wilder looks offended. "Sit down, Maggie."

I sit. "I don't want to intrude. And I should probably get back to Mystic. My friend Erika is getting married and—"

"I could use the company. Tell me about your students."

"Okay." As I detail my job at Darby, I can't help but feel Cam's mother scrutinize me across the café table in a similar style to that of Ainsley Perry across my desk. Perhaps more kindly, but it's an interview, nonetheless.

"Why teaching?" she asks finally, when I finish. In the midst of the smell of coffee and cafeteria food, I'm somewhat thrown by the philosophical question.

"I love kids." A lame textbook reply. "What I mean is, I love getting to know who my kids really are. And what they're good at or curious about. I like guiding them in the direction of their strengths."

She doesn't get sentimental like some do. But she doesn't glaze over like many others do, either. "Isn't it hard to give kids those kind of creative opportunities, given all the standardized testing in classrooms these days?"

Despite the fact that her only child is long out of school, Mrs. Wilder is abreast of educational trends. I sit up taller. "It can be. But assessments also give us valuable information. I guess it'd be nice to have more of a balance."

"Balance is good. If an unrealistic goal."

It's a sweeping statement.

Mrs. Wilder leans forward. "Maggie, has Cam shared much about his last year with you?"

I don't want to cross the line at divulging private conversations. But then, so many lines have been crossed already. "Yes, some of it."

"Then you know how he came to be a single father."

"I do."

"And you also know how special Emory is."

I glance outside. There are no clouds in the sky. I'm spiritual enough to take that as a good sign. "Cam told me about her heart condition. About the ASD. But he said she's doing well."

Mrs. Wilder smiles sadly. "She is, for now. But we don't know what the future holds, and Cam has already struggled so hard just to keep up with the present." She looks directly at me. "In the last year, he left his field of work, moved back home from across the country, and started a new business. All with a new baby. It hasn't been easy."

"For any of you," I rush to add.

"What I mean to say is that Cam's life has been full of surprises. Difficult surprises."

"I know." Though even as I say the words, I realize I don't know. Not like Mrs. Wilder must.

"Despite all the strides Cameron has made, there will always be the matter of Emory's mother." Mrs. Wilder does not call her by name. "She could come back at any time."

Lauren Peale, who, to my knowledge, is not coming today. I wonder how Mrs. Wilder feels about her. Whether she views Lauren as a missile gone off its trajectory, capable of shattering all that Cam has constructed for them, or as a missing piece to an incomplete puzzle.

She smiles sadly. "I'm happy that you're doing well, Maggie. You were always a bright girl. I want the same for Cam." She pauses, a stray tear in the corner of one of her eyes. "He deserves it."

On this we are united. "I couldn't agree more, Mrs. Wilder."

"Then please. Let him focus on Emory and his life here." Her expression is unyielding. I recognize it.

It's a version of the expression I've seen on my classroom parents' faces, when they are sharing a life-altering event with me: when a child is diagnosed with a learning disability, or the family is going through a divorce. Parents carry their children's hurts. And Mrs. Wilder is holding an enormous basket of her own hurts right now.

"Cam is an amazing man, Mrs. Wilder," I tell her. "He's going to get through this."

Mrs. Wilder's smile is gone. "Then you understand that he can't suffer any more disappointments. Not right now."

A flash of protest rises within me. I would never hurt Cam. And besides, we're not a couple of high school kids anymore. But when I look across the table at his mother, there is nothing I can argue.

"You've still got stars in your eyes," she says. "You're one of the lucky ones."

Set against the hospital, it becomes clear how my being here is brief and complicated, frivolous amid a backdrop rich with perspective. My intentions may be good. But perhaps they are also more than a little bit selfish.

Nineteen

The wedding party has landed in Mystic Village. Like a fleet of pastel soldiers, the girls arrive in choreographed union. The men are the opposite, rolling solo at unscheduled times, and their counterparts scramble to pick up forgotten groomsmen at T. F. Green Airport in Providence or the New London train station.

Trent's family, the Mitchells, are first to arrive, in two distinct units. But there are immediate changes to be made. Trent's father and the new Mrs. Mitchell, a rakish blond in her late twenties, are registered at the Inn at Mystic. Which, unfortunately, is where the first Mrs. Mitchell and her three sisters have also registered. Set atop a grassy rise overlooking the village, the Inn is rather intimate. And Trent is quick to point out that intimate will *not* work for the extended Mitchell family.

Evan and the groomsmen are all booked at the Marriott, which is unfortunately sold out, July being high tourist season. Since the first Mrs. Mitchell and her family have reserved three rooms between them, and Mr. Mitchell and his consort only require one, it is neither quickly nor quietly decided that Mr.

Mitchell will have to move his young wife to the Marriott. Evan has kindly agreed to trade.

"You didn't have to do that," I tell him when I meet him in his new lodging at the Inn that night.

"It was no big deal. Besides, you won't believe the room Trent's dad is giving up."

Apparently the new Mrs. Mitchell prefers largesse, as was apparent from the eight-piece Louis Vuitton luggage set that Evan helped to haul down to their car. The *room* from which she was displaced took up the entire upper east wing of the Inn, a legendary suite featured in lifestyle magazines. "Mags, we've got the place all to ourselves. A suite with a balcony overlooking the water!" I can only imagine the new Mrs. Mitchell's face when she lays eyes on Evan's standard double.

We drive over to the Red 36, a trendy spot at Seaport Marine, but it's an uneventful night by our Boston standards. Everyone's traveled in after a week of work, and tomorrow is Friday, with a full day of appointments, followed by a catered luncheon at Mrs. Crane's house and the rehearsal dinner.

The Chicago cousins have had too much to drink at the bar. Erika joins them, but even she is going at half her usual speed.

Evan and I find seats at the raw bar and order a couple beers and a platter of littlenecks. "So, how's the job search going?" he asks.

I shake my head. "I only just found out last week" I say. "But I'm working on a couple applications."

He shrugs and sips his beer. "No time like the present. I was reading this article in the *Globe* about successful work habits the other day, and it talked about how critical it is to keep moving. When one goal fails, start another. You know? You want to get out there as soon as possible." Evan enjoys reading health and motivation articles and staying on top of positive lifestyle trends, something I usually find charming.

When I give him a look, he seems confused. "What? I only meant that it's healthy to keep moving forward. You know, build the momentum instead of letting yourself get dragged down."

"I'm not getting dragged down," I say, prickling. "We've got the wedding this weekend, and I plan to start looking in earnest on Monday." The fact that I have to assure Evan that I'm on top of things bugs me. He should be the one reassuring *me*. I've barely had time to process Darby, beyond sharing the news and doing some desultory online searches. "You're going to be fine, kid," my father had said. "I know there's something great out there for you!" Then, retrieving his checkbook from the desk, "Here's a little something to tide you over." When I tried to explain to my dad that I was still getting my paycheck through the end of the summer, he'd pushed his check back across the kitchen counter to me, with a wink. "Then put it in a rainy-day jar." It was sweet and typical of my dad—not trying to fix the problem for me, but letting me know that he believed I could; and that he'd have my back until I did.

I'd expected more of the same from Evan.

"I'm sorry," Evan says now. "I'm just trying to be positive." He looks genuinely confused. And maybe even a little annoyed.

"I know you are, but right now all I need is a little encouragement. And maybe even license to wallow. Or complain a little. Is that okay?" Evan has always been so sensitive, so thoughtful. But it's been over little things: giving me flowers, ordering me a drink, calling to check in. We've never had to straddle something like this before.

Evan shrugs. "Okay, Mags. I just think it's more helpful to stay positive."

It's not a real fight. It's not even an argument. But it's largely disappointing.

By eleven thirty Peyton and Chad come over to say good night, Peyton stifling a huge yawn. "We're gonna hit the hay," she announces. It makes me realize how tired I suddenly am.

Erika squeezes between us and plops down on the free stool next to me. "I'm beat, too," she admits.

Evan throws up his hands half jokingly. "Is everyone packing up already?" he asks. "The night is young!"

"Actually, I think I'm going to head back to my parents' tonight," I tell him. "I'm tired, and all my stuff is there anyway."

I catch Erika looking at me sideways.

Evan shakes his head. "Don't be silly. I can drive you home first thing in the morning."

I should be thrilled for this night alone at the Inn together. I don't want us to be irritated with each other. "You're right," I say. "I'll be right back."

Erika reaches me before I get to the restroom door. "Everything okay?"

"Yeah. Just tired, I guess."

She trails me to the large bathroom mirror and watches me arrange my hair. She looks unconvinced.

Peyton has followed us in. "Is this about Cam?" Erika asks me outright.

With the sudden arrival of the wedding party, I haven't had

a spare second to pull the girls aside and fill them in. "Emory had her cardiac procedure yesterday morning in New Haven. I can't stop thinking about it."

Erika's got the nose of a bloodhound on the trail. "About Emory? Or about her dad?"

I meet her gaze in the mirror. "Both, okay?"

"Okay." She dabs some lip balm on her lips. "How are they doing?"

"I don't really know." Cam texted me late last night: two lines—*Em did well and she can go home tomorrow. Thanks for coming by*—a message that left me wanting more information, more *something*. "He said things went okay. But I don't know much more."

Peyton looks aghast. "She's just a baby, and she's having to go through heart surgery?"

"It's a catheter that they run through a small incision. It's not as invasive as open-heart." But still.

Erika touches my shoulder. "So, you went."

I nod. "Briefly. But I don't want to bother them." I don't add that Mrs. Wilder's words have been the only thing standing in the way of my contacting Cam since. As sharp as they are to hold, she's right. My life is not here anymore. And Cam's life is.

"I think that was best," Erika says. "It's sweet of you to want to help, but this is heavy stuff. It's not something you can rescue them from."

I look up at my friends; their voices are as soft as their expressions. It's the old joke among us girls come to life: I'm the rescuer. Of stray pets, of wayward students, of birds that fall from nests. I can't seem to help but stumble across their path.

Or maybe it's into them. Erika's just looking out for me, but still, it stings.

"Come on, you guys. I'm not trying to rescue anyone. I'm just trying to be there for him."

There's a beat of silence. Then Peyton pats me emphatically on the rear end. "And someone else is out there waiting for you. Let's go."

She's right. Evan is standing by the door holding my jean jacket. When he slips it over my shoulders, I let myself fall against him. It always strikes me how I fit just so against the crook of his shoulder.

"Everyone ready?" Peyton asks. She ushers us out in her usual mother-hen fashion. Erika laughs at something Trent says and loops her arm through mine. We walk out as a noisy group of friends into the warm night along the pier, each one of us linked with another. Like Mrs. Wilder said, there are stars in our eyes. And I can't help but wonder, why are we the lucky ones?

Twenty

The incongruity among the bridal parties is striking. As salon appointments and rehearsal timetables are dispensed to the women attendees, the men are somehow allowed free rein to wander in various recreational directions; the golf course, the club courts, and the hotel pool. "So unfair," Peyton complains. "I'd rather go have a beer with the guys than get a gel manicure with Trent's two mothers."

Trent pops by the Crane house mid-morning, where all the women have gathered for coffee before being dispatched to our nail appointment and dress fittings, and is received like a prince. That is, by everyone except Erika. Whipping from room to room with a notepad, ignoring her mother's pleas to eat something, she's already directed the cousins to call the salon and push back the manicures fifteen minutes and has asked Trent's mother to check in with the groomsmen who are supposed to be bringing their tuxes over.

I've been assigned the task of hanging Erika's gown, which has just returned from being steamed, along with her veil. Something I am more than capable of managing, but Peyton is hot on my heels on the carpeted staircase. "Be careful not to drag it," she cautions me.

She follows me right into Erika's room and watches as I unzip the garment bag and attempt to hang the veil alongside the dress. "No, no, you shouldn't put the veil in the dress bag. It needs to be kept separate so it doesn't wrinkle," she tells me.

"Erika said to keep them together. She's already lost it once," I joke.

Peyton isn't listening. "Plus, you don't want the veil to get stuck on the dress bodice. That happened to *my* veil," she adds with a cluck of her tongue. "Lost several pearls. It was disastrous."

I surrender the veil and take refuge on the window seat. "Sounds like it."

She drapes the yards of pearled tulle meticulously between hangers and hooks it a good two feet away from the dress bag with a flourish.

Below, Erika is walking Trent out to his car. Their voices rise up through the open window, and it becomes clear things are not as sparkling as the summer morning outside.

"What's going on?" Peyton asks.

Erika is standing on the walkway, arms crossed. "Can't the golf game wait? You've barely spent time with my side of the family. Or with me!"

"Isn't that what the next four days are about? Dinners, boating, the rehearsal night? Relax. I'll have plenty of time to sit with you and Grandma Elaine."

"*Ellen*," Erika barks back at him.

I close the window. Not that I blame Erika. While he's been acting like a tour guide for his friends and family, she has been left to manage all the details.

"Chad and I were the same way leading up to our big day," Peyton says breezily. "Don't worry, it's nothing."

Outside, Erika's face is flushed with anger. I can't hear what she's saying anymore, but I've got a pretty good idea.

"Are they still going at it?" Peyton asks.

I nod. She comes to stand beside me. Below, on the walkway, Erika is still talking. Yelling may be more accurate. Suddenly, she turns away from Trent and storms back toward the house. Trent throws up his hands and turns the opposite way—toward the driveway. But then he stops. We watch as he spins around in her direction.

"What's he doing?" Peyton says.

We have to crane our necks to see. Trent has caught up to Erika. He reaches for her arm, roughly, and grabs ahold. And before either one of us can let out the gasp that's in both of our throats, he pulls Erika against him and hugs her. I can see her arms go limp as she gives in. And just as quickly they're kissing like teenagers.

Peyton shakes her head and turns back to the closet. "Jesus. Nothing like a wedding to bring out the best in everyone."

Which makes me think about Evan. After waking up at the inn this morning, he wanted to lounge in bed and order room service. But I begged off, claiming our salon appointment was a couple hours earlier than it really was.

"Evan is sort of driving me crazy," I admit to Peyton now.

She finishes fussing over the veil and closes the closet door. "Is it because of all the wedding stuff? Because let me tell you, going to a wedding one year into a relationship is sort of like crossing a minefield." She sits next to me on the window seat. "I remember attending a college friend's wedding in Nantucket when Chad and I had been together around that same time. It was one of the most beautiful weddings, and yet the whole weekend was torture. Chad hadn't even popped the question yet, and all I could think about when I saw the bride was what my own dress would look like; or what my own menu would consist of. And Chad just wanted to get plastered and catch up with his fraternity guys."

"It's not like that," I say, with a sad laugh. "Believe me, I wish it were that simple."

Peyton contemplates this. "When we were at the bar the other night, Evan mentioned that he'd found a great apartment. It sounded like he's stressed about losing it."

I'm a little surprised to hear that Evan shared this with Chad and Peyton. Not the fact of the apartment search—they all knew about that already. What irks me is that he's complaining to our friends instead of confiding in me. "We have an appointment to see it this week, after the wedding. I just don't want to move into a place I've never seen. You know how Evan is. He's very pragmatic, and when he wants to do something, he wants to do it right away. I wish he'd be more patient."

Peyton draws her knees up to her chest. Sitting this close to each other, I can't help but notice that even in the humidity of the morning, not a single hair is straying from her casual chignon. Her cropped linen pants are wrinkle free. "Do you feel like things are moving too fast?"

I run a hand over my own sloppy ponytail. "Not really. I mean, this is everything I wanted: to move in together, and to have more time together. I still want all that. It's just that since I've been home I've been trying to catch my breath, and those wants seem to be somewhere off in the distance."

Peyton is as sharp as a tack. "I guess it depends which direction you mean—are those wants in the distant future? Or in the rearview mirror?"

When I falter, she hops up and extends a brisk hand to me. "Never mind." As much as her managerial style can sometimes get to me, this time I'm deeply grateful for it. She's letting me off the hook. "We've got manicures and dress fittings to get through this morning. Now, *that'll* make you glad you don't have to worry about a wedding anytime soon."

◆   ◆   ◆

On the way to the salon, I try Cam's cell phone. This time it goes straight to voice mail. It's not like him to ignore calls. His silence has filled me with a longing, leaving me jittery and distracted.

After eighty fingers have been painted in Bridal Bliss and eighty toes in Seaside Summer (Erika's "something blue"), there is still no word from Cam. Erika is beside herself with excitement to see us in our bridesmaid gowns, so I make a mental note to focus and have some fun.

Since day one of dress shopping, I had been nominated the official "mannequin" for fittings. But it was no compliment.

"You're perfectly average," Erika had gushed at the time. "Not too thin, not too busty." She went so far as to pat my tummy fondly as she said this.

Now Sarah, a tan young salesgirl, invites us to the back of the store. The dresses are hanging on a rack ready to be fitted by the store seamstress. But looking at them now, they aren't quite as I remember. The long cream sheath is more yellow than vanilla, and the green belt looks more office-fare than wedding-fabulous.

"It wasn't my first choice," Peyton whispers, as we follow Sarah toward a small dressing area behind a curtain, "but here we go."

Peyton and I step into our dresses and take turns struggling to zip each other up. Then we stand looking at each other, shaking our heads.

"I can't breathe!" I whisper.

Peyton struggles with the green belt to no avail. "Why didn't you mention that back on Newbury Street? This gown is like a straitjacket."

"It wasn't that tight. The sample size was an eight. I'm a four!" I remind her.

But she's on to other issues. "I'm sorry, but this yellow color completely washes us out. I look ashen."

I turn to face the mirror, feeling the same way. "I guess I was so relieved that Erika had finally picked out a gown, I overlooked the fact this dress is kind of . . ."

"Hideous!" Peyton sweeps the curtain matter-of-factly aside and steps out. Hideous isn't the only problem, however. When the seamstress motions me over to the fitting riser, I almost tip over.

"You'll need to take small steps in a mermaid design," she cautions us. I'm already picturing the four of us shimmying down the aisle, like wayward mermaids out of water.

"It's too bad there isn't a slit up the back," I say.

"There will be if any one of us tries to dance," Peyton huffs, as she, too, inches toward the riser. It takes her forever to get there, and we both burst out laughing.

Erika and the cousins come back and join us. "Look at you girls!" Erika cries, placing her hands on either side of her face.

"You're gorgeous." But when I try to turn around to face her, she narrows her eyes. "Why are you so stiff?"

I shrug, apologetically, and shuffle toward her.

"Oh, good Lord. You can't walk in this dress, can you?" She spins around to Peyton. "What about you?"

Peyton forces a smile. "Just need a little practice," she insists.

But Erika's not buying it. "Show me," she says flatly. Peyton hobbles closer.

Erika covers her face with her hands. "You'll never make it down the aisle. Or onto the dance floor!" She turns to her cousins. "Carly. Leslie. Go try yours on!"

Obediently, they disappear into the changing area with their dress bags. Moments later the curtain opens again, and there stand the Chicago cousins, their mouths zipped as tightly as their dresses. "It is a little snug," Carly admits finally.

Erika turns to the seamstress, her nostrils flaring. "Wait here. I'm calling my mother."

We wait in uncomfortable silence. I have no idea what kind of fashion consolation Mrs. Crane can offer mere days before the wedding, but moments later Erika's back with wet eyes and a wad of tissues.

Peyton gives it her best shot. "Look, I've been to several weddings where the bridesmaids all wore different dresses, but something in the same color scheme." She looks hopefully at Erika. "Shopping here in town might allow each of us to get something that suits our physiques and styles."

Erika sits down hard on her plastic folding chair.

Shopping last minute is our chance. I can almost feel the swish of a shorter, roomier gown against my legs. I can picture all of us hitting the dance floor and posing for pictures and actually eating wedding cake without feeling like we've been sewn into sausage casing.

"I don't know what to do." Erika lifts her face from the wad of tissues. "I just loved this gown so much," she says, running her fingers longingly across my skirt. "It would be a shame to give up on it."

Peyton flashes me a warning look. Even the cousins are watching me with intense interest. I know what they all want me to say.

"And the belt is the exact color of the bows on the reception chairs," Erika adds, in a small voice.

The belt. My least-favorite part of this dress. I can feel the possibility of a new dress slipping through our fingers.

"Mags?" Erika stands up. I can tell she's about to unravel. "Tell me the truth. You hate this dress, don't you?"

All eyes rest firmly on me.

◆　◆　◆

The Crystal Mall is part of our history. When we were both eleven, my mother took Erika and me back-to-school shopping there. In one week we'd be starting middle school. Erika offered me a swipe of her Bonne Bell root beer lip gloss as we discussed our wish list in the backseat of the family station wagon. "I want to get the pink-and-green Abercrombie rugby," she announced.

"The one that was in *Seventeen* magazine?"

She nodded piously.

I knew exactly which shirt Erika was talking about. We'd pored over the magazine's fall fashion layout, in which a lanky blond model wore the Abercrombie & Fitch shirt, while sitting on the bleachers and watching a homecoming game. I'm not sure if we ached more for the romanticized New England prep school scene, complete with football players and pom-poms, or the shirt itself. But the rugby was somewhat more accessible.

"Where should we start?" my mother asked, as we stood in the mall entrance.

"Mom, we need to go to Abercrombie."

Mom blinked. "Oh, okay. I guess we can try to find some sales there." It wasn't a good sign.

While Mom halted to eye a mannequin dressed in an orange triangle bikini, Erika and I searched the floor for the university-inspired rugby shirt from the magazine ad.

"That's the one!" Erika raced to the rack and whisked the shirt into the air. "What do you think?"

I grabbed the tag. "I think it looks expensive. Ninety-eight bucks for a shirt!" I was sounding like my mother.

Erika shrugged. "But I love it."

The bold watermelon stripes were hard to resist. I fingered the crisp canvas collar. Erika thrust it against my chest. "Wow, Mags. You should get it."

"I don't know." I was already imagining the multiple items my mother could pick out that would still total less than this one shirt.

"What's the matter? You look great."

I shrugged helplessly. How to explain to my best friend that my parents couldn't afford it, without feeling like I was throwing them under the bus?

"Just show your mom," Erika insisted.

She followed me to the lone clearance rack in the rear where we found my mother. "Mom, what do you think about this rugby?" Desperately, I tugged it over my head over my T-shirt.

"That's cute." Then Mom checked the tag. "Oh, honey." She looked at me apologetically. "I still have to take Jane back-to-school shopping, too. Maybe it will go on sale," Mom said brightly.

But I knew the truth. There was no second chance for the first day of school.

When it was Erika's turn to make her purchases, she piled her findings on the counter. Cargo shorts, tank tops, a red hoodie. Beneath it all the striped sleeve peeked out.

It was near the end of the week, during gym class, when it happened. We'd played tennis outside in the gorgeous late summer weather, and when we filed into the girls room to change, I opened my locker. There, hanging beside my jeans, was the Abercrombie rugby.

I glanced around. Erika was sitting on the bench, two girls down, unlacing her sneakers. My blue shirt, that I'd worn to school, was missing. "Erika?" I whispered.

She looked over at me. "Wow, Maggie," she said loudly. The girls around us quieted instantly, listening in. "I love your new shirt."

It was then I noticed the sleeve of my blue shirt sticking out of Erika's backpack. She zipped it up, and when no one was watching, flashed me her pinky finger.

Now, standing on the bridal shop riser, with my feet practically sewn together in this god-awful gown, I stand up straighter. "Erika. Do you love this dress?"

Erika nods, sadly. "But you girls can't move in it. I don't want you to be uncomfortable."

From behind me, I can feel the weight of Leslie's, Carly's, and Peyton's incredulous stares. But I shake my head. "It's not that bad," I tell her. "We'll put a slit in the back. Right?"

The seamstress nods in agreement.

"And you don't think the fabric is too heavy?" Erika worries aloud.

"Nah. It'll keep us tame on the dance floor."

Behind me Peyton sighs audibly.

"Are you sure?" Erika asks, trying to temper the excitement in her voice.

"I'm sure," I say, running my hand over the insidious green belt. "Besides, look at this."

Erika smiles hopefully. "The belt?"

I smile back as convincingly as I can. "The belt makes the dress."

Twenty-One

The bridal party is scheduled for a lobster dinner cruise aboard the *Mystic Whaler* tonight, courtesy of Trent's family. The schooner will take us out to Fishers Island, a place I've been excited to share with Evan since I first told him I grew up in Mystic. With the dress fittings complete, I want nothing more than to run home for a nap before I have to shower and get dressed in time to meet everyone at the pier. On the way home, I take a turn onto a side street too sharply. Something rolls out from under the seat of my car and hits my foot. Startled, I reach down to retrieve it and lift up Emory's bright green teething ball. It's all the excuse I need.

Cam's Jeep is in the driveway, and I'm relieved to see that his parents' cars are not. I park and jog up the walkway. No sooner have I stepped up to the front door than I notice a figure bent among the garden beds across the yard. It's Mrs. Wilder.

She kneels, her gloved hands working quickly as she carves small divots in the border. Beside her is a tray of pink and white pansies. "Mrs. Wilder?"

She turns, her trowel poised above the soil. Mrs. Wilder's expression is flat, her normally tidy brown bob frayed with the day's humidity.

"I guess you've heard," she says, sitting back on her haunches.

I hesitate, unsure of what she means. "Is everything okay?"

"Emory's back at Yale." She turns back to the garden bed. I watch her complete the row of divots she'd been working on, as I stand there trying to make sense of what she's just said—one, two, three more small holes. Then, discarding the trowel roughly, she reaches for the plastic tray of flowers. "She has thrombosis, but she's stable now. I just left them a couple hours ago." She plucks a clump of pansies from the tray and separates the roots.

"I had no idea. When?"

Mrs. Wilder tucks the flowers into a hole, patting them snugly into the ground. "Emory seemed fine after the procedure on Wednesday, but yesterday morning she starting showing symptoms of low oxygen and her leg was turning blue." She pauses, and wipes the back of her hand across her forehead. "They took her to Lawrence Memorial, then transferred her right over to Yale."

"I'm so sorry. Is she going to be all right?"

She seizes her trowel and looks at me. "She has to be."

I have never seen Mrs. Wilder looking like this. She has always been a somewhat intimidating, if polite, woman, a protective mother of her only son. Now, sitting among the vigor of her flower beds, she appears hollowed out. "Is there anything I can do to help? Would you like a ride to the hospital, when you go back?" I am babbling, unsure of what to offer, unsure of what the Wilders would even need right now.

"No, thank you. I was there all night. I just came home to rest."

I look at the garden bed and it's then I register the numerous piles of plastic flower trays, discarded and tossed aside, all around the yard. The borders of each bed are freshly over-turned, the dark soil baking already to a pale brown in the sun. "Why don't you come inside and have a glass of water?" I ask. She looks down at her shaking gloves, smeared with dirt. I al-most expect her to ask me to leave.

Instead, she rises uneasily. "Okay," she says.

She holds the back door open for me, and when I realize that she hasn't followed me into the kitchen, I hesitate. I find her in the living room, lying on the couch.

There is a pitcher of iced tea in the refrigerator. I fill a glass. But instead of bringing it to her, I start opening cabinets. I find what I'm looking for in a bottom drawer. It's the red tin tray that I have seen Mrs. Wilder use over the years to serve. To serve bowls of Jell-O, in every color, the Christmas that Cameron had his tonsils out. To bring us lemonade on their back porch, the first summer we dated. The red paint has faded and there are small dings along its edges. But now I pull out the familiar tray and place her iced tea on it along with a bowl that I fill with some yogurt. I find a banana on the counter and slice it quickly, adding it to the mix.

When I return to the living room, Mrs. Wilder's eyes are closed. They flutter open as I approach. She looks surprised to see me, but I motion for her to stay where she is and pass her the cold glass. Her eyes water when I press it into her open hand.

◆　◆　◆

I am two exits away from Yale. Mrs. Wilder is back at home, hopefully still resting on the living room couch. Erika is at the club with Peyton and Mrs. Crane, going over the menu one last time. Evan and the men will be playing golf until the dinner cruise. He does not understand what I am doing.

"What do you mean you're driving to New Haven? Where are you now?" he'd said.

"It's my friend Cam. His little girl, the one I told you about, is back in the hospital."

He'd hesitated, and I wondered which had given him more pause: the mention of Cam again, or the fact that there was a seriously ill child. "I'm sorry to hear that. But tell me again why you're going there?"

"Because it's serious," I'd snapped. *Because he may need me.*

Evan didn't argue, but his tone was curt. "So I take it you'll be back in time for the river cruise." It wasn't so much a question.

"I'll call you when I know more," I'd said, before hanging up.

◆　◆　◆

I take the elevator up to the pediatric cardiology wing. Cam's father is with him, Mrs. Wilder had said. As I walk down the corridor past patients' rooms, I wonder what I will say to them, but then I remind myself that I don't really have to say anything. I'm here.

The nurse at the main desk tells me in no uncertain terms that it's family visitation only when I stop to inquire about Emory's room number. I don't even hesitate. "I'm her mom," I lie. She looks at me funny, and I realize that I would know where my child's room was if I were truly Emory's mother. If I were Lauren, I would be in there already, with her.

But she points down the hall. "Eleven A."

I force myself to slow down as I reach the doorway. Outside I take a deep breath, and smooth my hair.

When I step inside the room, I'm surprised to see three silent figures hovered around the bed. Two men, Cam and his father, have their backs to me. But the third is on the other side of the bed, facing my direction. She looks up when I halt in the doorway. Her blond hair frames the angles of her face, her eyes a lucid blue against her pained expression. I recognize her immediately from the picture in Cam's room. It's Lauren.

◆ ◆ ◆

Cam sits beside me in the cardiac waiting room, playing with a stray thread on his T-shirt.

"How is she?"

"She's stable now," he says, his voice thin with fatigue. "Last night—" he begins, then stops. He returns his attention to the stray thread. I watch as he tugs it gently, then tears it off.

"I just heard," I say. "I was in such a rush to get here, but I should've run downstairs and gotten you a change of fresh clothes. Or something."

He looks at me. "You were at my house?"

"I was returning something." I fumble with my purse. When I hand Cam the green teething ball, his fingers shake. He presses it to his nose and closes his eyes.

I reach around the breadth of Cam's shoulders and squeeze. He doesn't cry. We sit in silence, side by side on the bench. Finally he clears his throat. "Dr. Weil did more imaging. The patch appears to be holding and the blood clot is breaking up. As long as she responds to the heparin, we should be out of the woods, for now."

I lean my head against his arm. "Thank God. All I could

think about on the drive here was seeing her." But Lauren is here now, I remember. And this is not my place.

After a while Cam runs his hands through his hair and stands. I let my arm fall away. "I've got to get back." He looks down at me. "Thank you for coming, Griff."

I nod. But it's too soon for me to go. There are too many unknowns. What does it mean that Lauren is here? And is she going to stay? They're questions I have no right to ask of Cam, especially not now.

Cam motions for me to follow, and I do, uncertainly. When I arrived and saw them standing over her bed together, I'd halted in the doorway. Cam had turned to me, then, and walked me wordlessly to the waiting room. I didn't even get close enough to Emory to see her.

But now, instead of stopping at the bank of elevators to see me out, to my surprise Cam passes them. He motions me back down the hall, back to Emory's room. His father is sitting in a corner chair, dozing. Lauren is still standing by the bed. "Lauren," Cam says, "this is my friend Maggie."

She looks at me warily.

But it's Emory I can't take my eyes off. She is sleeping. Someone has wrapped her snugly in a white blanket and she's wearing a pink pediatric gown, a cluster of tubes climbing up out of the neckline. A plastic oxygen mask is taped across her face, but I recognize the familiar curve of her tiny nose through it. One little arm is thrown up over her head, just like she does when she naps in her crib. The other rests by her side. Instinctively, I reach over the bedrail and tuck my finger into her hand. My eyes sting when her fingers flex around mine.

At that moment I look up. Lauren is watching me. She

doesn't smile or even hold my gaze. But it's not that that strikes me. It's the rawness of her beauty juxtaposed by the stillness of her body. I can't help but imagine Jane in this situation. In spite of the machines and IV tubes, Jane would be in the bed, or somehow perched on the edge of the bed, pressing some part of herself carefully but clearly against her child. There would be tears or whispers or humming. Some physical or audible melody of a mother's angst-ridden love. There is none of that with Lauren.

"I should go," I whisper.

Cam thanks me for coming. His father stirs in the corner chair. Lauren still says nothing.

In the doorway, I can't help but look back. The sun is high outside the window, bathing the sterile hospital room in light. There are two heads bowed together over Emory's bed. Her mother's hair the color of an angel's.

It's not until I reach the parking lot and climb behind the steering wheel of my hot car that I cry.

Twenty-Two

There's only one hour until the dinner cruise. But I simply cannot imagine putting on heels and tipping back cocktails as we set sail. Not after seeing Emory and Cam. And *her*.

How can there be such celebration and also such suffering in the same town, on the same day, just mere streets away? I've lived through such contradictions before: the death of my grandfather in the same year as the birth of my first nephew. I thought my heart would break when one of my students lost her mother to breast cancer, just a week after Erika got engaged. But I've never experienced two so closely, or in the same space of time and place. Right now I am drained; I want to crawl into bed and sleep until tomorrow.

Sometime later, my mother knocks on the door and pokes her head in. "Evan came by earlier."

I sit up. "He did?" I wonder if it was before or after I'd told him I was going to New Haven. "What did you tell him?"

"I didn't know where you were. We visited a little on the back porch. He was telling your father and me about sailing out to Fishers Island tonight. Sounds like fun."

"When was this?"

"A couple hours ago. When he left, your dad mentioned something about the Wilder baby being back in the hospital. Is that where you were?" I didn't realize my father knew this. But I also didn't realize my boyfriend spent the afternoon on my back deck with my parents. Mystic is a small town.

I roll over and make room for her to sit on the bed. "I went to see her."

I'm grateful when she doesn't question why, as Evan did. Instead she settles beside me. "What happened?"

"She had some kind of complication from her catheterization. Cam said it was a thrombosis—a blood clot." My voice cracks as I think back to Emory's tiny figure in the hospital bed.

My mom props herself up with one of my pink childhood pillows. "Is she all right now?"

"They have her on blood thinners, and Cam said she'll stay there for a few days for observation. But it sounds like they've gotten it under control."

My mother doesn't say anything right away. "Control is a funny word when you're a parent," she says, finally. "Children change everything. And control is something you come to find you have very little of."

Which makes me think immediately of Lauren. "Emory's mother showed up," I tell my mom.

"Is she back in the picture, then?" she asks.

I can't help it; a sigh escapes my chest. "I don't know. I don't think any of them know. Cam called her to tell her that Emory was going to have the catheterization, and she didn't come then. I was shocked to see her."

My mom thinks about this a moment. "I'm sure they all were. But she's here now."

"Yes," I say, thinking of the gravity of her words. "I guess she is."

My mother is not exactly a judgmental person, but she has strong opinions. Being liberally minded, for her there are plenty of gray areas. And she has raised us girls to recognize that, especially in the broader context of social issues, like single parenting, women's rights, and advocacy for children. But I have to wonder what her thoughts are about Lauren: a real-life woman who had the means and the ability to stay with her child, but chose not to. Until now, I've viewed her through the lens of someone in a fairly black-and-white situation. She could've chosen to stay. But since seeing her today, and on the whole drive home from Yale, I can't stop wondering what *her* gray areas are.

As if she's reading my thoughts, "I wonder if this will change how she feels," my mother muses. "Having a baby is not just a blessing, it's an earth-shattering responsibility. And some women find it hard to adapt. I guess there are a few who just can't. And maybe their children are better off not being raised by that kind of parent."

Then how does that explain the parents like Cam, a guy who's proven to be more than cut out to be a father, despite all the surprises and upsets along the way? "What about all that stuff about falling madly in love when you lay eyes on your newborn baby?"

"Well, I suppose that happens for some. It's certainly a lovely thought. But I would be lying if I said that was how I felt when I had you and Jane."

I turn over. "What do you mean?" My mother has never been anything but a sometimes overbearing hands-on mom, to the point where we were constantly wriggling away from her for a breath of freedom. Begging her to stay in the car at school drop-off and let us walk to the door ourselves. Telling her we didn't need her help when using the pair of big red scissors in the kitchen drawer. To this day, sometimes shunning her advice and insights, so sure of ourselves are we. This confession shatters the image I've always had of her bursting with pride in the nursery—a pink-faced Jane squalling in her firm embrace.

"Oh, I fell in love with you girls. Head over heels, make no mistake about it! But not right away. I'll never forget when that nurse handed me your sister, my firstborn. I looked at her plush red cheeks and her dark hair and I thought, 'Who is this little stranger?'"

"You did? Does Jane know this?"

Mom shrugs and laughs. "I'm sure we've joked about it in some fashion over the years. She was my baby, and I knew I'd love her. But it was not love at first sight that I most remember feeling. It was fear. And I think that's an honest reaction for many women. Perhaps this Lauren has come around. Maybe she's ready to be a mother now."

It occurs to me that my mother has more in common with Cameron right now than I do—or at least more of an understanding of what it means to love a child. It makes me realize how much I've taken her for granted; and how grateful I should be for having felt so safe and loved all my life. That golden ticket that lets you go out into the world and try to do and be what you want to do and be.

"Were either of us ever sick in a way that scared you?" I ask her now.

"Oh, you both went through the usual checklist: chicken pox, pneumonia. One spring Jane got the flu so severely when we were on a trip to Rhode Island that we ended up at Providence Hospital. We all spent Easter in the pediatric wing. Remember that? When the Easter Bunny came to visit—you were probably only three at the time—he scared you to death. You screamed so loud the nurses came running in, thinking something was wrong with Jane."

I stare at her in wonder. "I don't remember that at all. Are you sure it was me?"

Mom smiles. "Of course it was. Just like you were the one who fell in the Ocean Beach parking lot the following summer, racing to the ice cream truck, and skinned your knee. Four stitches and a few hours later, all you would talk about was getting your Rocket Pop. I think Dad drove you all over New London until we found the truck on its last run of the day." She chuckles fondly at the memory.

I run my hand over my knee—the scar is faded but still bumpy. "I forgot the ice cream truck part," I say. "How do you remember all this stuff?"

Mom rests a hand on my arm. "I'm your mother. Couldn't forget it if I tried." She lifts herself slowly from the bed and stretches. "You spend your whole life worrying about your children. But you come to realize that you can't put your kids in glass jars. We were lucky, I guess. You girls never had any serious medical hiccups. I'm just glad to hear that Cameron's little one is doing better." She pauses. "Now, what about you?"

The sun outside my window is that warm golden late-day

kind, and as it streams through my gingham curtains and across my bedroom, I can't help but notice that it highlights the grays in my mother's hair and the lines around her eyes. Standing in that light she suddenly looks much older to me.

"I'm okay," I say. "It's just been a long week. I need to get cleaned up and get down to the pier before Erika and Evan have a fit. And I need to land a few interviews, so that I can secure a job for the fall. And the apartment—Evan said he found a great one . . ."

The expression on my mother's face stops me. This is not what she is asking.

My mother and I talk about personal things all the time—as long as it involves others. Like Erika's misgivings when Trent first proposed to her and the fanfare of the ring had worn off. Or when my father retired and my mother's worried that he'd drive her crazy puttering around the house. Or the concern she had about Jane, having had three kids so closely together. But we've never been good about talking about ourselves. Lying on my childhood bed as she stands in my bedroom doorway, I feel suddenly vulnerable.

"I don't know," I say, finally, my voice cracking.

"You've grown pretty attached to Emory and Cameron."

I nod. "It just sort of happened."

"Well, that's who you are, honey. You've always wanted to take care of everyone. It's why you're such a good teacher. I remember, when you were just little, whenever you won a stuffed animal at the summer carnival, you always picked the one with the missing eyeball. Or the tattered paw. You've always had a soft spot for the underdogs."

I smile, in spite of myself.

"Can I tell you something?" she asks.

"Please."

"You're going to figure things out for yourself this summer. You may not know that now. But I do."

Later, as the *Mystic Whaler* pulls away from the docks and the sky overhead is strewn in pink and orange streaks, I whisper in Evan's ear that I'll be right back. The night is just starting out, and our friends are heady with anticipation as we set sail for Fishers Island. Mr. and Mrs. Crane have popped a bottle of Dom Pérignon, and Trent's father is already handing out cigars to the groomsmen. Evan is endearingly rosy-cheeked from a day on the golf course, and when he tucks his arm around my waist, there is no ill will remaining about my sudden departure to Yale. "I'm glad your friend is okay. Now, can tonight please be ours?"

I kiss him, to say *yes*. Tonight I will soak it all in. There will be lobster, toasts, and music. But for now, I steal away and find a spot on the rear deck away from the noisy celebration. When I lean out over the railing, I think of Mrs. Wilder alone in her living room, holding the untouched glass of iced tea. I think of Trent and the way he grabbed Erika's hand and pulled her hard against him on the walkway this morning. And I think of Cam and Lauren, a little girl with a patched-up hole in her heart between them. My mother is right. There is so much beyond our control, and so much we fear we cannot figure out. But what a difference it makes when someone else believes—not only that you can—but that you will.

Twenty-Three

Saint Edward's white steeple pops against the morning sky, a wedding beacon in its own right. We're doing an early rehearsal. Which started ten minutes ago. Evan and I finally find a parking spot and fly up the steps of the church, me holding the skirt of my dress and both of us laughing, only to find everyone in various states of disarray in the nave.

"Oh, good, you're here." Peyton is the sole picture of calm against the figures assembled. Her hair is pulled up into a sleek twist, as usual, and her suit dress is as crisp as the sky outside the heavy double doors. "Too much fun last night?" she asks coyly.

"Sorry, we slept late." I glance around. Erika's parents are standing near the pulpit speaking to the reverend. Trent and the groomsmen are standing around chatting. The younger members of the wedding party, the ringbearer and flower girls, are in various states of high-speed chase among the aisles. The Chicago twins are slumped in the first pew.

"So, let's run through the checklist."

This time I try really hard not to roll my eyes. It's the rehearsal, after all.

"You've got Erika's music for walking down the aisle?"

I dig through my purse and pull out the DVD. "Pachelbel's Canon in D."

"The vows?"

"Right here." I hand her an envelope containing printouts of their vows, just in case Erika or Trent forgets theirs.

"And your speech for the rehearsal dinner?"

I give her a look. "It's not a speech," I remind her. That's for the best man. "But yes, I do have a few words."

"And they are where?"

"In my head," I tell her flatly.

Peyton appraises me. "Well, look at you, Maid of Honor. You handled it. Well done."

For the most part she's right, I did. But honestly, if it hadn't been for her Norwegian calm and stealth sense of detail, I would never have pulled it off. "*We* handled it," I correct her. "Besides, don't tell me you weren't worried that I'd forget some appointment or lose a grandparent or something."

She shrugs as if she has no idea what I'm referring to. But I know better.

"Wait a minute. Give me your purse."

"What?" she says, feigning innocence.

"Hand it over!"

Begrudgingly, she does. I pull out a second copy of Erika's DVD. And a neatly creased set of papers, which I know are copies of the vows. "You thought I was going to screw everything up?" I hand her back the bag. "Thanks for the faith."

Then I notice a bundle of shiny ribbons peeking out of a gift bag in the corner. I recognize it immediately. "Is that Erika's bridal shower bouquet?"

Peyton shrugs casually. "Oh, that? I saw it back at the Cranes' house, and figured I'd bring it along. You know, in case Erika wants to carry it down the aisle for rehearsal."

I shake my head in wonder. That's exactly what Erika wants to do, and Peyton knows that. As tacky as the handmade paper plate and gift bow bouquet is, Erika would've had a fit if I'd forgotten it for her rehearsal. Which I apparently did.

"Peyton."

She waves me away. "It's not a big deal."

But it is. "Thank you."

At that moment the double doors burst open, sunlight streaming in. Erika sails through, all business. "Sorry, Reverend Astor, I couldn't find a spot." Seeing Erika, he breaks into a relieved smile and motions for everyone to begin the rehearsal.

Peyton hands me the gift bag. "Here. You give it to her," she insists. Reverend Astor has already lined up the groomsmen and corralled the flower girls, who are on the verge of twirling out of place with their tiny baskets. He smiles broadly. "Welcome, everyone. Tomorrow we have a couple to unite."

When the organ begins, Evan squeezes my arm. "Makes you wonder," he jokes quietly, as we take our places at the front of the line.

I smile at him, touched that he's the kind of guy who wonders about these things—unlike so many men who would rather chew glass than talk about the future of their relationship.

Everyone is in his or her place. Everything is as it should be. Ahead, the families have taken their traditional places in the front pews and are turned anxiously in our direction. Mrs. Crane is already dabbing her eyes. I peek over my shoulder at Erika, in the rear. She looks serene beside her father, who looks like he's about to take the last walk of his life. I blow Erika a kiss, and before I know it, Evan is guiding me down the aisle.

"I have some news," Evan whispers to me.

"Oh?" One of Trent's aunts smiles at me, and I wave. A teenager frowns as his mother snatches his smartphone away and tucks it in her purse.

"That apartment I liked? I signed the lease. It's ours."

I keep my eyes trained on the reverend, who is standing before us like a sentinel, assessing our procession. But I can see Evan clearly out of the corner of my eye. He's grinning like the Cheshire Cat. My heels wobble. "You what?"

"I know. Isn't it great?" We've reached the altar. Evan lets go of my arm and turns to the right, to stand beside Trent. But I halt, unsure of where to go.

"Left," the reverend whispers.

Mrs. Crane is crying softly. Which I suddenly feel like doing, myself.

The church is hot, despite the polished wooden fans whirring overhead. Before I know it, Peyton and the twins have joined me, and the flower girls are moving in zigzag trajectory, more or less toward us. One drops her basket. The altar feels crowded.

I swipe a trail of sweat that is working its way down my temple. "You okay?" Peyton whispers behind me.

I can't even nod.

Erika arrives and hands me her bridal shower bouquet. It prickles in my fingers. When Erika and Trent recite their vows, I try to focus. But I'm distracted by the wall of stained glass windows, the yellow and red panes as searing as my skin is beginning to feel. Overhead the useless fans whir louder.

It's then I notice the image in one of the stained glass windows: an angel, no more than a winged baby. Its cherubic body arched in flight, it extends its finger to a golden light above. And I can't help but think of Emory.

Suddenly everyone is clapping. The rehearsal is over. Trent and Erika are already holding hands, making their way victoriously down the aisle. Peyton nudges me. "Mags, go!"

Evan takes my arm in the aisle, but I can't meet his expectant gaze. It's all I can do to make it to the end, to the set of heavy double doors, where I burst outside and gulp the air.

Everyone spills out behind us onto the steps, thanking the reverend, issuing goodbyes and reminders to meet tonight for the rehearsal dinner. Aside from a final fitting, we have the rest of the day off, and everyone seems relieved to head off in separate directions. Erika and Trent pose for a couple of pictures and trot down the church stairs, seeming to float away from me. I linger on the top step, willing my breath in and out. Evan stands at the bottom and reaches for my hands. "So? What do you think about our big news?"

I keep my voice low, cognizant of everyone milling about. "I think that I said I wanted to see the place myself first," I tell him.

He looks genuinely taken aback. "You're mad?"

I'm about to contradict him, in my usual haste to keep peace, but this time I don't. "Yes, actually. How could you just go ahead and sign the lease without even asking me first? You know how I felt about it."

"All I know is that since you came home to Mystic you've been dragging your feet, Maggie."

I stare back at him, incredulous. "What does that mean? We agreed that I'd look at the apartment after the wedding."

"But we didn't have time. I had to make an executive decision, Maggie. I thought you'd appreciate that."

And there we have it. The executive part of Evan's thinking. For which he also seems to think I should be appreciative. "This is a partnership, Evan. We're not talking about ordering dinner. We're talking about making a home. Supposedly together."

Evan stuffs his hands angrily into his pockets and looks at me a long time. "I thought it would be a nice surprise for you. That's all."

Everyone else has gone ahead of us, dispersing down the sidewalks and climbing into cars. I stare back at Evan, at a loss for words.

Evan sighs. "Look, it's hot out and we had a late night last night. I think maybe you need to eat something," he says.

I try not to bristle. "I grabbed a bagel at the inn with you," I remind him. I'm not about to let him chalk this up to an emotional, hungry bridesmaid, which I am not. This is about so much more.

Evan shakes his head, clearly frustrated. "I'm sure you'll love it when you see it. Okay?"

But it's not okay. In his heart Evan believes he did a nice thing, but he's clearly unable to read my own. Which leaves us at a far more perilous intersection than just a real estate stalemate.

From across the street Peyton waves to us from Chad's car, and I raise my hand and force a smile. "See you at the dress shop," she calls. We are the last ones standing in front of the church.

And then, over the tops of the cars parked along the curb, I see a blue Jeep. Time stalls, like that drizzly night on the bridge. Only this time Cam is the one driving by. He slows in front of the church, and looks directly at me. Just as Evan takes my hand and draws me up the sidewalk.

Twenty-Four

The hideous bridesmaid dresses fit. Only this time the tears do not belong only to the bride.

"I can't believe he just went ahead and did that," Erika says to me, as she unzips the back of my dress. Peyton is shaking her head, too.

"I totally agree with you—the lack of a pet clause is a pretty selfish oversight," Peyton allows. "But show her the photos. It's an amazing pad."

I hand Erika my phone and she scrolls through the real estate link that Evan sent me. "Wow. Hardwood floors, marble kitchen. Is that a double vanity?" She looks at me. "Hate to say it, but this place looks nicer than Trent's and mine!"

"I know, I know. And my parents would take the cat for me in a heartbeat. But Evan knows how I feel about my pet, just as he knows how much I wanted to see the place first. It's like he overlooked a whole part of me."

"What are you going to do?" Although I know Erika's genuinely concerned about me, I'm sure there's a part of her that's also wondering just how much of this calamity will seep into her wedding day.

"I don't know yet. But don't worry, I promise I won't let it get to me this weekend."

"Please," she jokes. "It wouldn't be a wedding without something falling apart." But I can tell she's a little relieved.

While Peyton and the cousins bring their dresses out to the front, Erika lingers behind in the dressing area with me. With all of the events and activities and family around, I haven't been able to get two seconds with her to myself.

"So how are you doing?" I ask her now.

She tucks my bridesmaid dress into its bag and zips it up. "Honestly? I'm happy. It's been a crazy week but a great week, and tomorrow I'm marrying the man I'm supposed to marry." She looks at me. "Thank you for everything you did to make this happen, Mags. Trent and I are both so grateful."

"Me? I think Peyton kept that wheel turning."

She laughs. "I know. But when things turned sour—like when the venue fell apart and the dresses weren't right—you were the one who steered things back on course." Erika's complexion is as bright as her eyes. She really does look happy. I give her a big hug. Tomorrow she will not be Erika Crane anymore. In a move that surprised us, Erika has decided to take Trent's name. "It's my wedding gift to him," she explained to us on the river cruise last night. "I want to have the same last name as our kids. I want us to be like a little tribe." After today, she will be known as Mrs. Erika Mitchell. A move that, Peyton argued, would only change her in name, but I'm not naive.

"Have you heard anything from Cam?" she asks me now. "How are they doing?"

"He promised to let me know if anything happened. Until

then, I'm giving them space." After leaving the hospital and talking with my mom, I've decided to do what Mrs. Wilder had suggested I do when I first came home this summer: to live my life and let Cam live his own. But since seeing him outside the church, that prospect seems harder each minute. "It's better this way," I add.

Erika puts a hand on her hip, like she doesn't believe what she's hearing. "Maggie, are you telling me that or yourself? It's not like you to just walk away."

Her words surprise me. "This, from you? You've always hated Cam."

"I didn't hate him."

"Yes, you did," I insist. "I could never understand what happened between you two, or why you didn't like him. But all those summers you guys made my life miserable. I always felt like I was choosing between the two of you."

Erika sinks onto the narrow bench and pats the seat beside her. "You'd better sit down."

This doesn't sound good.

"Remember the summer you guys first got together, after our freshman year?"

I nod. "It was the only time you seemed to get along. I could never understand why that changed."

She nods, sadly. "Well, that was kind of my fault."

A bad feeling parks itself in my stomach. Suddenly I feel like I'm nineteen again and about to receive bad news about my boyfriend. "Oh, God. Did he try something with you?"

Erika stares at the floor. "No. I tried something with him."

The whole dressing room starts to spin. It doesn't matter that it's her wedding weekend, or that my own boyfriend, who just signed a lease on an apartment, is a few streets away at the inn, or that ten years have passed. I leap up. "You did what?"

Now she's looking at me, cheeks flushed with shame. "I know! I'm sorry. I begged Cam not to tell you."

"When? Where did this happen?" Then, more important. "Why?"

Erika looks like she's about to cry. "We were all at Ocean Beach one night, having a bonfire. I'd had a couple beers and I'd just broken up with Mike."

I shake my head, unable to recall Mike, but viscerally remembering the bonfires we went to at Ocean Beach. "That's no excuse. Tell me what happened!"

"You went home early that night. I was lonely and probably pretty drunk, and a small group of us was left sitting around the fire. I leaned over and kissed him. But he pushed me away. And when I asked him to go for a walk with me down the beach, he turned me down."

"I was your best friend," I remind her. Erika grabs my hand and pulls me back down onto the bench.

"Maggie, please. Cam was cute, and funny, and smart. And he wanted nothing to do with me."

"That doesn't make sense, Erika. Why would you care how he felt about you?"

She holds up both hands, at a loss. "I don't know. Maybe because for the first time, you had something I didn't. And I was jealous. Remember that night in our apartment when we were looking at old pictures for my wedding board?"

It was the same night I'd taken the picture of Cam back to my room.

"Well, I wanted to tell you that night, and then again when

I confessed about cheating on Trent. I've never *wanted* to keep this from you. But it was so petty, and so stupid. I figured after all these years it wouldn't matter."

I put my hands over my eyes and take a deep breath. "But it does."

I think back to that night in our apartment when we went through her old photo box together fondly—how vulnerable and teary Erika got talking about our past—and the way she remembered our friendship. I had always felt like the one in her shadow. It never occurred to me she might ever have had reason to feel the same about me. "Why now?" I ask, unable to keep the anger from my voice.

"Because tomorrow is a big day, and I have my loved ones standing up for me. You're one of them, and I don't want you standing there with any regrets or any secrets. Being back here, in Mystic, and seeing Cam—I had to tell you. I'm sorry."

I need time to absorb this. Suddenly the years of strained silence between Erika and Cam make sense. But the fact that Cam never told me, either, is another soft blow. "It was really shitty of you," I tell her. I look her right in the eye as I say it.

"I know. But it was nothing, Mags. Cam only ever wanted you."

I feel silly at how stung I am all these years later, but I can't help it. "I'm glad you told me," I say finally.

"Do you forgive me?" Erika's eyes are wide and watery.

We were both nineteen. Drinking beers in our bathing suits on a sandy beach without a care in the world beyond ourselves. It was the perfect recipe for disaster.

"I don't want to hold this between us," I tell her. But I'm still stinging from her confession.

Erika knows better than to hug me right now. She takes my dress bag and swings it over her tanned shoulder, her lips pressed tightly. "Thank you, Mags. It's the best gift you can give me."

We meet the others, who, to my relief, remain completely unaware of our conversation, at the front of the store, where they're busy looking through the racks. The cashier rings up my alterations. "Let me," Erika says, but I wave her away.

On the way out, she turns to me. "Are you still thinking about what I said?" she whispers.

"No, actually, I'm thinking about Lauren," I tell her.

Erika looks relieved, but she gives this some thought. "That poor baby," she says, finally. "What if Lauren leaves again?"

As I follow her out into the sun, it's a very different thought that rattles around my head: *What if she doesn't?*

Outside, we loiter in the parking lot beside our cars. The sun is high and hot, the lunchtime hour fast approaching. "I'm starving," Peyton announces. "But if I want to belt that dress tomorrow, I should stick to my diet."

"Don't be silly," Erika says. "Let's grab lunch while we're in town. My treat."

I'm hungry, too. The bagel I grabbed earlier at the inn barely put a dent in it. "Mystic Pizza, for old time's sake?" I suggest.

Peyton drops her diet like a hot plate. "Let's go."

"I'll drive," Erika says. But as I start to follow them all toward her car, she spins around to face me. "Not you."

"What do you mean? I'm starving."

"No." Her voice is as firm as her expression. "You have somewhere else to be."

And then I know what she means. "Erika, I can't go back

there." It's too much. And it's also her last afternoon with us as a single girl. Despite everything, I'm not harboring ill will. In fact, I have the sense of being somehow lighter. "I don't want to miss hanging out with you guys. Besides, I've got my own stuff to figure out with Evan."

"It's been almost ten years. I think you need to figure this one out first." Erika holds up her pinky finger. "Promise me you'll go."

In the end, it's all the permission I need. I link my finger around hers.

Twenty-Five

This time, when I stand in Emory's doorway, Cam is not there. Nor are his parents. Or, thankfully, Lauren. Emory is sound asleep again, and I marvel at how pink her cheeks are. When I run my index finger down her arm she stirs and makes a little gurgly sound. Her long lashes flutter, and she sleeps on.

"Doesn't she look good today?" A nurse comes in behind me, and moves briskly to the IV pole. I notice as she taps the IV bag that her fingernails are painted fluorescent blue. She checks the fluids, makes a note, and comes around to check Emory's vitals. "What a little trouper, huh?"

"She sure is," I say, stepping closer to the bed.

"Do you know where Mom and Dad are?" she asks, smiling brightly. "I have a new doctor's order for dosage that I want to go over with them."

I falter. "Uh, no. I only just arrived myself," I stammer.

"I'm here." I turn at the sound of her voice, a voice I have never heard but cannot mistake. Lauren enters the room quietly, sets down her purse, and comes to stand beside me at the bed. The hairs on my arms rise, we are so close.

The nurse glances at me, uncertainly. "Would you like me to go over them now?"

"Yes, that's fine. I'll share them with her father."

I'm flooded with the sense that I have been caught. Caught here, in Emory's room, by her mother. Listening to medical information that is intended for a parent's ear. And keeping vigil by a child who, no matter my interest, is not my own. I glance at Lauren out of the corner of my eye. Her eyes are fixed on the young nurse; it's as if I am not even present. But for some reason I remain at Emory's bedside, my fingers clenched on the stainless steel railing that has grown warm beneath my sweaty grip.

The nurse finishes her explanation and goes. We are left in the breeze of her wake, shoulder to shoulder, looking down at Emory. Lauren reaches down and adjusts the blanket over Emory's shoulders. Her arm, unlike my own, is deeply tanned and flecked with tiny blond hairs and freckles. She wears a silver cuff bracelet and a sporty diver's watch. When I brave a glance in her direction, I see her face is void of any makeup, her skin the color of a peach.

"Hi," I say unevenly. "I hope it's all right I came to visit."

It's not lost on me that I feel the need to ask her approval, a woman who while biologically connected has never had any custodial say over the little girl in question, but it feels respectful.

Lauren does not glance at me sideways, as I did. She turns fully to me, despite our close proximity. The tip of her nose is sunburned. "You're Maggie."

I nod.

And that is all. She reaches past me to retrieve her bag from the chair, and proceeds to sit down in the corner. The same corner where Mr. Wilder snored softly, exhausted, the last time I was here. Where is Cameron?

Lauren crosses her arms and leans back in the chair, her gaze turning to the window.

"Is Cameron here?" I ask.

"He's finishing lunch downstairs. Does he know you're here?" It's just a question. But the fact that I have to say, "No, he doesn't," makes me uncomfortable. Cameron is not expecting me. I wonder if this matters to her.

Lauren looks like someone who spends all her time outdoors. Lithe and lean, she is exactly the sort of person I would look twice at on the sidewalk. Someone who would make me conscious of my freckled knees and unruly hair.

There is an air of cool assuredness about her—something disjointed in the confines of this hospital room. While I didn't really know what to expect of her, I imagined some level of sheepishness or awkwardness. Some fitting sign of a woman having returned, or having been summoned, to her own baby's bedside from across the country. But there is no sense of that.

"How is she doing?" I ask.

"Very well, actually. They've been able to break up the clot and move the blood flow out of her groin." She comes to the bed and lifts the blanket, exposing Emory's legs. "See? The bruising is diminished." Emory shifts, and I fight the urge to cover her back up. Eventually Lauren does.

"That's great news." I offer a smile. "You must be relieved."

She returns to the chair. "Of course. We all are."

I can't help but notice her use of *we*. I wonder if Mrs. Wilder has this same sense.

And then Cam is with us. He is far more surprised to see me than Lauren. "Maggie? What are you doing here?"

At which Lauren looks at me expectantly. Despite her polite responses to my question, is she wondering the same thing?

"I had the afternoon free, and I wanted to see how she was doing."

Cam glances over at Lauren. "Much better."

Lauren stands. "The nurse came in." I can tell she wants to share the information the nurse told her, and there is no reason for me to stand and listen. Emory is sleeping and doing well. I've heard what I came here for. But then she puts her hand on Cam's arm. "They've changed her dosage."

It's all I need. "I'll leave you guys to talk," I say. I pull my purse quickly over my shoulder and turn to Cam. "I'm so glad she's doing well. Please tell your folks I said hi."

I glance at Emory once more. Her little lips are moving in a slow, dreamy sucking motion. It's the same sweet sound she made the night I babysat and fell asleep holding her in the rocking chair. "I think she's hungry."

When I turn, Cam is smiling down at Emory. But Lauren is not; her gaze is fixed on me, and it has hardened. Emory stirs. She turns her head toward us, blinking, and kicks one foot out from beneath the blanket.

"I think you're right," Cam says. He turns to Lauren. "Want to pick her up while I get the nurse?"

"I'll get the nurse," she says, striding for the door.

I've said my goodbyes. And yet I can't bring myself to go. It's the first time I've seen Emory awake all week. Gingerly Cam moves the blanket aside and adjusts the IV tube. Careful not to tangle it, he lifts her up out of the bed and nestles her in the crook of his arm. "Hi, sweet girl. Are you hungry?"

Emory is flushed, and her head wags back and forth impatiently. Cam laughs. "This feistiness used to make me panic. Now it's such a relief."

I can only imagine. As Lauren returns with a nurse, I move to the doorway. Bottle in hand, the nurse checks the IV tube and helps Cam adjust her blanket. Emory lets out an impatient wail. "That's what I'm talking about!" the nurse says, looking pleased. "Let's get this girl her lunch."

But instead of settling into the chair with her, Cam looks to Lauren. "Here, why don't I let you feed her this time?"

Lauren stiffens. "Oh, that's okay."

But Cam repeats the offer. "It's fine, really. As soon as she latches on to the bottle, it's smooth sailing." And before Lauren can object, he holds Emory out.

Emory is not having it, however. She's angry in the way only a hungry infant is, and she arches her back and cries. The nurse looks between them impatiently. "Let's get her going," she says, "before she tires."

All eyes rest on Lauren. "Here," Cam says again, gently.

"I said no." Lauren steps abruptly aside, leaving Cam a clear path to the chair.

"Okay, let's sit her down, Dad," the nurse says. Her efficiency saves them, and Cam does as he's told. The focus becomes one of propping up Emory and positioning her tubes, and soon her plaintive fussing sounds are replaced with silence and the rhythmic *thwack thwack thwack* pull of the nipple.

"I'll be back in five to check on you," the nurse says, keeping her eyes on Cam.

But he is looking at Lauren, who has moved to the window. The farthest reach of the room.

I follow the nurse out, feeling as if I've witnessed something too personal. Erika was wrong; it's too late to settle any business with Cameron now. In fact, the only business Cameron has is the two other people, besides me, in this room. It's time I stop inserting myself here. This time I don't interrupt them with a goodbye.

The elevators are slow to come up to the cardiac floor. When one finally does, I'm relieved to see the car is empty. Just as the doors closed someone calls, "Please wait." Quickly, I punch the button to hold the doors. When they open I look up to see Lauren Peale.

The car stops on the next floor and a doctor steps in, between us. As we ride down, I wonder where Lauren is going. Emory is still working on her feeding. The car stops again, on the next floor, and the doctor exits. It's nearly agony standing side by side in silence.

The cafeteria is one floor above the lobby. At the last second she reaches past me and hits the button. The elevator stops abruptly. When I turn, her cheeks are streaked with tears. During the labored pause as the elevator doors open, I hear her say it.

"I'm not a monster." And then she's gone.

Twenty-Six

A wave of clapping erupts, and I join in, a beat too late. Erika and Trent have finished their toast to all the guests at the rehearsal dinner. We're seated outside on the shaded upper decks of the Oyster Club, in what locals call the "Tree House," overlooking the Mystic River. Trent's parents have reserved all the Tree House for our party, and despite the lush leafy coverage and the salty breeze wafting across the decks, I'm flushed.

"I need a drink of water," I say, rising from the bridal party table. Dinner is over, but I've barely touched my plate. Evan has finally given up trying to get me to, and has helped himself to several of my oysters.

I'm still troubled by the ride over. Evan had picked me up at my house. It was early, still, so I asked him if we could take a quick drive along the back roads. We drove past the library and my old elementary school, places I wanted to point out to him and he seemed grateful to see, but soon he worried that we'd be late to dinner and suggested we head back to town. On the way back, along River Road, I asked him to pull over.

"Now?" he'd asked, glancing nervously at the clock.

I pointed to the stately white house up ahead. "I want to show you someplace special," I said.

"But we're going to be late."

"It won't take a minute," I said, feeling some of my excitement quelled. "See? Up ahead, on the right."

He sighed, but pulled over obligingly in front of the Edwin Bate house. I rolled down my window. "What do you think?"

Evan leaned across me and peered up at the house. I watched the expression on his face. "What about it?"

"This is the oldest house in town," I explained. "It was my favorite house when I was a kid—Jane and I called it the Wedding Cake House. It was just renovated."

"How old is it?" he asked. I appreciated he was making an effort, even though I could sense that the house didn't have quite the effect on him I'd hoped.

"Over two hundred years old. It was a whaling captain's home. Can you imagine all the changes this house has witnessed through Mystic's history? I think that's neat."

Evan cringed in his seat. "Can you imagine all the dust and dirt in those floorboards? God only knows what's in the attic. Or down in the basement."

I shook my head. "But it's all redone now. The builder kept the original plan, but gutted the walls and ceilings." I pointed to the roofline of the house. "Look, he even made reproduction moldings to match the originals. Isn't it beautiful?"

Evan looked at me curiously. "You sure seem to know a lot about it."

As we reversed out of the gravel drive quickly, Evan glanced at me. "That's what I like about new construction. Sleek, modern, and new. No one's 'history' to worry about, except my own."

He flicked his wrist to look at his watch. "Perfect. We're still on time."

◆ ◆ ◆

Now, Peyton is on my heels as I head across the Oyster Club deck to the small bar. "You feeling okay?"

The server pours me a glass of champagne but I realize I'm not actually thirsty, or feeling terribly celebratory. Despite the jaunty red, white, and blue table settings and the nautical striped linens. Even the starfish set against the glass votive candles, which flickered in the breeze up here on the decks. "Just look at this place. It's perfect." I point out Erika, who is whispering something in Trent's ear at their table. "She's perfect, this night is perfect. How can some people be so . . ."

"Perfect?" Peyton asks. "Knock it off. If you're going to start using Erika as a measuring stick against perfect, you're worse off than I thought." I let her drag me over to an empty corner of the patio. Below us, the Mystic River is glasslike in its stillness. Unlike the currents in my head.

"Look, we've all made it to the rehearsal dinner in one piece. Couples crisis averted. Cousins accounted for. Bridesmaids toasted. So, why are you in such a funk?"

"I can't stop thinking about Cam."

Now she's listening. "Go on."

"I let Cam walk out of my life almost ten years ago. So why can't I leave him there?"

Peyton lets out a long breath. I notice her glance over at our table, where Evan and Chad are finishing up dessert plates of chocolate framboise. "Maybe you guys aren't done with each other."

"There's no way. His life is messy. And mine was finally

going well. I mean, just look at him." I nod toward Evan. "He's pretty much perfect."

She follows my gaze but looks unconvinced. "All right, listen. If you want to do this, let's really do this." She scoots closer. "I've got news for you. You don't do perfect very well."

"Excuse me?"

"I'm serious. Remember when we all first moved to Boston and none of us could afford to eat out, but none of us could cook well?"

I could barely boil pasta. "So?"

"You insisted we come over for Friday-night dinners. You had all these big ideas, but you never had the right ingredients. Or utensils. The kitchen ended up a disaster, every time, and the fire alarm usually went off. But none of that mattered. Because somehow you took what you had and made it work."

I smile at the memory. "Olive and tuna melt nachos?"

"Exactly. Just like when you started at Darby. Remember how nervous you were about teaching science? You almost didn't take the job."

I cringe. "I was a literature major." The thought of trying to teach the scientific method to a class of nine-year-olds paralyzed me.

"So you convinced the dean to get you those crab-things."

"Crayfish."

"Whatever. They stunk like hell. But the kids liked it, right?"

I nod.

"And then one day the dean popped in to do a surprise evaluation, and the kids had the crab-things crawling all over, and the floor was soaked."

I put my head in my hands. "This isn't helping."

"It was another mess. But the dean loved the hands-on nature of your lesson. He ended up ordering those creatures for the rest of the grade."

"Yeah. My friend Sharon wanted to kill me."

Peyton reaches over and grabs both my arms. "That's what I'm trying to get at. You don't do perfect, Maggie. You excel at messy." She points across the deck at Evan. "He's not messy."

A cry catches in my throat. "He can get messy."

"No. No, he can't, honey. He's as squeaky clean as they come. For crying out loud, Maggie—he was an Ivory soap model."

We both burst out laughing, but just as quickly I'm crying.

"God knows why, but you're attracted to all things that need help. I used to think you wanted to fix things that weren't yours to fix. But now I realize it's just part of who you are."

I look at her. "So, what's that supposed to mean?"

"It means, don't be afraid of messy."

The tears are spilling down my cheeks now and Peyton hands me a napkin. She is one of the last people I would have expected to give me this little talking-to. But she's got me.

"Where have you two been?" Erika sweeps in behind us. "You're missing dessert. Wait, why are we crying?"

"I'm making a mess," I tell her.

Peyton grabs my hand. "Don't worry. She knows how to clean this one up."

◆ ◆ ◆

An hour later, Jane pulls up in front of the restaurant. "How'd it go?" she asks, as we pull away from the Oyster Club.

"It was beautiful. Erika and Trent are going to have a great day tomorrow."

She glances over at me. "So, why aren't you staying at the hotel with the girls tonight? Or Evan?"

I roll down the window and tip my head back. "Did you ever want something so badly that you just pushed through whatever obstacles were in your way, until you had it, never slowing down to really ask yourself if it's what you really needed?"

She turns onto our old neighborhood street and slows the car. "You mean that once you get it, you're disappointed? I guess so. Probably more when I was younger." She smiles, ruefully. "These days I have so little time to think about anything I want, it's all about needs. None of which are my own."

I look at Jane out of the corner of my eye. For all the teasing I do about her mom's-uniform yoga attire, or her harried state, or her cluttered minivan, she has accomplished so many things. Beautiful things.

She rolls to a stop in front of our parents' house and puts the car in park, but neither of us makes a move to get out. "You're unhappy with Evan."

I nod.

"Then tell him, Maggie."

"But he's such a great guy, Jane. He's the guy I've been holding out for. He's thoughtful and smart. He orders me my favorite drink before I even arrive at the restaurant. He doesn't complain when I'm late. And he's got this amazing job. My friends and family are crazy about him."

Jane nods, in agreement, her gaze level. "Yeah, but are you?"

"I want to be. He fits all the boxes. I'm afraid that it's me who's the problem. And that if I let him go, I might regret it."

She sighs and looks past me through the window at our family's cape. "When Toby and I were first married, I thought that we'd have smooth sailing because he checked all my boxes. We wanted kids, but first our careers. We both loved to travel, but hated to camp. We share the same politics and loved old movies. On the surface, it was sunshine all around." She shakes her head. "But it's the deep dark stuff that matters. Like, when you're in the middle of a heated argument, he knows that all I really want is a hug. And despite the hideous thing I just called him, he still hugs me. Or when I'm up with a crying baby in the middle of the night, he can tell when I'm about to lose it and relieves me. Or when Grandma died, and I wouldn't talk to anyone, for days, he didn't try to make me. He gets me. It's those unspoken understandings that save you."

I wonder if Evan and I have any understandings. Or if all we've really acquired are merely polite habits. He puts toothpaste on my toothbrush every night before bed. And he doesn't mind my staying up late to read when he falls asleep. But when I told him about Darby, he quickly pointed out all the private schools in the area and narrowed down the ones with the closest commutes on a map. In red pen. Missing entirely how I felt about it. And not bothering to ask me, either.

I open the car door.

"Hang on a sec." Jane nods toward our house. "When we were growing up here, remember how great this neighborhood was? You could throw a rock in any direction and hit a kid that you could play with."

"Nice, Jane."

"No, really. But when we got older, it didn't matter as much that this was the best hill to sled down. Or that we could hit thirty houses on Halloween night. Remember how we used to get embarrassed, living in such a small house? We had to share a room. And so many of our friends were living in those new-construction neighborhoods on the southern end of town."

I nod, recalling with a pang how we complained as teenagers. Thinking our house was too small and plain, the yard too narrow. The furniture too old. And how we cringed over the big Chevy my mom drove around in, a model practically as old as we were.

"But when we got off the bus every afternoon, Mom was home with snacks on the counter and pencils sharpened for homework."

I can see it now—a plate with two cookies, two glasses of milk, and a sliced apple on the side. "And dinner on the stove," I add.

Jane laughs. "Remember how Dad would walk into town with us on weekends and let us buy Vanilla Cokes at the diner? But he didn't want us to tell Mom."

I look at Jane, with narrowed eyes. "Careful, this is bordering on sentimental for you."

Jane shrugs. "It was a no-frills childhood. But it was the best. And I think it's funny that tonight, with all your Boston pals home for the wedding, and all the ritzy plans they've made, this is the place you most want to be." She punches me lightly in the arm.

◆ ◆ ◆

Upstairs in my bedroom, I slip out of my dress. The night is warm and the old bedroom window creaks in protest as I tug it open.

Evan is in the village at the Oyster House, probably having another drink. Later, he'll spend the night across town at the Mystic Inn. I wonder if he's angry that he'll be stretched out across the king mattress alone. When I said good night to him at the rehearsal dinner, he didn't protest. Instead, he walked me out, and while we stood solemnly on the sidewalk waiting for Jane, he loosened his tie. "I think you need to figure things out, Maggie," he said finally. By the time her minivan pulled up to the curb, he'd already gone back upstairs to the party.

Twenty-Seven

The morning of the wedding began much the way the previous night ended: an unsettling swirl of pink and orange stretches across the horizon, this time in sunrise. Unable to sleep, I'd been up since five o'clock. There are three completed teaching applications on my laptop: two for positions in Boston, and one for a position in Mystic. Like my mother suggested, I've decided to leave all my options open. Who knows—the MFA graduate program flyer is still in my purse.

Last night, before I went to bed, I climbed up the narrow ladder into the dark confines of our attic, the air rank with dust and the smell of hot shingles. It took me a while to find what I was looking for. When I finally carried it down, my father was standing at the bottom of the steps in his bathrobe, watching me curiously. "What are you doing up there at this hour?"

I held up the crumpled art portfolio for him to see.

"Ah. Traveling down memory lane." He leaned forward and kissed me on the forehead. "Don't stay up too late. Those memories will still be here in the morning."

That's the trouble with memories. Whether they are painted in soft strokes by a watercolor brush across a canvas, or are written in the dreamy teenage scrawl of a best friend who holds a secret: they fade over time, but their imprint lasts. After reading through the letters that Erika and I had passed to each other in middle school, and having sifted through the collection of paintings my mother so painstakingly arranged by date and composition, one thing is sure. Some memories of the past, stored away all these years in my parents' attic, are still very much alive in my mind.

There is the memory of a first friend; the firm hand that grasped yours on the first day of school, and pulled you up the steep stairs of the playground slide. Then wrapped around your middle as the two of you slid down in one shrieking sweep, landing at the bottom in a heap of skirts and back-to-school buckled shoes. Those same hands are the ones you pass a bridal bouquet to in the church today. Despite the rifts that have been caused, or the secrets kept. They are the same hands whose pinky finger wraps securely around your own, before you walk down the aisle on her wedding day.

Then there is the memory of color. The hazy blue that captured the river that ran through your childhood when you entered your first painting in the high school art show and came in second. There are the fiery reds of first loves, and family love, and the kind of love you spend your life wishing for. And there is the gold of a sun setting over a chapter in your life before a new one starts; the same golden hue of a baby's downy hair.

◆　◆　◆

When Erika walks down the aisle on the July afternoon of her wedding day, my heart is full of these memories. Mr. and Mrs. Crane are watching their only child with tear-filled reverence, while beside me, Peyton dabs at her eyes. But mine are on my best friend: on the shimmering ivory skirt of her wedding dress, the tilt of her head as she kisses the man to whom she has just pledged her partnership, and on the congregation whose applause we turn to face, a smattering of all our shared loved ones gathered to celebrate her big day. This time, when Evan meets me in the aisle, I meet his gaze with a warm smile. I am grateful for him. For his love and his trust and his good intentions. He is not the man I will walk down the aisle with someday, myself. And I will gently tell him that before this weekend is over. But now, I take his hand, and we follow our friends down the center of the pews. Past my parents, who both wave a little too enthusiastically. Past Jane, and Toby, and their children, who have not quite sat still for the entire ceremony, but leap up and call out my name as I sweep by. Lastly, I rest my eyes on the blue sky overhead as we surge through the double doors of our small New England church. This summer day is ripe with possibilities. And tonight, as we dance the evening away at the country club along the Mystic River, as someone once said, the stars overhead will compete with the ones in our eyes.

◆　◆　◆

When the last song of the reception plays, Erika and Trent move onto the dance floor one last time. Watching them from the deck door, I am sated with the celebrations of this delicious summer day. The rest of the bridal party are slumped in ball-room chairs, rubbing their sore feet as guests scrape the remains of wedding cake off their plates. Evan is among them. Seated off to the side, he will be going back to his room alone tonight. He understands that now. He thinks I am making a big mistake; and I don't blame him for walking angrily away from me when

I told him just now, outside on the deck. But I'm sure he'll come to realize that I did us both a favor. Evan is not home for me. And he deserves to take the next step in life with someone who is. But as I stand on the edge of the dance floor watching the way Trent looks at Erika, I know then that there is one more thing I need to do.

Soon, I am dashing up the stone walkway to the gate, the moon barely illuminating object from air. The front door is locked, but it's no matter. I know the way. I slip between the arborvitae and along the side of the house to the rear. At the foot of the stairs, I begin my ascent.

The white balcony takes on a ghostlike glow in the moonlight. I am alone, and yet I feel as if I am not. As if there is also someone from before, someone who has not left, and whose spirit will never quite leave. And yet it doesn't scare me. Because someone very real is coming.

From up here the Mystic River is a mercurial ribbon in the moonlight. To the east, there are the dots of lights and shadows of rooftops. Somewhere among them is the club, music probably still emanating from its deck doors. My friends will be on the dance floor. And up the river, Erika and Trent are just now sailing aboard the beautiful white schooner that swept them away from the reception, moments before I took my own leave, white lights glittering up and down the mast.

But here, at the Edwin Bate House, there is only silence, save for the peepers and the whoosh of evergreen branches in the breeze. I wait, holding my breath. Moments later, headlights appear on the road below. They swing up toward the house, and there is the crunch of gravel beneath tires. I close my eyes. A car door slams.

Soon, footsteps sound on the wooden staircase behind me. I turn as he steps on to the balcony.

Cameron pauses. Even in the pale light I can see him. His expression is uncertain.

"Maggie. Is everything okay?" he asks.

"It is now."

He comes to stand beside me, but I can sense his hesitation.

"Thanks for coming," I tell him. "I'm sorry I called so late."

He waits for me to speak, but I can't. "What's going on?" he asks.

Cam's hand is soft and warm when I reach for it on the railing. I fold my fingers in between his. "Lauren is gone, isn't she?"

Cam shifts his gaze away toward the grove of hemlocks, but I keep hold of his fingers. "She's flying out tomorrow. How did you know?"

A breath leaves my chest, a mix of sadness and regret. "I had a feeling after I left the hospital. I'm so sorry, Cam." No matter what Lauren represented for Cam, she is still Emory's mother.

"It's done now," he says. Then, "Why did you call tonight?"

I inhale. "When I first came home this summer and ran into you, I never thought I'd be standing here now. So much has happened in these short weeks. And this last week, at the hospital, I caught a glimpse of just how full your life really is."

Cam looks at me. "My whole life is Emory. It's the way things have to be right now."

"I know. Which is why I've tried to stay away from both of you, to leave the past where it is. But when I heard Emory was sick, I couldn't. I hope I didn't intrude by coming to the hospital, but I had to see her."

Even in the darkness, I can feel him turn toward me. "You

didn't intrude. What happened with Lauren would've happened anyway; she doesn't want to be a part of our lives. But you're right—my life is full even without her."

"I'm glad," I tell him.

"And you have your own life, too, Maggie," he adds. "I saw that for myself."

I know what Cam is referring to. Seeing me with Evan and all of our friends around town. Listening to me talk about how great Boston and city life are. What a fool I've behaved like this summer.

"It's not so full," I tell him, a sad laugh escaping my throat. "A lot has changed. I'm not seeing anyone anymore. I'm no longer teaching at Darby. Hell, I don't even know where I'm going to live after this weekend is over."

Cam doesn't say anything for a long time. Behind us the peepers have picked up again. I imagine they've grown used to us; as if we, too, are just another part of night.

Cam clears his throat. "When I saw you at the church yesterday, in your white summer dress . . ." He shakes his head. "Maggie, ever since I ran into you at the pier, I haven't been able to get you out of my head."

It's all I need to hear. "Yesterday, during the rehearsal, I was feeling so strange. Like I couldn't breathe. I had to get out of there. And then you drove by the church, like some kind of a sign."

"I don't believe in signs, Maggie."

"That's okay, because there are real things, too. Things you can put your thumb on: like history, and friendship. Like the foundation of an old house that just needs to be shored up."

Cam is so close I can feel him. "Is that why you called me here?"

I lean out over the railing. "This is where I first felt it this summer. Before I really understood about you and Emory. Before I lost my job. Or realized I was in the wrong relationship."

"And now?"

I reach for him. This time when our lips touch, there is certainty. And so much more. He envelops me, and I let him pull me against him, the whole summer exhaling around us. I don't want to let go. When we finally part, Cam pulls me close to his side and we stand entwined overlooking the river. I wonder if Edwin Bate ever stood beside his wife like this. I bet he did.

Finally, Cam speaks. "So what are you going to do about a job, Griff?"

I shrug, but the question doesn't scare me. "I don't know. I guess I'm going to have to figure that out."

"Any leads on a new apartment yet?"

"I'm thinking of widening the search. Outside of Boston," I say, looking at him out of the corner of my eye.

There is one thing I still have to ask. "Do you think you could ever let someone back into your life again?" Below, the river is iridescent beneath the moon. Standing up here, with only the sound of the night and our own breath surrounding us, we could be any two people at any point in time. But we aren't. Lucky us.

Cam takes a deep breath and lets it go. "I like to think so. One thing I've learned from Emory is to take things one moment at a time. All we have is today."

I squeeze Cam's hand. "What are you doing tomorrow?"

ACKNOWLEDGMENTS

They say third time's a charm, but our second time around has proven that one wrong. It has been both a joy and a privilege to work with my editor, Megan Reid, once again. She has done no less than champion my work, sending *The Lake Season* out of the gates and into the heart of the pack. And I'm honored to hand her the reins for this one, too. From the heartfelt handwritten notes that land in my mail with galleys to the brilliantly rendered suggestions on edits, Megan remains a gentle but constant voice of encouragement. She trusts me to run the distance and set my own pace—but she's always waiting at the finish line. Wrapping a book together feels like landing in the winner's circle every time. I can't thank you enough.

MacKenzie Fraser Bub, of Trident Media, remains my scout. Don't be fooled by that soft southern accent—she's the New York agent stuff of dreams. Always abreast of the market and expectations, she provides the measuring stick against which we all line up. She keeps me ever mindful not of the book I'm working on but the book that I want it to be. I'm forever grateful for her partnership, her sharp ear, and the questions she's not afraid to ask.

I can honestly say that I talk more about my team at Emily Bestler Books than I do about my books. Another tremendous thank-you to Emily herself, whose keen eye and fabulous team have made it possible to deliver two novels in two years. Hugs and high fives to Ariele Fredman, publicity fairy godmother, who called, messaged, promoted, and ultimately garnered more media and print exposure than I ever imagined possible. Huge thanks also to Arielle Kane, who in one lengthy, laughter-filled phone call talked social media marketing, tossed me into "the Twitter," and oversaw the videotaping with Studio4. Thanks to Jin Yu, who so kindly assisted in all things web related. And to Matt, who entertained me during my visits with all things crochet-animaux. (I'm still waiting for that chicken!)

Friends and family are where it all starts and ends. Cheers to my New York "sisters" who put me on the right train and also come along for an adventure: A.C., J.R., and J.J. A toast to the C.C. Ice Fishing crew, whose laughter and cheer sustained me during the writing of this book. To B.B., fellow Camel and tour guide extraordinaire, who so generously shared Mystic with me and helped bring it to life for Maggie. And to Sherman, the little town big on love for this resident writer. You know who you are.

It's been so rewarding to connect with my readers online, and I must thank all the bloggers, reviewers, librarians, book clubs, Indie bookstore owners, and readers who reach out to me. Your support has been inspiring.

To my family, who still call me and shout into the phone

when they see my name in print. Most of all, to my girls, Grace and Finley, who remain the stars in my eyes and the reason I do what I do each day, and with each book. You'll always be my most important works. I can't wait to see the stories you write with your own lives.

Mystic Summer

by Hannah McKinnon

A Readers Club Guide

EMILY
BESTLER
BOOKS

∧P
READERS
CLUB

Introduction

When she's blindsided by a trio of seemingly unconnected events—her best friend's summer wedding, a heartbreaking potential layoff, and a chance run-in with an ex-boyfriend—Maggie Griffin has no idea that she's just embarked on a summer that will change her life and cause her to question everything she holds dear. A devoted Boston resident, she returns to her hometown of Mystic for the summer, where the past and present collide. Her journey of discovery impacts others' lives as well, and when a vulnerable child is suddenly in danger, Maggie must make a choice. Should she hold tight to the life she's built, or let go—and allow room for something even better? Critically acclaimed novelist Hannah McKinnon spins a warmhearted and thoughtful story of summer, friendship, and self-knowledge that is sure to charm women's fiction fans everywhere.

Questions and Topics for Discussion

1. Maggie and Erika are two best friends who prove that opposites attract. Despite how they exasperate each other, what are

the ties that bind these childhood friends, and how does their relationship change throughout the novel?

2. On page 5, Maggie notes: "I have always taken pride in my skill to find good in all of my students . . . Even when I have to dig deep." How does she apply this optimistic spirit and goodwill to other characters in the novel? You might consider the Cam, Jane, Erika, and Peyton as examples.

3. Jane is a constant sounding board for Maggie as an older sister (a role she's played their entire lives), and Maggie's parents are likewise close confidants and advisers. What are some of the bonds that have held this family together? Find examples in the text to support your answer, in addition to discussing the more emotional side.

4. Change and stability are two of the major forces that drive *Mystic Summer*'s plot, but the author never makes them simple opposites. For instance, for Maggie, Boston represents change in that she must navigate finding a new home, but it is also the stable, safe choice when she considers returning to what she knows. How do other elements of the book embody this duality? Discuss Maggie's relationships with Cam and Evan, her friendships, and the town of Mystic itself.

5. One of the most charming parts of *Mystic Summer* is its description of parenting—the good, the bad, and the ugly. Compare and contrast Cam and Jane's approaches to raising kids. Which did you relate with most?

6. Erika gives Maggie a lot to think about when she tells her about her difficult summer with Chase, her old high school boyfriend. Do you agree with her decision not to tell Trent about her infidelity? Why or why not?

7. Maggie makes the decision to forge a reconnection with Cam impulsively. Discuss this decision with your book club. What does Cam represent to her? Why is this so important at this point in her life?

8. Why does the Edwin Bate house evoke such nostalgia for Maggie? What does it come to represent for her?

9. Lauren, Cam's ex and Emory's mom, is one of the novel's most complex characters. What are her struggles and motivations? When does she feel most sympathetic to you?

10. Peyton, Erika, and Maggie are a close-knit group, but each has a distinct part to play in their friendship. Discuss the role each woman holds in their trio. How do their approaches to crises (like Erika's wedding venue meltdown) reveal their personalities?

11. Hannah McKinnon makes the interesting narrative decision to never show Erika and Trent's wedding, though it's arguably the focal point of the book. What effect does this have on how you experience Maggie's story?

12. "This is not my style. I am not the girl who shouts after old boyfriends in the street" (page 112). In what other ways does

Maggie challenge her own expectations of herself and her relationships throughout the novel?

Tips to Enhance Your Book Club

1. Research atrial septal defect, the congenital heart condition that affects baby Emory (the American Heart Association's website at heart.org is a great place to start). Ask your book club members to bring contributions to one of the many great charities that supports children with this life-threatening defect, like the Children's Heart Federations, the AHA, or the International Children's Heart Foundation and make a group donation on your club's behalf.

2. Even if your book club is chilly and landlocked, there's no wrong time of year to evoke a Mystic summer. Serve New England beach–themed snacks like mini lobster rolls, corn on the cob, and spicy shrimp, and make sure to have lots of chilled white wine on hand! You can even try your hand at making homemade mini-pizzas inspired by the real-life namesake of the film *Mystic Pizza.*

3. A summer wedding is at the heart of *Mystic Summer,* just like in *The Lake Season,* Hannah McKinnon's debut novel. Bring in some of your favorite wedding pictures—whether they're from your own nuptials, or those of your friends and family. As you peruse each other's photos, tell your best wedding stories, and give a prize to whoever can share the funniest mishap!